DESPERATE MAN

Morgan pulled back, letting Devilin take a little-used trail that wound out of town toward the river. A half mile later, the trail ended abruptly at a green field. Morgan sat on his horse as Devilin pulled the rig to a halt. They were 40 yards apart. There was nowhere for Devilin to drive except through open country along the Grande Ronde River.

Morgan and Devilin stared at each other for a minute or two.

"Morgan, what do you want?"

"I want you in jail on murder charges."

"I have solid cartridges, now loaded with six fresh ones."

"No chance, Devilin. I saw your piece back in the saloon. It's a percussion just like mine. Only I have four rounds left in mine. Ready to go back to jail?"

In reply, Devilin slapped the reins on the horse and jolted the buggy directly at Morgan....

The *Buckskin* Series:

#28: APACHE RIFLES
#29: RETURN FIRE
#30: RIMFIRE REVENGE
#32: DEATH DRAW
#33: .52 CALIBER SHOOT-OUT
#34: TRICK SHOOTER

Double Editions:
**SILVER CITY CARBINE/CALIFORNIA
   CROSSFIRE**
PISTOL GRIP/PEACEMAKER PASS
REMINGTON RIDGE/SHOTGUN STATION
**WINCHESTER VALLEY/GUNSMOKE
   GORGE**

Giant Editions:
GUNSLINGER'S SCALP
NIGHT RIDER'S MOON
SIX-GUN SHOOTOUT

PISTOL WHIPPED

35

BUCKSKIN

KIT DALTON

LEISURE BOOKS   NEW YORK CITY

A LEISURE BOOK®

May 1993

Published by

Dorchester Publishing Co., Inc.
276 Fifth Avenue
New York, NY 10001

Copyright © 1993 by Chet Cunningham/BookCrafters

The name "Leisure Books" and the stylized "L" with design are
trademarks of Dorchester Publishing Co., Inc.

Printed in the United States of America.

Chapter One

The sun flashing off metal 50 yards ahead came almost too late. Jed Bradburn dove toward the side of the rickety seat of his buckboard. The roar of a rifle in the dry high country of eastern Oregon came at almost the same instant as a bullet blasted into the underside of Jed's left arm. The hot lead bored a neat hole through half an inch of flesh and kept on going out the other side.

Jed rolled off the seat before the bushwhacker could snap off another shot. He got one knee under him as he hit the ground and spread out on the dirt behind the rig. Without the command of the reins, the horse pulling the buckboard stopped.

"Whoa, there, Maud. Easy girl. Easy."

The rifleman fired another round at Jed. It showered half inch splinters off one of the wooden spokes on the buckboard's skinny front wheel and slanted away. The wheels weren't much protection. The body of the rig gave him a little cover since the shooter lay in the rocks 20 feet above the trail.

Jed felt for his six-gun. The trusty 1860 Army Percussion revolver lay safely in leather. He pulled open the strap and eased the weapon into his hand. His rifle was perched uselessly in the buckboard box over his head. Before another shot came, Jed rolled to the side where he saw a small gully carved out by runoff water from the trail.

Another round slammed through the dirt just over his head. Jed crawled down the gully which became progressively deeper. It seemed like an hour of crawling on his stomach, pulling himself along with his elbows and pushing with his toes.

At last the little ditch was deep enough so he could lift up and crawl on his hands and feet without exposing himself to the rifle fire over the top. The next 30 yards went quicker, then he was in the brush of a small creek.

He felt a sudden rush of terrible hatred for the man shooting at him, knowing that he wanted to track him and kill him.

He had done it before and had promised himself he would never do it again.

Two more rifle shots came slapping through the brush around him. The gunman was good. He knew approximately where Jed was, but knowing where the target was and killing it were two different practicalities.

Now Jed did the waiting. The gunman would figure he had him pinned down or had wounded him.

Jed lay near a cottonwood tree that stretched

50 feet into the air. He was a man in his early thirties, tall, rangy, Texas-thin yet well-muscled. When he moved it was with a mountain lion's quickness and a lithe economy of motion, swift and sure, and when the occasion demanded it, deadly. His eyes glowed pale green, set deep in his craggy face. An inch long, half-moon scar over his right eye glowed softly white against the surrounding skin.

His clean shaven face gave way to a trimmed moustache matching his nearly black hair. Tendrils of black curls escaped beneath the back of his low-crowned cowboy hat. He had pushed it back in place after he lost it diving out of the buckboard.

Something moved by the rocks where the puffs of powder smoke pinpointed the gunman.

"He's coming to get me—he thinks," Jed whispered half to himself.

He lifted the revolver and steadied it. Five shots against a rifle. He could reload if he had time. He dreamed of a revolver with solid bullets. Some of the European hand pieces were made that way. He'd try to find one. What an advantage that would be.

For just a moment a blonde wraith clouded his vision and frowned. "There's always a better way than using a gun," Virginia said softly, intense and concerned. Then she faded, and he concentrated on the rocks.

The bushwhacker stood up and ran from his cover, evidently convinced that his victim had no rifle. He was still nearly 70 yards away.

A better way than with a gun? Jed thought about what Virginia had always said. What better way was there right now? He was damned if he could think of one. A bushwhacker was a hard person to sit down and reason with. A killer seldom wanted to investigate intellectual solutions when the problem at hand could be solved quicker with a lead slug through the brain.

Jed had put down his iron three years ago and had not fired a shot in anger since. He hadn't used his gun to solve a single argument, problem or confrontation. Sure, his iron was cold, but he could heat it up again. Yes, he had lost that quickness of draw he once had, but the old dog never forgets his old tricks. Three or four rounds and he'd be in top form again.

The problem was, could he live long enough to use his cold iron?

The rifleman leaned around a rock 50 yards away. He wore no hat and had on a blue shirt and a brown vest.

Damned bushwhacker! No man worth his hogleg would fire at a man from ambush, especially with a rifle. Why? Who?

Jed knew he was not in the best tactical situation and should advance. He had learned that the hard way. Never just lay back and let some bastard walk up and shoot you dead. So the bushwhacker had a rifle, which was only 20 yards of advantage. Jed could use his six-gun at 40 feet and knock the cork out of a bottle of whiskey and never spill a drop.

At least he used to be able to—before Virginia.

Jed surveyed the area immediately ahead. The bank of the creek was four feet deep here, gouged out of good soil, rock and sand. The bushwhacker was still 50 yards away, and another ten from the creek. Meet the bastard at the creek. The soft chatter of the water over the rocks made enough noise to cover part of his move.

Jed slipped away from the tree crouched over low so the top of the bank was hiding him. He moved cautiously, never taking a step until he was sure he could do so silently. Six steps, then a look over the bank through a healthy sage. The gunman was still glued behind his rock.

As Jed watched, the shooter made another rush, this time ten yards closer to the creek where he dropped behind a fallen cottonwood.

Jed hurried silently another 20 feet through the sandy creek's dry side to where a cluster of willow grew on the bank above him and offered lots of leafy concealment.

Through the leaves, he could see the bush-whacker checking his rifle. It was a breechloader, not a fancy repeater like a few Jed had seen.

Jed surveyed the terrain. Ahead the creek took a slight turn toward the ambusher. Willow cloaked the near side of the bank. Perfect concealment, but no protection from hot lead.

The bank continued three to four feet high. He could still move there, but once the bushwhacker got to the same ditch, there was no place to hide for either of them.

Twenty feet down stood a maple with wide leaves. It had a gnarled trunk nearly three feet in diameter. Jed sprinted the 20 feet, heaved up and over the bank and lay on the grass behind the sturdy tree trunk.

He parted some leaves and looked for his vic-tim. The man lay on the bank 30 feet ahead. He scanned the brush near him and down toward

where Jed lay. He had no protection. Jed lifted the
.44 and sighted in on the gunman's chest. Then
he shifted his aim to the man's gunhand. At last
he concentrated his sights at the bushwhacker's
right shoulder and squeezed off the round.

The bushwhacker's right shoulder spouted
blood, and he bellowed in rage, rolling away.
Jed fired at the man's legs which were rapidly
vanishing in some light brush. Another scream
of pain billowed through the trees near the small
creek.

"Bastard! You shot me!" the man brayed.

"What did you expect? I'd offer you a drink?"

There was only silence.

He waited. Ahead he heard a gasp, then nothing. Jed watched the brush where he had last seen
the man. It moved slightly as the bushwhacker
worked toward the stream.

If he had lots of hard cartridges, Jed could put
a few rounds into the brush and reload. Now just
the thought of having to reload his percussion
revolver irritated him. He'd find a solid cartridge
handgun as soon as he could.

He might have time to get the linen cartridges
out of his pouch with their measure of powder
and lead ball all wrapped together and ram them
one at a time in each of the cylinders and then
put the little brass detonating caps on the five
nipples. But that took a lot more time than he
had right now.

The brush moved again. The wounded man
was coming forward, advancing. Jed waited. The
bushwhacker was less than 20 feet away now but
still hidden in the copse of willows. Jed had just
three rounds left.

He wasn't going to waste one now. Besides, if he fired he would give away his position.

Old talents and well-honed practices settled down over him. Jed relaxed, sure of himself now, of his ability, of his performance.

Ahead, the rifle fired and a round thwacked into the maple tree. The small cloud of white smoke rose from the young willows. Jed edged lower where he lay now behind the big tree. The smoke lifted lazily higher over the thick willow brush. It was amazing that the lead got past all the dozen of willow shoots to hit the tree.

Just then the brush ahead of Jed exploded. The man barreled through the concealment of the brush with a six-gun in each hand and charged forward toward the maple.

Jed's sighting the target and firing took only a fraction of a second.

Jed's big .44 boomed. The slug hit the man in the left thigh and stopped him short. He roared in pain, firing twice at the maple tree as he fell.

"Drop the iron or you're a dead bushwhacker!" Jed barked.

The gunner lifted up and fired at the voice. Jed had two rounds left. He aimed automatically at the gun hand and squeezed the trigger dead on target as the hunter tried to pull the hammer back with his right thumb.

Jed's round tore into the cylinder of the six-gun which broke apart, and half of the hot lead ripped into the bushwhacker's knuckles where his fingers wrapped around the weapon's grip.

For a moment there was no sound, only the echoing of the gunfire down the twisting ribbon of trees.

Then the bushwhacker's voice came high, keening in intense pain and anguish. The round had driven him flat on his back, but now he lifted up, pushing on his right elbow and aiming the gun in his left hand. Jed shot him through his left wrist, and the man roared in anguish and lay still.

"Move an inch and you're a dead man," Jed rasped.

"Hell, I counted. You fired five shots. You carry one piece. You gonna stomp me to death?"

"If I have to. I use the linen cartridges. Fast to reload. I charged up three more rounds as you wasted time. Who the hell are you?"

"Don't matter none, but the name's Elroy Jamison."

"Why you gunning me?"

"Your name's Jed Bradburn. Got a wanted poster on you from California."

"Oh, damn, that paper's no good."

"They all say that until they hang. You're wanted in California, dead or alive, and that's for damn certain. You're worth two thousand dollars."

Jed had been checking the area. Both six-guns the man used lay on the ground. His hands were useless.

Jed stood up behind the maple, then stepped out quickly cocking his empty Army Percussion .44 revolver as he did. Jed kept the weapon trained on the bushwhacker as he moved toward him. The man was shot up and hurting bad.

Jamison was bearded. He appeared harmless and held his right hand with his left. He looked up. Blood pooled in his hand, dripped to the ground. "You shot me four times. Ain't that enough?"

"Don't appear to be, since you're still breathing and talking. No bushwhacker deserves to live."

"Hell, if you wanted me dead you could have killed me at least twice. You didn't. So what happens now?"

"Jamison, you go to jail in La Grande as a guest of the county sheriff on attempted murder charges, assault with a deadly weapon, and whatever else I can figure out."

"Won't stand up in court, not with the wanted poster out on you that I got."

"It's no good. I told you that. Now get on your feet. It's time to move."

"I can't walk."

"Lay there and die then." Jed lifted the barrel of the .44 until it centered on the man's chest. Jamison groaned, stood up and started to limp.

Ten minutes later the bushwhacker lay in the back of the buckboard, his hands tied securely to the side rail, his horse on a lead line behind the rig.

"You forgot my rifle back there," Jamison said.

"Where you're going you can't have a rifle. Don't let it bother you."

"I've got a judge in Texas I do a lot of work for. You won't get away with ramming some conviction through a backwoods legal system with a paid-for judge."

"You keep talking that way in Oregon and you'll need all of your high-powered friends."

Jed had tied up the man's wounds so he wouldn't bleed to death before they drove into town. La Grande had just one doctor and felt lucky to have him. He was an older man who didn't want to work too hard. The 200 people in town and the

surrounding area seemed about right to him. Doc
Fetterman had been in town as long as Jed had.

Jed followed his usual trail down Catherine
Creek until it turned north, then he struck out
northwest another five miles to town.

When he pulled into the edge of town near the
Grande Ronde river, four small boys chased after
him the two blocks to the sheriff's office.

"Who you got there, Mister. Some dangerous
killer?"

"Why you got him tied up?"

"You shoot him, Mister?"

Jed waved at the boys, looped the reins over
the rail outside the county sheriff's office and
stomped inside.

He'd known Sheriff Larson for the three years
he'd been on his ranch. The man was over 60
years old, never wore a gun, and admitted that his
right hand didn't work the way it used to. He was
as liable to drop a six-gun as he was to aim one.
He never touched a gun any more. He claimed
his iron was cold. Larson was a small man with
a pot belly and gray fringe hair around a mostly
shiny pate. He flashed his friend a warm smile as
Jed walked in.

"Jed, just in time for some fresh coffee." He
looked out the window at the wagon. The three
boys hung over the sides looking at Jamison.

"You got some business for me out there?"

"Rightly so, Sheriff Larson. Bushwhacker. Put
one through my arm, so I repaid the compli-
ment."

They sipped the coffee for a minute.

"Guess we better get him in here and let him
have his say," the sheriff said.

"Reckon. Sheriff, you need to know that this man says he has a wanted on me. I know there's an old one out, but it ain't good paper. Happened six, seven years ago and wasn't a true bill then. Ain't any better now with six years of dust on it."

Sheriff Larson lifted his brows. "I'll be. Jed Bradburn on a wanted. Never would have thought it. Well, looks like we better get to the bottom of this one."

They brought Jamison into the office and the sheriff gave one of the small boys a nickel to run over and get Doc Fetterman to come as quick as he could. The bushwhacker pulled a folded paper out of his inside shirt pocket.

"You better take a look at this, Sheriff. Bradburn here is a wanted man with a two thousand dollar price on his head. I want you to lock him up until we can contact them in Hangtown, California."

Sheriff Larson looked at the much-folded piece of paper. It had a name and description but no picture. The lawman took the paper behind his desk, sat down and spread it out.

"Mr. Jamison, 'pears we have a slight difference of opinion here. Mr. Bradburn says the wanted poster is not valid. We'll have to find out about that. I do know a felony was committed in my county. Attempted murder. I'll be holding you on that charge until we clear up this matter of the poster."

"You can't do that, Sheriff! A wanted poster is a license to go get a man any way I have to."

"Not in my county, Jamison. You come on back to cell number one and the doctor will be over directly to get you wrapped up. Don't look like you're in much shape to do any traveling all the way to California anyway."

"This is crazy, Sheriff. You just can't do this!"

Sheriff Larson's mouth set in a grim line. "Young man, don't tell me what I can't do in my own county. Your cell is right back here."

Doc Fetterman came a few minutes later, dug out one slug and wrapped up Jamison's other wounds. "You'll live. What were you? Target practice for somebody?" Doc shook his head, adjusted his wire-rimmed spectacles and closed up his bag. The sheriff locked the jail cell behind him.

"Send the county a bill, Doc."

"Been doing that for three years now. County is near six months behind in paying me."

The sheriff nodded. "Sounds about normal. Stay healthy, Doc. We need you in this county."

"Sheriff, I know this doesn't look good for me," Jed said, "but all I ask is that you send a letter to the sheriff of El Dorado county in California and ask him if this wanted poster is any good. I know it isn't. If he's honest, he'll say the same thing. The whole thing was a political ploy to get me out of town."

Sheriff Larson sat in his chair and rubbed his whiskered chin. He hadn't shaved for two days and the white stubble was showing.

"Dang me, but you got a point, son. This jasper shot you from ambush, you say?"

"Right. Me sitting on my buckboard coming to town. I finally persuaded him to come in. Look, Sheriff, I could have killed him half a dozen times. I didn't because I figured he had one of those old wanteds. I knew it had to be a mistake. Would I ask you to send a letter to California if I thought that paper might be legitimate?"

Sheriff Larson pushed a boot against the desk and leaned back in his chair. He rubbed his jaw again. "Dang me, Jedediah. I guess if'n I was in your spot, I'd do the same thing." His foot came down, his mind made up.

"I'll keep the wanted poster. I'll send a letter today to the sheriff of that county in California. And you, Jed Bradburn, will fill out a complaint against this man for attempted murder and assault with a dangerous weapon. I can hold him two weeks on that until the circuit court judge comes around."

"Done," Jed said and reached for a piece of paper and pen.

When he had the paper filled out, the sheriff looked it over and approved it.

"Sheriff Larson," Jed said. "On that letter to Hangtown, I hope you can make it urgent. Two weeks ain't much time to get a letter there and back again, and you said that judge will be here by then."

"True, Jedediah. I'll get it out on the evening stage."

Jed thanked him. Now he had to get over to the general store to pick up the goods for the ranch.

Chapter Two

Lee Buckskin Morgan stood by the window in Portland, Oregon, and watched the rain drenching the street outside. He had come there on the promise of a job, and now he wasn't too sure that he wanted to take it on.

"I can't just shoot him in a fair fight and call it good."

The man sitting behind the desk was one of the biggest businessmen in Portland, owning half a dozen enterprises including one of the large banks. He tapped the ash from a 50-cent cigar into a gold-trimmed tray on his desk.

"Mr. Morgan, I know your reputation. I can hire a dozen men right here in town to go out and shoot down Chance Rivers, but I don't want him dead. I just want him to face justice for once in his life and find out what it means to serve his time in prison."

Kiel Rothmore was a rich man. He had offered

Buckskin $5,000 to go bring Rivers back to Portland to face the criminal charges waiting for him. Rothmore's size matched his reputation. He was six feet tall, square shouldered, solid, in his mid-fifties and the proud father of four daughters.

"I simply will not abide his getting away with what he's done. The details are all in the folder I gave you. I understand that you've heard of Chance Rivers. I know he's had his way with town after town, intimidating the sheriff and taking over the whole county. He didn't try that here—Portland's too big a place—but he did violate my daughter, and while I have managed to keep the fact a secret, he did terrible damage to the sweet young thing and she'll forever be scarred by his attack."

"But a trial . . ."

"No, I'm not bringing him back for trial for rape. He also murdered a man in a downtown bar in front of a dozen witnesses. The man had no weapon. He sloshed some drink on Chance and that set off the beating that resulted in the man's death. For that crime I want him tried and convicted so he will spend at least thirty years in prison. That way he'll be paying for what he did to my daughter as well."

Buckskin wished it would quit raining, but this was April in Portland. They told him all of this rain was what made the Northwest the garden spot of the nation—green grass, green flowers, and hundreds of miles of forest green fir, pine and hemlock trees.

He turned toward the industrialist. Buckskin had wired $500 to a bank in Portland before he had arrived from Denver. He didn't want to be obligated to take the job because he was broke. Now he could take it on its merits or walk away from it.

"I'd wager that Chance Rivers won't come back to Portland peacefully."

"Granted. That's how you'll earn every cent of that fee."

"You wouldn't object to a few bullet holes in his hide, as long as they aren't fatal?"

"Certainly not. I might even be pleased if the shots caused him a lot of pain."

"Perhaps if I could see the young lady and talk to her . . ."

"No!" The reaction came swiftly. "Not possible. She's confined to the house right now. Her doctor say she'll get over the trauma but it will take time. Your seeing her would serve no purpose."

"You think Rivers has moved on to eastern Oregon, Pendleton, perhaps, or Baker, maybe even south to Klamath Falls?"

"I know he went as far as Pendleton. That was where he almost killed a private detective I had tracking him. He may have hidden somewhere for a time, knowing I will still be hunting him."

Morgan held out his hand. "I'll take the job with one stipulation. If it comes down to gunplay I'll kill him before I let him kill me. If that happens, I still get half of the fee. Fair enough?"

Kiel Rothmore stood and smiled for the first time since he had met Morgan. "Good. I like the way you do business. If you get him here alive he's worth twice what he is dead. I like that."

After Rothmore advanced Morgan $200 for expenses, he walked out of the office building on his way to the stage line. The next coach leaving for Pendleton moved out in less than an hour.

It stopped raining. Morgan had not taken a hotel room until he talked to Mr. Rothmore so he still had his traveling carpetbag with him. He caught a hack and rolled down to the stage depot.

As he waited in the depot for the rig to load, Morgan read over what material Rothmore had given him on Chance Rivers. Morgan figured the first thing Rivers would do after he found out someone was chasing him would be to change his name, so he couldn't count on the name for any clues.

He probably left Pendleton the day he clobbered the detective who must have been an expert in domestic disputes and petty thievery, not in brawling, killing gunmen.

Morgan had heard of Chance Rivers. He came out of California where he was wanted by several law agencies. Chance had always touted himself as a gunsharp, but nobody could name any fast draw expert who had gone down to Chance's firepower.

He was a gambler, a womanizer, a thief and a low-down outlaw, but never one to get many wanted posters out on him. Now Buckskin had the dubious task of bringing him in alive, back to Portland to stand trial. Catching a man was hard enough, but transporting him even 400 or 500 miles usually turned into a nightmare with dozens of chances for escape or violence.

Morgan remembered what a crusty old farmer had told him once when they were faced with a tricky problem.

"Hell, son, the fresh cowpie is right there in front of you. All you have to do is make sure you don't step in it as you dance around." By the sound of the description, Chance Rivers was going to be a damn big and ugly cowpie.

Lee Buckskin Morgan stepped down from the stage in Pendleton and looked around. The coastal clouds were 100 miles to the west. The sky was high and dry, the street dusty. Small whirlwinds generated their tiny tornadoes down the middle of the street, and the sun beat down at over 75 degrees. It was still April.

Morgan carried his carpetbag into the Umatilla County Sheriff's office in the courthouse and talked to a deputy.

"Chance Rivers? Yep, he was in town. Caused a big fight in a saloon the afternoon he arrived. Beat up three men and the next day he was gone. Nobody around here's seen or heard from him. Most of us are glad to be quit of him."

"Any idea which direction he headed?"

"Not back toward Portland. He's got big trouble there. We got a flyer on him. He's wanted in connection with a murder. Beat some poor son of a bitch to death with his fists."

"Obliged," Morgan said and walked outside. He tried to remember the Oregon map at the stage line office. There was not much choice where to go from Pendleton, only south into the dry lands of central Oregon. He wasn't even sure if a stage line went down there. Or he could keep going on the old Oregon Trail and head southeast to La Grande, about a 50 mile jaunt. After that there was a little town called Baker and then on into Idaho Territory.

It wasn't like Chance Rivers to simply hole up in a house somewhere and have someone bring him food and drink. He was a social animal, a violent social animal who liked his way with women and drink and good food. No, Chance would be moving, probably with a different name.

Morgan made it back to the stage before it pulled out for Baker. There had been a half hour layover to repair a wheel, and he threw his bag onboard just in time.

When he arrived in La Grande some six hours later, the sun was still up but there was a soft evening chill in the air. It felt good.

He remembered a little about La Grande from a previous visit. It was on the old Oregon Trail and served as a retail center for ranchers and a few small farmers and a growing lumber industry in the surrounding mountains. The mill men lobbied for a railroad to get their lumber out to market.

The little town began in 1861 as Brownsville and had grown slowly as more and more people stopped there on their way to the coast. Oregon was an established state, but sometimes in these outlying towns the law was spotty and hard to enforce. Often an ineffective sheriff meant that the law degenerated into who had the fastest gun, right or wrong.

Might be just the place for a man like Chance Rivers to change his name and try to melt into a small town and go unnoticed. The idea made Morgan grin. That was not Chance Rivers' style. If he was around, he would never melt into the woodwork. He'd be out front and obnoxious. That's why Morgan hoped if he was in La Grande, somebody would know him.

He registered at the Grande Ronde Hotel, named after the river that ran through the county.

Morgan figured the sheriff would be home by five o'clock. It was that time when he finished checking in at the hotel, washing the traveling dust off his face and upper body and donning a clean shirt for supper.

From time to time he had found out that waitresses often knew more about what went on in a small town than the authorities did, so he strolled down Main Street until he found a likely looking eatery and went in.

He ordered beef stew, and when the waitress brought it he smiled.

"Sally, wasn't it? Sally, could you tell me if this is a quiet town or is there some wild stuff goes on after dark?"

Sally was almost as square as she was tall, and she put down his plate of stew and two side dishes and sat down in the other chair across the table.

"Wild? I tell you this sure is a wild town. Once last week Lem Schiller lost his pig and had a dozen men chasing it down Main Street. Then we had a cat that got caught up a tree and couldn't get down. The town rowdies came out and started shooting their six-guns to try to shoot off the branch this kitty was holding onto. Sheriff came and stopped them. Said they didn't even have a blanket out to catch the kitty. So we spread out a blanket and six folks held it, but the cat never did fall down. Brightened up the whole afternoon, though."

Morgan sampled the beef stew, which was good—potatoes, carrots, cabbage, parsnips, turnips as well as savory chunks of beef.

"Good stew?" Sally asked.

"Great, yes. Good stew."

"You want seconds you give a yell, you hear. We like good eaters in here."

Sally wasn't going to be much help in tracking down anyone like Chance Rivers.

After his meal, he hit the half dozen saloons he saw along Main Street. The first one had barely made it past the barrel style with sawdust on the floor and the bar a pair of planks set on 50 gallon barrels.

The second one was called the Wildcat Saloon. He had a cold beer and watched the action. A dozen poker tables filled one side, with the other taken up with different gambling tables. One woman circulated around the tables. She wasn't one of the whores, who kept to the back except to meet and drink with regulars and then vanish up the open staircase to the back rooms. The place was about half-filled with drinkers and gamblers.

The woman made her way to his table and paused.

"You new in town, aren't you?" she said.

He nodded and started to stand up.

"Don't stand up. The men in here wouldn't be impressed. Mind if I sit down a minute?"

She was 30 or 40, he couldn't tell. She didn't have as much fancy woman paint on as most whores used, but she had on some. She was solidly built, no bag of bones, with a thick waist and fleshy arms, but she was in better shape than most women her age.

"Please sit down," Buckskin said. "I'm Lee Morgan."

She held out her hand. "Pleased to meet you. I'm Nancy. I own this place."

Her hand was cool and her grip firm for a moment, then she let go and slid into the chair. Her dress top showed a slice of cleavage but not as much as most whores show.

"New in town, clean-cut, square shoulders, no scars. You must be a lawman. U.S. Marshal?"

Morgan chuckled. "Way off the target, Nancy. I'm just a cowpoke looking for a ride. Anybody hiring around here?"

Nancy laughed. "You a cowboy? Look at your hands. No rope scars, no broken fingers. You're not sunburned below your hat line or on your hands. You're no cowboy."

Morgan nodded. "True, and you're no dummy. Can you stay a while and talk?"

"Why not? I told you I own the place."

"You must know a lot of people in town."

"Most of them. I don't know a lot of the uppity bitches who cross the street when they see me coming, but then, I damn well don't want to know them."

"I'm looking for a man."

"But you say you're not a cop. A damned bounty hunter?"

"Not a chance. I hate wanted posters."

"So you're a detective hired private by somebody to chase down some poor lost soul."

"Nearly right. Only he ain't poor or lost. He's a sidewinder who takes what he wants and punishes anyone in his way. He takes women the same way."

"This hombre have a name?"

"Yep, but he probably ain't using it. He's known as Chance Rivers."

Her eyes squinted and she cocked her head. "You talking about *the* Chance Rivers."

"You've heard of him. A snake of the first water. You know him?"

"Thank God, no, but I've heard of him."

"Then he isn't around town. He was in Pendleton a month ago. Figured he might have come this way."

She shrugged. "You want another beer or a shot of some good whiskey?"

"What are we celebrating?"

She signaled the barkeep who brought over a bottle from under the bar and two shot glasses.

"I'm the welcome to La Grande committee. The drink is on the house."

"Obliged."

He let her pour, then sipped the whiskey. It was better than he'd had lately. He tossed it down and closed his eyes, letting the taste of it burn all the way down.

"You know what Rivers looks like?"

"Somewhat. I have two eyewitness descriptions of him. They agree he's a big man, maybe six-one, a hundred and eighty pounds. No flab. Hair might be brown or black. He might have a moustache or be clean shaven."

"So he could be half of the big men in town," Nancy said. "Not one hell of a lot of help."

"Nobody in here fits that description," Morgan said. "You remember a man who could be him during the past month?"

"Yeah, two or three of them. One got himself

killed in a buggy accident. Another one has lived here ten years and is a church deacon. The third one came in about a month ago and picked a fight with a cowboy, but before any punches were thrown, they bought each other drinks and left. I ain't seen the big guy since."

"What did he look like?"

"Six-one or two. Near to two hundred pounds, I'd say. Black hair, likes to play poker, hard drinker, quick temper. Could be right-handed. I never saw him draw, but his iron was on his right hip."

"Could be Rivers."

"Could be don't pay the rent, Morgan. Also could be just another gambler or saddle tramp."

"True."

"So, you through working for the night?"

" 'Pears as how."

"Ask you a personal question, Morgan?"

"Fire away, Nancy, but be sure to use blanks."

"You ever paid for love?"

Morgan laughed, staring at the woman in front of him a moment, then down at her cleavage. She noticed his stare.

"Well, have you?"

"Not since I was fifteen up in Idaho. A first time folly I called it. She was the only fancy lady in town. Cost me a whole dollar and I got cheated at that. Ten minutes."

Nancy laughed. "Since then you've never been with a whore?"

"Didn't say that. Said I'd never paid for any since then. I've known a dozen or so ladies of the evening. Some I helped, and some helped me when I needed it. All loved me long and well."

"So you don't look down on whores?"

He poured another half-shot and downed it, then looked up.

"Most women are whores. They exchange their bodies and sex for money, or for marriage and a ring and security. What's the difference? Bought and paid for."

"I'm a whore."

"Congratulations. I like to see women work for a living."

"Used to be, that is. Retired. I own this place. Won it on a poker hand you wouldn't believe."

"Congratulations again. You want to tell me all about it? We could take this bottle and the glasses up to your rooms and be a lot more comfortable."

"My idea exactly. You can go out the back door and come up the outside stairs if you want to."

"Why, Nancy? You ashamed to be seen leading me up the stairs?"

She grinned, poked him on the shoulder and stood up.

Her place upstairs was three rooms—a sitting room, a bedroom and one reserved for her clothes. They stopped in the sitting room and had another shot of the whiskey. She came back with three apples and chunks of bright yellow cheese.

"Some girls get hungry after, but I always get ravenous before. Have a bite."

He watched her and saw that she had opened one more button down the front of her dress so he could see the swell of her breasts on both sides.

"This big guy with the short temper—did he use a name?"

"Never heard it. He was only here about an

hour, and I move around a lot when the place is busy."

"The man he left with—you remember who he was?"

"Oh, sure. Ripper Johnson from the Running R ranch. Big outfit out north of town on the river."

"So there's a chance this big guy signed on as a hand?"

"Or signed on as a shooter. Been some trouble with rustling out there. I heard that old man Johnson is hiring a few guns to do battle with the rustlers if he ever finds them. Oh, Ripper Johnson is the oldest son of the Running R ranch owner Malcom Johnson."

"Sounds like a spot I should check out tomorrow. Maybe I can locate our friend Rivers and get this job done in a hurry."

"Maybe. They aren't exactly friendly out at the Running R—never have been—and this rustling has them more tense than ever. I wouldn't want you to get shot just riding out there."

"Thanks." They sipped the whiskey and nibbled on the cheese and apples.

"Anybody else in town who might fit my description?"

"La Grande isn't a big place, Morgan. Maybe six hundred people all told. Not a lot of tall men around. Hell, the average height of men these days is only about five feet and eight inches."

He sipped the whiskey. "One thing bothers me about that hombre riding to the running R ranch. If he is Rivers, how could he stay away from the gambling tables and your fancy ladies for a month?"

"He might be going to another saloon."

"Yeah, he might. I'll be asking them tomorrow."

"Not tonight?"

Morgan reached over, unfastened the last two buttons on the front of her dress and folded back the cloth. Her breasts were large and red-tipped with darker red nipples starting to flush with hot blood and harden.

"Not tonight, Nancy. I figure that we have a hell of a lot more fun things to do tonight than take a tour of the bars."

"Like take a tour of me?"

"Figured you'd get around to giving out an invitation sooner or later. It's always better to be asked."

"I think it's about time that I show you my bedroom," Nancy said.

Chapter Three

Nancy led Morgan into her bedroom. It wasn't a whore's room, but tastefully decorated, with proper painting and wallpaper, a border around an 18-inch deep drop around the ceiling, and a bed with four posts and a canopy over the top. The bed itself had an expensive spread over it and half a dozen pillows scattered around.

She let go of his hand and turned, buttoning one fastener on her dress. Nancy pivoted back and smiled.

"I always tell my girls that a female form is ever so much more enticing and alluring if it isn't naked. Look at me. My dress covers most of me, but you can see the swell of my breasts and just the edge of one nipple. Isn't that sexy?"

"Absolutely." Morgan reached for her. She stepped away and slipped out of the top of her dress.

"Is this more sexy with my boobs hanging out?"

Morgan chuckled. "Hey, you're a damn sexy

woman, either way. Staying covered is good if
you're trying to make the sale. After the gent is
hooked, then he's gonna want to see the whole
package."

"You telling me how to run my business?" There
was a snap to her words, then she giggled. "Hey,
I'm just teasing. Come over here and let me
undress you. I still get a kick out of stripping
a man's clothes off and getting down to the good
parts."

She did.

They lay on the bed both naked now, curled
together in a kiss. He came away from her lips,
and she snuggled against his shoulder.

"You don't know how many times I wished a
man would just hold me. Now it seems like ages
ago. I don't pick up a man like you often, only
now and then when I get a real strong urge and
see a man I can't keep my hands off.

"Hey, just because I was a whore for a few
years, don't mean I lost all my sexy feelings. Hell,
that was just work. Didn't mean no more than
shaking hands or nodding at somebody on the
street."

Morgan curled one hand around her breast and
began to caress it, working slowly up to the nipple, then pinching it and twanging it. He bent and
kissed the orb, and she rubbed her hands over his
hairy chest and smiled.

"Hey, I like that. First time a man, a boy really,
ever kissed my titties I exploded all over him and
he thought he'd hurt me. Ran home so fast he
almost didn't get his overall straps over his shoulders. I was raised a farm girl so I knew all about
breeding, just never seen humans do it. Almost

did. Saw my older sister and the hired hand once in the hayloft, but then at the last minute she got scared and used her hand on him and pumped him off but never would let him inside her."

He pushed her away and onto her back, then he moved to her other breast and licked and nibbled at her nipple until she moaned in pleasure.

"Glad you like that. It's on the expensive list of services," he said. She punched him in the shoulder, then her hand went lower and found his crotch.

"You could cause problems down there," he said. "I sometimes get this large swelling."

"How large?" Her eyes sparkled.

"Bigger than anything you've ever seen."

"Show me."

"Soon," he said, and they both laughed.

She rolled on top of him then and lowered a breast into his mouth. He chewed with pleasure, finding her other orb and massaging it gently before switching and pulling it into his mouth as well.

"Damn, nobody's done that for me for years. You sure you know who I am?"

"You're a wonderful, marvelous, sensitive woman. What more is there to know?"

He could feel the heat that came from her now, as if it had been long confined and denied and now suddenly let loose.

"That feels so good, Morgan. I'm not used to getting something back from a man. You understand what I'm saying to you?"

"You're a woman with feelings and desires and ambitions just like any other woman. The problem is that you're as tight as a just wound seven day clock. How long has it been since you last had a good man?"

"Too long, damn you. A year at least."

He brought his hand up her inner thigh, and she yelped and moaned, gasping as his fingers reached her swatch of soft pubic hair.

"Oh, damn, Morgan, but that feels good. No man has pretended to seduce me since I was sixteen. They just took, never giving, just took me fast and furious like I was a chunk of meat and wanting more."

His hand brushed her nether lips and she sighed. He moved back and found her small, hard node and twanged it. She grinned. He hit it again and again as she smiled at him.

"You think I'm gonna pop just like that? You got to get me warmer than this."

"What's your pleasure? It's your party."

She slid down his body until her breasts touched his lance. Nancy pushed her orbs around his erection, then moved lower and kissed the purple tip of his prick.

"Careful," he said.

"I'm hungry near to starving." She looked up at him a minute, then licked him tip to roots before taking him in her mouth. She bobbed up and down a few times, then sucked hard until he felt the pressure. His hips jerked, and she grinned, coming off him.

"You are alive down there, after all." Nancy turned on her side facing him and lifted one leg in the air, "Now, darling Morgan, right now. I'm ready."

They came together like a pistol shot, and Nancy let out a long satisfied sigh, clamping his hips tightly with her legs and humping forward to meet his thrusts.

"Oh, yes, this is fine. My favorite position. Go, you fucker. Do me good. Poke a hole right through me. Make me feel like a real woman again."

Morgan knew he couldn't wait for her. He pushed her over on her back, lifted her legs to his shoulders and drove in deeper at this new angle.

By that time, he couldn't stop. He slammed at her and she humped back, then the sudden explosion came before he was aware it was on the way and burst from him like a cannon. He finally fell on top of her, completely spent.

She let him rest for three or four minutes, then she stirred under him and he sat up and helped her up.

"Now that was fine," Nancy said. "You got me interested there at the last. A couple more warm-ups and I think I might be able to pop myself."

"You don't make it often?" Morgan asked.

"Trained myself not to, and just fake it. The guy is happy and I get him out of my crib in half the time. More men, more dollars."

"You still have that cheese?"

Nancy laughed. "Men, you think first of your cock, then about your belly." She lifted her brows. "Hell, I guess that's about in the right order. Lots of cheese and apples. Let me cut them in half and take out the core."

He watched her, coolly efficient with a paring knife. He wondered where she came from and how she got into the business. Morgan knew from long experience that was the one thing most whores would never talk about.

"You mentioned that there was some rustler trouble. Is it bad? Lots of beef raised around here?"

"Getting to be good cow country. Not many farmers have moved in, and the dry weather farming is new to most of them. So we have ranches on most of the good valley spreads around here. Some of the ranchers have been bitching to the sheriff about losing some cattle. Not a lot, fifteen or twenty at a time, but over the months that adds up."

"What's your sheriff like?"

"Sheriff Larson? He's about sixty-two, I hear. A widower. Comes in once a month for a pop. Girls say that he usually cries. He talks to his dead wife as he's humping away and cries and complains about his hands. He doesn't wear a gun anymore. Says his right hand just won't hold on to a six-gun now."

"So he hasn't done much about the rustling?"

"He can't. Only has three deputies to cover the whole county. He's got the town to worry about and a batch of little places and ranches and a few farmers to look after. Too big a job for the sheriff, I'm afraid, but he does the best he can. At least he's an honest man."

"Sounds like just the place Chance Rivers would lite. A weak sheriff, not a lot of people. Wonder if that is him out at the Running R?"

"One good way to find out," Nancy said. "Ride out there looking for work. But that's tomorrow. Tonight you're gonna have another go at me until you get me over the goddamn hill and I blow apart."

"Tonight's the night."

"For me it is. Can your dick stand the wear and tear?"

"Be interesting to find out."

Nancy made it at the end of the fifth go-round.

The next morning, Lee Morgan woke up early, dressed and slipped out the back door of the saloon without waking up Nancy. She needed the rest. He found a café open and had the morning special—two eggs, two flapjacks, country fried potatoes, toast, jam and two cups of coffee.

A little after eight o'clock, Morgan walked into the sheriff's office. At first he thought no one was there. It was the usual: one big room with a counter across the front, two desks behind it and a door that must lead to the cells.

"Hello, anyone here?"

A silence stretched out, then a voice came from the open door.

"Just a dang minute until I get my britches on."

The voice was old with a slight crack in it, and Morgan figured it must belong to the Union County sheriff. A man came through the door a minute later with white frizzled hair, a day's growth of beard and soft blue eyes that took in Morgan in a minute, evaluated him and evidently decided he was not a threat.

"Yes, sir, young fella. What can I do for you today?"

"First get the coffee pot on that little stove before you pass out. You the sheriff?"

The older man grinned. He nodded and went to the stove where he struck a match.

"Deed that I am—Sheriff Larson of the great

county of Union here in the Grande Ronde river valley. Anything I can do for you?"

"I'm out skunk hunting and wondered if you've been smelling anything foul around your county lately?"

"You a bounty hunter?"

"No. Got no patience with that kind."

"Good. Me, too. Who you hunting?"

"Chance Rivers."

"Him? That damned gun sharp, grave robber in my county?"

"Last sniffed him in Pendleton. Figured he might be hereabouts somewhere."

"Ain't seen nor heard of him. Hope he kept going into Idaho."

"I hear the Running R is bringing in some hired guns. Rivers wouldn't be one of them, would he?"

"Hired guns? Not in my county. Won't allow it."

Morgan grinned. "Nice try, sheriff. We both know there's no way you can keep out hired guns if somebody is hiring them. Is the rustling situation that bad?"

"Rustling? Where you hear that? Not much. Just a few strays here and there."

"Fifteen or twenty a month add up in a year's time. You got cattle, you have rustling. Just how bad is it?"

The sheriff squinted at Morgan from one eye and blew on the fire. "Sure you ain't some kind of range detective or something out here to cause trouble?"

"Just looking up my old friend Chance Rivers, that's all."

"Sure you are, and I'm a gunsharp about ready

to take on Billy The Kid." He closed the door on the firebox and positioned the coffee pot. "Should be ready in about ten minutes. Now, let's sit down and put our cards on the table, young man. If you've got a badge, I want to see it. If you're something else I want to know. Then maybe, just maybe, we can do some work together on this. I like the way you got that six-gun hung low and tied down. Just maybe we can do business."

Morgan sat in the chair beside the desk, and the old sheriff slid into the other one. Morgan explained that he had a job to bring in Chance Rivers to stand trial in Portland.

"Well, now, I can't say as I see how that's any different than being a bounty hunter, but I'm not a man to quibble. If Rivers is in the county, I'd just as soon see him gone, one way or another."

The sheriff looked up and combed his fingers back through his white hair. "You really think you can take Rivers back to Portland alive?"

"That's my job and I aim to do it."

"You think Rivers might have hired on out at the Running R?"

"Possible. Cheaper to hire a couple of good gunmen than to lose fifteen cattle a month. Course the Running R is the biggest outfit in the area, right?"

"True."

"So is it possible that this Johnson could be doing the rustling himself, mixing in the cattle with his and shipping them?"

"Possible, but I know Malcom Johnson, and it ain't gonna happen. He's tough as an old mule skinner, but he's no rustler."

"Worth a shot. How do I find this place?"

Morgan listened while the sheriff showed him on a county map how to get to the Running R ranch.

"About five miles out along the river. Can't miss it. I hear there might be outriders along the road, so don't be surprised if you pick up a warning rifle shot over your head. Just a friendly warning to hove to and let them ride up to you."

"Sounds reasonable," Morgan said. They shook hands.

"I don't aim to give you no trouble while I'm here, Sheriff Larson. Just wanted to get the lay of the land a little."

"Much obliged. Good meeting you. Best of luck with Chance Rivers. Things get too sticky, I got a pair of deputies who can handle shotguns right well."

Lee Morgan nodded and walked back to the street. He looked around for the livery stable which was usually at the edge of a town, one end or the other. He stared one way, turned the other and ran smack dab into someone.

"Oh, sorry!" Morgan said. His hands shot out and grabbed the other person's shoulders. It turned out to be a pert young lady with a blue hat and a blue dress and dimples that seemed never to stop.

"Oh, my goodness," she said. "It was my fault. I heard a friend call and looked back. I wasn't looking where I was going."

He still held her shoulders, and she grinned and looked down at his hands.

"I think I can stand up now unassisted," she said, her grin growing into a full-blown smile. He saw teasing green eyes, thick black hair and a perfect nose over lips that he suspected had been enhanced just a little with some raspberry juice. She made a picture pretty enough to paint.

"Oh, sorry." He let go of her shoulders and edged back a little. "It was my fault. I was looking for the livery stable."

"You're new in town. Welcome to La Grande. We try to make visitors feel at home here. My name is Priscilla Parmley."

She looked at him and held out her hand.

"Oh, I'm Lee Morgan. I'm pleased to meet you, even if it had to be through a collision here on Main Street."

She laughed, and the dimples came back. When she shook his hand, he wasn't keen on letting go.

"It was good to run into you, Mr. Morgan. Now, I really must go see my friend up the street." She turned, took two steps away, then looked back. "Good-bye, Mr. Morgan."

"Yes, good-bye, Miss Parmley."

Morgan grinned as she walked away. He swore that she put a little extra wiggle into her hips as she moved down the street. She was slender, the pretty blue dress setting off her small waist perfectly. Maybe he'd see Miss Parmley around town again.

He saw a sign at the south end of town that touted the Wilson Brothers' Livery and headed that way.

Ten minutes later he had hired a horse and saddle, mounted up and took further directions from the stable hand how to find the Running R ranch.

"Don't think they're hiring right now, but it

ain't a long ride," the young man with the pitch-
fork said. "Maybe five mile out there along the
river. Can't miss it."

Everytime he heard the phrase, "Can't miss it,"
he paid special attention to the particulars. Too
often he had missed the mark.

He rode due west following a wagon track along
the Grande Ronde river. The high dry Oregon
eastern plateau took on a decidedly green tinge
along the river which rose in the Blue Mountains
west of La Grande and the high Wallowa Mountains to the east. The river picked up drainage
along the route and soon headed due north, then
northeast, and after another 150 miles dumped
into the mighty Snake river.

He soon saw cattle roaming the land, working
back from the greener grass along the river to the
spring fresh grass of the flat lands. He was headed
for the junction of the Grande Ronde river and
Catherine Creek, a smaller stream from the south
that drained the western sides of the Wallowa
Mountains before feeding into the larger river.

He passed one small operation on the far side
of the river and then rode around another larger
outfit before he came to the gate on the end of
the wagon track that said, "Running R Ranch".

Morgan turned into the lane and could see the
ranch buildings a half mile ahead.

When he had proceeded another 100 yards a
rifle round slammed over his head, and he ducked
and stopped his horse. He certainly hoped that
it would be the welcoming party that the sheriff
spoke about.

Chapter Four

Jed Bradburn rolled into La Grande about ten o'clock. It was the first time he'd been in town two days in a row in over a year. His arm was giving him lots of pain, and he'd forgotten to get shotgun shells the day before.

Doc Fetterman took off the bandage and examined the wound. He probed a little and shook his head.

"Damn if I didn't miss a piece of lead in there. Figured the round went straight through." He told Jed to grit his teeth and used a thin wirelike probe that he pushed into the bullet hole. Jed almost passed out. By the time Jed had his senses about him and opened his eyes, the chunk of lead was out of his arm and Doc had cleaned out the wound and put some salve on it. Then he put on a new bandage.

"No heavy lifting with that left arm for two weeks," Doc told him.

"Yeah, sure, Doc. No heavy lifting. None required on a ranch, especially a small spread like mine with only three hands and a cook." He paid the medic a dollar, drove the buckboard across the dusty street and parked the rig in front of McMurphy's General Store.

Jed tied the reins and went inside the establishment. McMurphy's was the first store in town when it was little more than the river crossing on the Oregon Trail. The store had started small, developed slowly, moved from a tent to a cabin and then to a frame store. Later they added on and even bought up a small store next door and knocked out the wall.

Oliver McMurphy had two sons who helped him with clerking and running the store. They were stocking shelves and pricing new goods when Jed walked in. The boys waited on customers when their dad was too busy.

"That man or woman who walks through our front door is the most important person in our store," McMurphy had drilled into his two sons. "Without that buyer, all of our other work here is for nothing."

True to his principles, McMurphy hurried forward as soon as he heard the little bell ring that he had attached to the front door.

"Ah, it's the up and coming cattle baron, Mr. Bradburn. How goes the beef production today?" McMurphy was short and thickset, with a red beard that was three shades darker red than his hair which had faded near to reddish brown in his forty-second year. Green eyes snapped, and he showed a big grin as he held out his hand. McMurphy was a toucher, enjoying the physical contact of a handshake or a hug from the ladies.

"Beef are growing every day, but it's another year to market time. Forgot to get shotgun shells yesterday. Damn rabbits are driving me crazy. I hear somebody is talking about making fence wire with twisted little barbs on it every few inches. You hear about that, McMurphy?"

"Deed I haven't. But if it comes out in the next few years, I'll get some. What you need with fences, anyway? You gonna become a sod buster?"

"For about half an acre. I try to fence in the garden down in that low place by the creek. Biscuits got furious this spring when half of his sweet corn crop got eaten just before the ears set on."

McMurphy laughed and looked. "You used them three-tined pitchforks you bought yesterday? You going into the hay business, Jed?"

"Thinking on it. Got some low places along the creek we could mow and then have winter hay if the snow gets too deep. More of that is going on, these days."

"Even the cows are getting finicky," McMurphy growled. "I like them pure Texas Longhorns. They're so mean and tough they can live over the winter on a handful of sage brush and some weeds they paw up out of the snow."

"That's progress, I guess. I just wish you could figure some way to feed out one of those Longhorns in less than three or four years. Then I'd get some of them. I'm happy with the cross bred stock I have now."

Jed waved and headed out to the buckboard. He drove the rig down to the blacksmith who also ran the livery stable.

Jed had come out from Portland three years ago with enough money to start his small ranch. He moved into what he considered prime grazing land with water along Catherine Creek and ran advertisements in the newspaper every week for six weeks, claiming possessory rights to the lands for 20 miles along the creek and 20 miles on each side of the stream. The ads had no legal standing, but they looked like legal ads and they worked.

As soon as he got situated, Jed signed up for his homestead along Catherine Creek. He had two entrymen homesteads, adjoining 160 acre parcels with the understanding they would sell out to Jed on demand for one dollar. Both were actually cowhands on his ranch. This was a well-established practice.

The homesteading parcel itself was unusual. He had his land survey laid out along the flow of Catherine Creek, one acre wide, 200 feet by 160 acres long. The strip covered a little over 6 miles of the river. The three homesteads they put together end to end, reached up Catherine Creek for 18 miles. Jed controlled the water, so he controlled the use of the land for grazing.

Now with the help of his lawyer he owned all 480 acres of the homesteads. There was a commutation clause in the homestead act that permitted any homesteader to buy up the land after he has lived there six months. He paid $1.25 per acre to the federal government and owned the land outright without having to prove up on the homestead for five years.

Jed had provided the entrymen with the $200 each to buy up their homesteads, then after the papers came through, Jed had bought the land

from the men for the agreed upon price of one
dollar.

Jed pulled up in front of the livery stable and
went in to see the blacksmith. Big Gus evened up
a horseshoe on the anvil with a few whacks with
his heavy hammer and looked up.

"Hey, Jed, I got them new branding irons for
you. Making that damn circle is more trouble
than it's worth."

Jed paid him for the six new branding irons
and loaded them in the rig, then he drove the
loaded buckboard back half a block and parked
near the Wildcat Saloon. Right next door was his
lawyer's office. Jed got down from the rig, tied the
reins and went to see his long-time friend and
counselor.

His name was Larry Sheeler, but over the years
he had found so many ways to get around the law,
legally, that he had been nicknamed Loophole.
The name stuck. Jed pushed open the door and
waved.

"Come on, Loophole, looks like you could use
a cold beer."

Sheeler glanced up from some papers on his
desk and threw his pencil into the air as he pretended to faint. "Lord Almighty, he's risen from
the dead! Haven't seen you for two months, so I
figured you cashed in your chips in that big poker
game in the sky."

"You do need a drink," Jed said. "Come on."

Sheeler laughed and stood up. He was a big man
at six foot two and 220 pounds. A thick, brown
moustache covered his upper lip and matched the
color of his neatly cut hair. He wore dark-rimmed
spectacles and had a small muscle tic on his right

cheek that usually got going when he was in the courtroom.

"Hell, why not? I don't understand this case. Maybe a break will give me a fresh look at it. What the hell you been doing for loving, sneaking up on those young heifers out there on the range?"

"Loophole, you know how fast they are. Not a chance."

Loophole closed his door, locked it and put up a sign that said he'd be right back, then they walked next door to the Wildcat Saloon.

It looked the same. It had a floor that needed sweeping, a bar that had been polished and varnished and repolished again. There were half a dozen tables for drinking or playing cards, but no house games. Three fancy girls rested at a table in back, and when they saw who the new patrons were, they waved and went back to chatting, knowing neither man would be a customer for the cribs upstairs.

Nancy waved at them from the tall stool at the end of the bar. It was her throne and nobody else sat on it.

"Nancy just keeps rolling along and raking in the cash," Loophole said. "She's got her fortune made right here, you know that?"

"Is it true she won this place in a poker game?" Jed asked.

"Hell, yes. She was a whore here before then, a damn good dance hall girl. For a year now she's been running the place."

Nancy slid off the stool and walked toward them. She was nicely dressed, like any matron on the street. Jed guessed she was about 35 but she looked older. She wore only a little make up and kept her hair set and combed out so it gave her a blonde halo around her face.

"Hi, gents. Looks like a convention or a revolution. Count me in if it's a revolt."

Jed and Loophole stood up at once. She smiled, sat at their table, and then they dropped back in their chairs. A tear rolled down her cheek.

"Damn, I can't remember when a man stood up for me that way. Must have been in Laramie about ten years ago. True. Us whores don't get that kind of respect very damn often."

"Watch out, Jed, she's in a mood again," Loophole said half in jest. "Whenever Nancy calls herself a whore, your ear bones are in for a beating."

Nancy wiped the wetness from her cheek, frowned slightly at Loophole and turned to Jed.

"Hope things are doing well for you out on the Circle B, Jed. This is what—your third year out there?"

"Halfway through the third."

"Getting started is a killer. I know cattle. No steers ready to sell for three to four full years, right? So what are you doing for income? Takes some cash money to buy groceries."

"Had some savings."

"That takes a damn lot of ready cash." Nancy frowned. "Next July you can make a drive. You able to hold out until then?"

"Hope so. I'm bound to have a tab run up here and there around town."

"Come on, Jed. You don't have to do that. You need a few thousand, you come see Nancy. You hear?"

Jed lifted his brows. "Well, thanks for the confidence. I'm not at that point yet, but I'll sure remember it."

"Good." Nancy waved at the barkeep, Zack, and he brought over three cold bottles of beer.

"On the house," Nancy said. She sipped her beer and looked at Jed. "Some people say whoring and drinking money is dirty. Hope you don't think so. My cash is just as clean as a dressmaker's or a boarding house lady's or a guy running a general store or even some damn shyster lawyer.

"Hey, you guys remember Charlene, the little redhead who looked like she was about fourteen? She was really twenty-six. Anyway I got her married to a guy over in Bend. He used to live here and moved over there with some critters. Damn glad for little Charlene."

"You ever getting married, Nancy?" Loophole asked.

"Hell, too late for me. I'm a whore and a madam and a saloon owner. You know I never played a hand of poker since I won this place? I figure I got to quit while I'm ahead. What a damn winning streak that was!"

"You really won this place playing poker, Nancy?" Jed asked.

"Really. No cheating. New deck, shirt sleeves rolled up, and we stood up at the bar. Old Will had lost two hundred dollars to me, and he figured he had to get back at me. He goes in with a full house on five card draw game, aces over kings. I caught a fourth deuce on a two card draw for four of a kind. I bet all I had, six hundred, and Old Will put up the saloon to cover me and called. I laid down my hand. Will looked at my four deuces, near had a heart attack, then laid down his hand face up, gave me the keys to the front and back doors and walked away. Nobody in town ever saw him again. Went to Portland, I hear."

They all sipped their beer.

"You gents talking business?"

"My only business now is one more cold beer," Jed said. "I don't have an ice house."

"You should make one," Nancy said. "Then you could keep fresh meat for a week, keep your milk and cream and butter from spoiling. Hell, make a little box and put it in your kitchen to hold the ice in the top on a metal rack. Then below put your milk and meat."

"Maybe next year," Jed said. It was a good idea. They had plenty of ice in the winter. They could dig a little pond and let it fill up.

"I heard they're talking about running you for mayor, Loophole." Nancy said. "That true?"

Loophole laughed. "Not a word of truth in it. In a small town I'll never be mayor. That office makes too many enemies. I want to be everyone's friend, so I can get enough business to stay alive."

"Thinking business," Jed said. "A guy in jail now might need a lawyer. He bushwhacked me five miles out of town. I'm charging him with attempted murder."

Loophole kicked over his chair he stood up so fast. "I better get right down there and talk to him before somebody else does."

"Finish your beer, Loophole," Nancy said. "You're the only lawyer in town."

"True, but you never can tell." He took another pull at the beer, thanked Nancy and hurried out of the saloon.

"He's half-crazy," Nancy said.

"Have to be half-crazy to live in La Grande. Hot summers and cold winters." Nancy nodded. He finished the beer. "I better get moving. Thanks for the brew."

"Welcome. Nice to talk to a real person for a change. You come back."

Jed waved and walked out to the street. As he went toward his rig he saw a woman standing there tapping a small foot on the boardwalk near his buckboard. It was Priscilla Parmley, daughter of the town's only banker and one of the men who founded the city. She saw him and watched him walk up as if she had been waiting for him for hours.

"Mr. Bradburn, I'm glad you came back, I've been waiting for you."

"Yes, Miss Parmley, I can see that. Am I over-drawn on my account or something?"

She laughed and shook her head. She was small and cute as a ladybug on a petunia. "No, nothing like that. It's not business, it's social."

She looked up at him and smiled while he just stood there and watched her.

"I'm having this dinner party for sixteen Saturday night. Actually my mother is having it, but I'm going and we've come out uneven. I mean, we have one more woman than we do men." She looked at him again but he said nothing. "So, I'm wondering if you'll come to our dinner and even out our sixteen? All of the best people in town will be there."

Jed scratched the boardwalk with the toe of his boot, then looked at her. "Miss Parmley, I'm afraid I'm not much good at dinner parties. Definitely I'm not one of the town's best people. I wouldn't know what to do or even what to say."

She took a step toward him, and he could smell some kind of interesting perfume. Her thick black hair shined in the sunlight, and her eyes sparkled.

"Now, Mr. Bradburn, there's nothing to it. All we do is eat and talk. I know you can do both. It would be a real big favor to me if you could come. A special favor."

Jed cleared his throat and looked at his rig, then back at the pretty girl. He'd seen her around town and decided she was the loveliest little thing in the county. But a dinner party?

"Sixteen. Sounds like people are paired up. If I did say I might come, who might this extra old maid be I'd have to sit beside?"

"I know it would be a strain on you, but the old maid is me." She laughed and looked away. "Now you're going to embarrass me. I really want you to come. When I heard you were in town, I tracked you down. I'll be just so embarrassed that I'll die if you don't come. Then you'll have to attend my funeral and it'll be all your fault. My daddy will probably run you out of the county or maybe bring in a hired gunsharp."

Jed laughed. "Let's not let it go that far, Miss Parmley. Sounds like I'll save us all a lot of trouble if I come."

"Oh, that's just grand! I'm so glad."

"Do I have to wear a suit?"

"Probably. The other men will."

"Do I have to wear shoes, too?"

"Yes, and even your britches!" She laughed and grinned at him. "I'm so pleased you'll come. It's Saturday night at six-thirty at Daddy's house on the slope. I'll watch for you." She reached out and touched his shoulder. "Thanks, Jed." Priscilla turned and hurried up the boardwalk toward the La Grande First National Bank.

Jed looked down at his clothing. He hadn't bothered to get dressed up to come to town. He had on his old boots, a pair of dirty blue jeans, an old blue shirt, his roundup sweat-stained leather vest and his working hat. Damn, he must look a mess. Now being so close to a pretty girl he felt sweaty and dirty. He was sure he hadn't washed well when he left the ranch and he hadn't . . . Jed shook his head and swung up on his buckboard seat. He was acting like some love sick calf.

Jed snorted and whacked the reins on the back of the roan to urge her forward. It had been quite a morning. Now he was anxious to hurry back to the Circle B and get on with his ranching.

Chapter Five

Lee Buckskin Morgan sat motionless on the horse as he waited. Two or three minutes later he heard the sound of hooves pounding toward him. He turned his head and saw a mount coming at a trot. The man astride carried a rifle pointing at the sky.

He reined in 15 feet away and stared at Morgan.

"Don't know you, stranger. What the hell you doing riding down the Running R lane?"

"Looking for work. Somebody in town said Mr. Johnson might be looking for some hands."

"Ain't likely. We got enough help now."

"Is it possible that Mr. Johnson has some plans you don't know about?"

The cowboy frowned, moved the rifle from the sky position and poked it into the boot.

"Yeah, I reckon it's possible. But the ramrod told me to turn away any saddle bums who come sniffing around."

"I look like a saddle bum to you, cowboy?"

"No sir."

"Then I suggest that you lead me through any other booby traps you have out here and take me up to the ranch house so I can talk to Mr. Johnson."

"Can't do that. Just flat out can't do that and keep my job. The ramrod said—."

The cowhand looked on in amazement as Morgan's hand darted to leather. The cowboy tried to draw as well, but Morgan had his six-gun out and centered the muzzle on the other man's chest before the rifle cleared leather.

"Ease the iron back in your holster and let's ride up to the big house," Morgan said. "No offense, since you were just following orders. They happen to be orders I don't like and won't abide."

The half mile ride to the ranch house went smoothly. The cowboy didn't say a word. Morgan had him ride ahead and slightly to his right. When they neared the house, Morgan put away the six-gun but the cowboy didn't know it. The two mounts stopped short of the back door.

"Go tell the owner I'm here. The name is Lee Morgan."

The cowboy slid off his horse and hurried up to the door without looking back.

A few minutes later, a lantern-jawed, dark-haired and pot-bellied man came on the porch and stared at Morgan. He wore spectacles, had red suspenders holding up his jeans, and a rusty colored shirt.

"What the hell you doing on my ranch?"

"You must be Johnson. If you are, I hear you're

looking for a man who can work a horse and is good with a six-gun and rifle. I'm both."

"How good, how fast?"

"Ask your lookout."

"He told me." Johnson frowned, then shrugged. "Hell, light a spell and get out of the hot sun."

Morgan stepped off his mount and walked up the six steps to the porch.

"You been riding long?"

"Long enough to put a few notches in my rifle stock."

"Where abouts?"

"Here and there, around and back again."

Johnson chuckled. "Like a man who's close-mouthed, plays his cards next to his vest. No big trouble around here, but could be. Somebody making off with cattle. Few at a time, but every few days. Counts up fast. Lately they've been rustling prime steers ready for market."

"Fast turnover."

"Too damn fast. I'm about ready to set some traps, but I need good men."

"How much you pay?"

"Going rate for gunhands. Twenty dollars a month plus found."

Morgan stood from where he had sat on the step. "Sorry, not my kind of deal. I don't get shot at for no twenty dollars a month. Your cowhands make thirty."

"So how much do you want?"

"Going rate from where I come from is a hundred."

"Out of the question."

"That's what you paid the last gun you hired." Morgan was fishing but playing a hunch.

"He's a special case."

"He have a reputation?"

"Nobody I'd ever heard of, but he put on a demonstration. Impressive."

"Fine, I'll meet him in a shoot-out at targets. Who can knock over the most cans at thirty feet with a six-gun. Then we keep backing up until somebody wins."

Johnson rubbed his long jaw, then his face and wound up shaking his head. "Nope. He's good. He stays. I can't afford two. I don't back down on a deal, so you get to move on."

"Fine, I'll find him in town and beat him there."

"Won't matter unless you kill him. Then you'll wind up in jail and I won't have no gun at all."

"Want to think it again, Johnson?"

"Nope, said my mind was made up. Best you ride back to town. Oh, my man won't be spending any time in town. I got everything he needs right here."

"A woman?"

"I got him two. Now you best be moving back to La Grande."

Checkmated, hogtied and knocked out of the saddle. Morgan nodded, walked down the steps and out to his horse. He mounted and rode out, knowing that he had lost the best chance to discover if the gunhand who Johnson hired was Chance Rivers. Now he'd have to do it some other way. Exactly how he hadn't figured out yet.

The ride back to town seemed longer than going out. What the hell did he do now? He had a possible lead, but the man was ensconced behind armed guards roving the ranch, evidently housed somewhere with hot and cold running women and all he wanted to eat and drink. But who was he?

Gunman, gunsharp, killer, brawler, rapist? Yes, Chance Rivers might settle for women and food and whiskey and ease off a little. He wouldn't have to worry about his trail or about any lawman coming from Portland to find him. No wanted posters out on him yet. Hell, why not sit there and see if there was going to be a range war? He was making a hundred a month for having all the good things and probably didn't do a lick of work.

Morgan had a strong hunch he had found his man, but how did he make certain, then go in and haul him back to Portland?

Back in town he turned in his horse at the livery, then stopped in the Wildcat Saloon for a cold beer. Nancy wasn't there. He drank his beer and headed for the hotel. He hadn't had a good hot bath in a week. It would feel good.

After his long bath, it was food time, so he walked the street for half a block and turned in at the Ochoco Café.

He was about to sit down at a table when the young girl he had bumped into that morning came up to him.

"Mr. Morgan, I wondered if you could help me. I have a friend who's having trouble with rustlers, and from the looks of you, I figured you're the kind of man who could help him."

"Miss Parmley, nice to see you again. Rustlers?"

"Yes, come and meet him. He's just heading out of town, but he has to come past here and we can catch him." She paused, her pretty face turning anxious.

"That is, if you're interested."

"I am interested in the rustling. Where is this young man?"

On the street they saw a rig coming toward them. Priscilla Parmley walked three steps into the dusty roadway and held up her hand. The rig slowed down and came to a stop.

"Jed, I need to talk to you," she said, and the young man tied the reins and stepped down from the light wagon.

"Yes, Miss Parmley, what's the trouble?"

"Oh, Jed, no trouble really. I want you to meet a new man in town I thought might be able to help with your rustling problem." She turned and motioned Morgan forward.

"Lee Morgan, I'd like you to meet my friend Jed Bradburn. He has a ranch outside of town a ways on Catherine Creek. Jed, this is Lee Morgan."

The men shook hands and then both looked at Priscilla.

"Well, it seemed like a good idea." She pouted prettily for a moment, then she set her jaw and hooded her eyes. "Now, Jed, you know you're having some trouble with the rustlers. You don't have enough men to go after them. I thought maybe Mr. Morgan could ride out and take a look at what happened and maybe give you some advice or some help." She turned pleading eyes toward Morgan.

"Jed, I'm not real busy right now. How many head have you lost?"

"Mr. Morgan, I have a small spread. If I lose twenty head it puts a big dent in my herd. I lost five two nights ago. This is the third time. From what I could read on the tracks, three riders cut them out and drove them to the east, up into the fringes of the Wallowa Mountains. Can't figure that out."

"What's up there?"

"Nothing but about sixty miles of wilderness all the way over to Wallowa Lake. No roads or trails, no cabins or ranches. Nothing but wild country."

"Must have a holding area," Morgan said. "Gather bunches from all around, then make a run for a market."

"The railroad is a long way off," Jed said. "Have to drive them nigh into Portland to find a buyer."

"Mr. Morgan," Priscilla said, "would you ride out to Jed's ranch and look at the tracks? Maybe you could make something out of them."

"Well, If Jed wants me to."

Jed toed the dust on the boardwalk and nodded. "Reckon I'd appreciate it. I can't pay you, understand. Me and cash money are nigh on to strangers."

"Nobody said anything about pay, Jed. I'm interested in this cattle rustling from another angle. Yes, I think I might like to go out to your place and see where those cattle vanished. Can you wait until I rent a horse down at the stable?"

"Sure, Mr. Morgan," Jed said.

He tipped his hat to Priscilla and started off toward the livery. This might be one way to get inside the Johnson place. If he could come up with the whys and hows of the rustling, old man Johnson would be glad to talk to him again and even show off his gunman since there would be no more use for him.

It turned out to be a ten mile ride to Jed's place. They wound along a scratch trail southwest of La Grande until they hit Catherine Creek, then it was only a half mile more. The country was green near the stream, still chattering and full from the spring rains high in the Wallowa Mountains and from the melting snow pack.

"Gives us all the water we need all summer for the herd," Jed said. "We have about seven hundred head now with the spring drop. Next year we should move close to a thousand. Then we'll make a drive with our market-ready steers— if we have any left by that time."

They drove the wagon into the ranch where a man with an apron around his waist and a greasy shirt came out, waved when he saw no supplies on the wagon and went back inside the cook shack.

"I'll get a horse and we can go out right now before it gets dark. You can bunk in here for the night and have supper."

Morgan nodded and looked around the spread. It had two small barns, a pole corral that had seen some horse breaking, and a fenced area down by the creek which must be the ranch garden. The place had been well cared for. In time it could become a big ranch.

Jed came on a bay, and they rode due west toward the blue ridges which must be the foothills of the Wallowa Mountains. Some of them were over 9,000 feet high. La Grande sat in a valley of 2,700 feet.

"Any other ranches around here?" Morgan asked.

"One downstream near where Catherine runs

into the Grande Ronde. Guy by the name of Yank Vanderzanden lives there. A Dutchman. Good rancher. He's been losing some cattle, too."

They rode in silence. Morgan had been seeing cattle for the past hour. Now he saw some that were sleek and fat and looked nearly ready for market.

"Most of these steers will be ready in the spring," Jed said. "I'll probably make a drive over through Pendleton and see if I can contact some buyer over there. Somebody said there was one there last year. Wish we had a railhead there, but it's all tied up in politics somehow."

They rode another four or five miles, came to a small ridgeline and turned northwest.

After another half mile Jed got down from his mount and pointed at a small trail beaten into the grass and sod.

"Near as I can tell there were five or six head in this line moving north and west along the edge of the foothills here. I followed them for a mile and a half, and they just seemed to vanish into thin air.

"Did you find a spot near there with more droppings than usual on the trail?"

Jed scowled, then nodded. "Come to think on it, I'd say that there were lots more droppings than normal."

"Like several of the steers had been kept there for an hour or more, maybe three or four hours."

Jed nodded. "So?"

"So, it means that the rustlers probably herded them there, then roped them and took them one at a time in a different roundabout way to a holding pen. Makes it look like the trail ends right there, and it does, but there are half a dozen smaller trails leading out from it. Let's go have a closer look."

A short time later, Morgan looked at the droppings and went out 20 yards and began making a half circle around the northwest side of the manure.

Within five minutes he picked up the first sign. He whistled, and Jed came running up. Morgan pointed out the shod hooves of the horse and the dragging steps of the steer.

"See how the steer hooves scuff the dirt in a forward direction?" Morgan asked. "Usually means the animal has been roped and is being half-dragged forward. After a hundred yards or so the steer will give up resisting and trot or walk along behind the horse with little resistance, and the scuff marks will vanish."

Morgan tracked them on foot, and Jed ran back for the two horses. A quarter of a mile out, another set of tracks met and laid down over the first set.

A half mile farther on, Jed saw a new set of tracks coming in from the side, and they soon overlapped the first two.

"Shouldn't be far now," Morgan said. He was wrong. A mile farther along they found all six sets of tracks had merged back into one trail and the animals had been bedded down for the night. Beyond the bedding down spot, they saw where the trail picked up again with six head of steers and three riders.

The sun had rimmed the far peaks of the Blue Mountains far to the west.

"Time we head for home," Jed said. "We'll pick

up the trail tomorrow if you have the time."

"Think I'll take the time, Jed. If I can find the rustlers, it should solve a problem of mine."

On the ride back, Morgan inquired about the pretty little brunette.

"Is this girl, Priscilla, sweet on you, Jed?"

"Never thought about it much. Guess she is. Invited me to a dinner at her house with some other folks. I got to wear a suit."

Morgan chuckled. "Might not be so bad. All you do at one of them fancy dinners is eat and talk. I'd wager that you can do both."

"I reckon, but I need to wear a suit. Got one, but it's nigh on to four years old."

"Should work."

They rode the rest of the way in silence, and when they got in, the cook had chow ready for them. Supper was potatoes, beans and ham hocks, and biscuits with lots of black coffee.

"There's a spare room in the house for you to bunk in," Jed said. "No sheets but got plenty of blankets. I'm right glad that you'll be looking for them damn rustlers. You got farther already than I did or could have."

Morgan turned in with a groan. He figured he'd ridden more than 30 miles that day, and he went to sleep at once.

They rode out of the ranch the next morning just after daybreak with sandwiches in saddle-bags and a canteen filled with coffee they would heat up for lunch.

The spot they stopped at the day before still carried the trail, even though the wind had faded the prints a little, filled in a few more and wiped them out on a rocky stretch.

The trail wound around a small hill, slanted behind another one and up a small valley, then over a little rise into another valley, but there the tracks really did vanish.

This time there were no droppings or faded hoofprints. Sheetrock covered this end of the valley, as if some mad builder had put down a rock floor for a gigantic building that remained uncompleted.

The granite sheetrock covered the valley for half a mile in two directions. There might be prints on the far side, and there might not. From this small valley there were three directions the cattle could have been driven. One was up the valley past the sheetrock into the grassy turf, but no cattle were visible. There seemed to be no outlet on that end where the land sloped up into the foothills.

To the left, the sheetrock ended in an abrupt cliff that lifted 200 feet straight up from the floor. No way out there. The only other route was to the right, which would go back the way they had come only farther east and deeper into the mountains.

"Only chance we have is to try to the right," Morgan said. "Let's take a look."

They worked over the sheetrock slowly, and when they came back to the sod, both got off their mounts and studied the edge of the rock and the grassy valley. No tracks leaped out at them. Morgan worked slowly along the 200 yards of rock edge and grass but found no steer or horseshoe tracks.

He took off his low crowned hat, wiped away the sweat and tried again.

Nothing.

He sat on the grass and chewed a stem of grass. Jed came up leading the two horses.

"Where the hell did they vanish to?" Jed asked.

"We'll take a look at the other two possibilities, but the chances of finding any tracks are less than good. How about moving over there to that little grove of trees, make a fire to heat up that coffee and have our lunch?"

After lunch they rode to the far end of the grassy valley that lifted into the foothills and searched the timbered far slopes. Again they could find no trace of horse or steer hooves.

The land rose sharply into a ridgeline that was part of a towering peak that must go at least 7,000 feet. They retraced their tracks to the third possibility.

For ten minutes they stared up at the sheer rock wall. Nothing could go up there. The end of the valley was choked with brush and the start of pine and fir, but there were no tracks anywhere.

"End of the line," Morgan said. "How often do you lose stock up here?"

"Three times so far. Near as I can tell it was about a week apart each time."

"The last time was four days ago?"

"About."

"Then the only way I see we can nail down these rustlers is to leave someone up here along the known route and wait for them and then follow them right into the holding pen, wherever the hell that is."

"Let them rustle another bunch?"

"Only way I can see. But that shouldn't be for three more days. You have a man who could handle that? He'd have to come out just at dusk, find himself a good spot, hide in some brush, then sit and wait and not go to sleep. Night work."

"I can ask, but I don't think I have a man who could do it."

"That leaves me, I'd say," Morgan said with a snort. "Reckon I can invest a night or two out here waiting and watching. Now about all we can do is get back to the ranch."

"What day is it today?" Jed asked.

"Friday."

"Oh, damn. That makes tomorrow night Saturday and I have that dinner party."

Morgan laughed. "Don't worry about it. Put on your suit, comb your hair and enjoy yourself. The food should be worth the trip. Also there is the lovely Miss Parmley as well to enjoy."

Jed nodded, a slow smile spreading over his rugged face. "Yeah, that's going to be the best part of the evening."

Chapter Six

Back at the ranch, Morgan arranged to come out Sunday afternoon to set up for his night watch on the cattle. He'd take food along to keep him awake and have an afternoon nap.

As Morgan headed for town, Jed watched him go and thought about his first days on the ranch. Three years ago Jed had ridden over half the country around La Grande. He had been hunting for the ideal cattle spread and found what he considered the best location in the whole area. One big cattle operator also looked at the area at about the same time, but decided there wouldn't be enough water in Catherine Creek during a dry summer for the 20,000 head he figured to have in a few years.

He moved on, and Jed pounded in his stakes with Public Notice signs that the land was occupied and controlled by him and the Circle B ranch. Any and all trespassers would be dealt with harshly. Then he pounded in his first homestead stakes and had it surveyed and legally filed.

When he drove in a herd of 200 brood cows and 16 range bulls to service them from a place over in Montana, he decided he was in the ranching business. Two of the men who helped him on the drive stayed on including Kit Cranston, his foreman.

Kit was only 24 but grew up on a ranch and learned to ride as soon as he could walk. He knew the cattle business from breeding to shipping and had become a good friend as well. Kit was one of the two who had been entrymen for homesteads that helped give Jed control of 18 miles of the river.

Kit was short and stocky, tough as weathered leather, a top hand, an excellent rider and got along well with the other cowboys. He was also left-handed and had red hair which made him the butt of a few jokes which he took good-naturedly. By the time he was 21 he figured he should be foreman on his father's big spread in Montana. The elder Cranston told him no, not until he was 25.

When Kit said he was leaving, his father said not unless he could whip his old man. So Kit did. He picked one evening when his father just got back from a long ride to town and was exhausted. Then it was no contest. Kit's father admitted defeat, gave his son $100 and told him to write his mother every week. Kit had done so for three years now.

When he started the ranch three years ago, the first thing Jed did was use the chuck wagon to haul in logs from the pine timbered slopes of the

Wallowa Mountains to the east. It was a seven mile trip one way, but within a month they had enough logs to build the ranch house. Jed hired a carpenter from La Grande who had made log houses before, and the 20 by 40 foot structure went up quickly and without any problems.

It had a kitchen, a living room and three small bedrooms. A big fireplace on the side of the living room heated most of the house. The kitchen had a small cast-iron kitchen range and an indoor pump to a well the men dug the second day they were there. The plank floor in the kitchen had a trap door the same size as the well for access to it when needed.

After nearly three years they had built a barn, two corrals, the ranch house and the start of a bunkhouse that would be 16 x 30 feet with room for 20 to 25 hands if they ever needed that many.

Jed went back to the kitchen for another cup of coffee. They called the cook Biscuits, since that's what he wanted them to do. He said it was because that was the best thing he ever baked. He was of medium build but shrinking with age. He wouldn't tell them how old he was, but Jed guessed he was well over 60. He limped on his right leg and said his knee didn't work none too good anymore.

Biscuits wore a full gray beard which he trimmed once a year. His eyebrows were shaggy as well, and he let his gray hair grow long around his shoulders so he sometimes looked like a whirlwind. He had lost most of his teeth but was what he called an expert gummer when it came to food.

Biscuits had green eyes that sparkled when he

told one of his long-winded stories. He filled Jed's cup again and squinted up at him.

"Say, did I ever tell you about the time in Billings that I collared this gent who was weighing short? He worked in this feed store next to the livery, and city folks bought hay and oats there for their horses. One day this old maid come in to get her usual ten pounds of oats. Nobody knew why the old maid had a horse, but some folks said she took him out at night and rode him astride bareback without her underpants on and got herself a real thrill. Anyway, she come in to old Bartholemew's place and asked for her ten pounds of oats. Bart weighed them out, then threw in an extra handful. . . ." Biscuits watched as Jed stood and eased away from the table.

"Gol dangit, where you going, Jed? I'm just coming to the good part."

Jed grinned. "Go ahead and tell it, Biscuits. I can hear you."

"Can't either! Gol dangit, sometimes a body just don't feel appreciated around here. I could go cook for a real big spread somewhere." Biscuits shouted this last sentence, then shrugged since Jed was out the kitchen door by then. He picked up the empty coffee cup and took it to the wash pan.

A big yellow cat sat on a stool in the kitchen. Biscuits put the cup in the wash pan and turned to the cat.

"So the old maid said, 'Bart, why you throw in that extra handful of oats?' " The big yellow cat yawned, jumped down and ran out the open back door.

"Gol dangit! Yeller, you come back here when I'm talking to you."

Biscuits gave a big sigh, went to the stove and checked on a stew he was making.

When Jed came back in and changed his shirt, Biscuits saw the bandage around his arm. Jed told him about the scrape with the bounty hunter.

"Gonna get me a paper from Hangtown that straightens this all out."

"But what if it's the same sheriff there in Hangtown? Then you'll be in trouble."

"That sheriff was too crooked and too ugly to live this long. I'm sure there's a new one there by now."

Biscuits warmed up beans and bacon for dinner that noon, along with slabs of fresh baked bread and coffee. Biscuits was still grousing about not being able to finish his story.

"Biscuits, we've heard that same damned story thirty or forty times," Kit said. "Hell, we know it better than you do. Fact is the feed man gave the old maid only seven pounds of oats not ten, cause seven was all she needed. She fed her horse a pound a day and never knew the difference."

Biscuits snorted and went back to the stove where he added some more water to his beef stew.

Jed grinned. "Kit, let's go look at the tall grass down by the water to the north. We could go in there with scythes and cut down a bunch of that grass in a day. Could be right good to put in the haymow for the milk cow and the horses this winter."

"Take a lot of it, but we might be able to put up enough to feed the herd during a hard winter. If we had a mowing machine we could cut it for half a mile upstream, let it dry and then stack it outside the barn.

They rode north to check on the field right after the meal.

"Where are Bill and Wally?" Jed asked.

"I sent them out to the east range to check on that calf we thought we saw down. Probably just sleeping but we don't want black leg to jump us this summer."

They rode a mile north and sat on a small rise looking at a low place along the stream. In the spring this little side valley flooded when Catherine Creek overflowed its banks as the snow melt and a heavy rain combined to speed the runoff from the mountains.

Soon after the water went down the grass shot up like thunder, and it was a favorite grazing area. But soon the grass got beyond the cows and grew three feet tall.

The two riders moved on down into the tall grass and stepped off their mounts to inspect the growth.

"Don't seem too stiff for good hay," Kit said. "We used to cut a little over in Montana, mostly for the milk cows."

"Let's try it. We'll get out those old scythes I bought and cut some and see how it dries. If it works out, I'll see if I can rent or borrow a power mowing machine. I saw one somewhere that had a windrower on it so all you have to do is shock it up to dry."

"Damn, you're trying to turn me into a dirt farmer, Jed. You know us cowboys don't do farm work."

Jed swung back on his horse and grinned.

"That's why I made you foreman. Foreman's got to do whatever needs doing. If it means cutting and hauling hay to keep our animals alive in some three foot high snowdrift, that's damn well what we do."

"I was just shuckin' you, Jed. Hell, I'm nigh to being married to this outfit. Remember them two hundred head of brood cows and sixteen range bulls we drove over here from Montana?"

"I recollect something about them."

"You didn't think I was gonna let some greenhorn get away with a prime herd like that, did you?"

Jed laughed. "Glad you got me straightened out. Tomorrow, early, you and me come up here with those two scythes and get to swathing down this grass."

Supper was better that night. They had potatoes that hadn't been frozen half the winter, carrots out of the garden, fried chicken from the hen house, chicken gravy and a good-sized watermelon straight from their garden.

"Eat up that chicken. It won't hold till noon tomorrow with this heat," Biscuits commanded.

"Yes sir," Bill said, saluting the grizzled old cook and stabbing the neck and a wing.

"Reminds me of the time we was after some horses running on Pedro Sandoval's ranch across the Rio Grande down in Mexico," Biscuits said. He glanced around the table and nobody started to move.

"Never told you this one. Ten of us went across the river that night. We always raided Sandoval at night because he had bad eyes and couldn't see much at all at night. We rode right into half a dozen of his men coming over to our side to raid our cattle. Well, I'll tell you, we all cut loose with our six-guns and knocked two of them greasers off their cayuses and run the rest of them halfway back to the Sandoval ranch. Then we rounded up about fifty head of horses and drove them back across the river to the U.S. side of the border. Next morning we found that half of them horses we had rustled had our brand on them. Sandoval had rustled them from us the night before!"

"How long you steal horses across the border, Biscuits?" Wally asked.

"Long about two, maybe three years. Then one night Sandoval caught us flat with our guns down, and he went ahead and hung all six of us."

Nobody said a word. Wally looked at Biscuits. "But . . . but if you was hung . . ."

"Easy, Wally. I cut myself down, spurred my horse forward and drove about thirty of them Mex horses across the border before old Sandoval and his Mexes knew what I was doing. Never went back after that."

"But I don't see no rope burns on your neck, Biscuits."

"Course not. I worked so fast I got moving before they kicked my horse out from under me."

Kit couldn't hold in any longer and burst out laughing. Jed joined in, and then Wally realized that he'd been set up to take the joke.

"Aw, damn," Wally said. "Just for that I'm gonna eat the last piece of chicken."

He did.

Kit watched Jed who had taken down the tally book and was doing some figuring. Kit had never had much schooling. He respected a man who could read and write and do ciphers.

"What you figuring?" Kit asked.

"Checking the tally. We came with two hundred brood cows and sixteen bulls, right?"

"Right as rain."

"First year we dropped a hundred and eighty calves and ninety-two was heifers and we cut eighty-eight for steers, so we then had three hundred and ninety-six head and two hundred and ninety-two head of cows and heifers. Next year we got a hundred and eighty more drops from the brood cows. Which means right now out there on the range we have five hundred and seventy-six critters. Three-hundred and eighty-two are brood cows, heifer calves and two year-old heifers. Then we have our sixteen range bulls and a hundred and seventy-eight steers, some yearlings, some two year-olds. Next spring our yearling heifers will produce their first drops."

"Yeah, these critters breed good, even better than me," Kit said. "So what's this all mean?"

"Next fall we should have some steers ready for market, the first eighty-eight which might be down to eighty by then. Or maybe we can throw in a few two year-olds that are big enough and make a hundred. That, my friends, means forty-five to fifty dollars an animal down in Portland."

"How the hell we get them to Portland?" Bill asked. "That's almost three hundred miles from here."

"True, Bill. Heard there was a buyer in Pendleton, but that's halfway to the river. I also know for a fact there's a dock down at Hat Rock landing on the Columbia River. That's only a hundred miles away. We drive our herd to Hat Rock, get them on board a cattle barge, and I can ship them to Portland for two hundred dollars. Two dollars a head."

"Beats old Ned out of driving them three hundred miles," Kit said.

Wally frowned. "Then every year after that we'll have more and more steers to sell as they get big enough?"

"Right you are, my boy," Jed said. "We'll be rich before we know it. Which is to say between now and September next, we might run a bit short of hard cash."

"Your credit's good with me," Kit said.

"Hell, yes, if I had money I'd just gamble it away," Billy agreed.

Wally looked a bit hesitant. He'd only been with them for six months.

"Besides," Jed tossed in, "all three of you get to keep your jobs this winter when there won't be a tinker's damn of work to do."

Wally shrugged. "Yeah, I'll risk it. Who wants to get stinking rich, anyway."

Saturday night came much too fast for Jed. That morning he took a bath, then in the afternoon he sent the hands out to check the south range. Then he took another bath and washed his hair again. It had been at least four years since he'd been out with a lady, especially a beautiful one like Priscilla.

Biscuits came in and gave him a haircut which wasn't perfect but was as good as the old ragamuffin could do. Jed looked in the one glass they had in the place and saw his reflection. He had been

near clean-shaven for two years now with side-
burns only halfway down his ears and a medium-
sized moustache with no droop at the ends.

His face was burned brown on the lower half
and gradually got lighter until around his eyes it
was almost pure white. It was called a cowboy tan
because the wide hat protected the upper part of
the face from weathering.

He shrugged. Jed Bradburn was what he was.
If those city folks didn't like it, too bad for them.
He took out his one suit and had Biscuits fire up
the stove and warm a sadiron and press the blue
serge. When Biscuits was done he shot a stream
of tobacco juice out the back door and shook his
head.

"Ain't the best, but them creases been in there
for some time."

"More than two years."

"Leastwise it's clean."

Jed rode into town early. He stopped by at the
barbershop for a store-bought haircut, taking a
little more off the top and sides so the brown
forest didn't get out of hand. When the barber
finished he put some bay rum and rose water
on Jed's face, parted his hair on the left side and
called it a done job.

The whole thing cost him a quarter, but it was
worth it. Jed checked his Waterbury and saw that
it was only five o'clock. He had an hour and a
half. He stopped by the livery stable and talked to
Mr. Ingram who sold buggies, wagons and some
farming machinery as well.

"A hay mower, standard sickle mowing machine, is what you're talking about. Nope, ain't
seen one around here. Could get you one from

Pendleton. Some folks using them up there on the dry wheat land. Might cost, oh, thirty dollars. That would be with an extra sickle bar and lots of extra blades. You could do a lot worse."

"I'll let you know, Mr. Ingram. I'm testing some of the grass up by my spread. If it works out I'll probably cut it for hay to feed with later on when the snow flies."

"Good idea. No sense letting them critters starve to death in a snow drift."

By 6:20 Jed walked north on Main Street toward the small hill that ran up to the better houses in La Grande. The banker's was the largest with a veranda around the front and both sides. It was a three-story frame house painted white and the best looking place in town. It even had a green lawn and a bed of flowers. He'd never noticed that before.

When he rang the twist bell on the heavy door that had a large pane of glass in it, he saw Priscilla coming toward him.

She opened the door and smiled, her face so beautiful he wanted to shout about it.

"Oh, boy! Great, you came!" Priscilla said with so much emotion in her voice that it wavered and almost broke. She laughed self-consciously. "You see, I didn't know for sure if you'd come or not, with me being so pushy and all." She held the door open and motioned for him to come in.

"Now don't you be nervous or worry about a thing. Everyone here is nice and you know them and all we'll do is talk a bit and then have dinner and talk some more."

She put her hand through his arm and pulled it tightly against her. For just a moment his arm touched the swell of her breast. Then she eased away and smiled at him.

"First, you get to talk with the men in the study. It's what they call their cigar time. It smells just terrible in there, but maybe you can stand it." She laughed softly and left him at the den door.

Seven men turned and looked at him. Loophole Lawson hurried over. "Well, Jed, I hardly knew you in a suit. You're getting into the social swim here."

Loophole grabbed a cigar and handed it to Jed who bit off the end and lit it from Loophole's match. He puffed out two drags of smoke, squinted against the fumes and shook his head.

"Not really, Loophole. Actually I'm only doing this as a favor to a friend. You work out that case that was giving you fits?"

"Not at all," he said. Two more men came up.

"Well, now, here is a man who should know." The speaker was their host and the town's only banker, Broderick Parmley. "Now, Jed, we were talking about the price of beef. Tim Waldron here says he has a tip that beef prices are going down. He says the market is shrinking and pork is taking over. What's your reaction?"

"If that's true, I may need that bank loan sooner than I thought," Jed said and everyone laughed. He shook his head. "From what I can find out, the whole country is eating more and more beef. Some places are even grinding it up and making little patties out of it and frying them for sandwiches. Roast beef, beefsteaks, beef ribs are all selling like wildfire. I really think that Tim is reading the wrong newspapers."

The crowd laughed again.

Tim Waldron shook his head. "I saw it in the *New York Times* and I don't take their opinions lightly."

"I don't care what they eat in New York," Jed said. "It's La Grande and Portland that I'm interested in. What's the price of slaughter beef in Portland?"

"I don't know. I don't get those quotes." Tim turned away and the discussion was over.

Oliver McMurphy, the general store owner, came up and nodded at Jed. "How is it going out at the Circle B, Jed?"

"Fine, so far, but this first four years is the hardest. I wish now that I had started out with some brood cows and some yearling steers. Then I'd have had some steady income earlier."

The den door opened, and Priscilla stood there in her shimmering white dress that accented her figure. Jed hadn't noticed how pretty she looked in that dress before.

"Gentlemen, the ladies are at the table. Now it's your turn because dinner is served."

She nodded at the men as they walked past her and waited for Jed who was the last one out of the room.

"There now, that wasn't so bad so far, was it? This part is easiest. If you don't want to talk, just pretend that you have a mouthful, although from what I heard you did very well in there with the men." She grinned, caught his arm and walked into the dining room.

Jed Bradburn's knees shook so he thought he might stumble. Priscilla flashed him her prettiest smile and held his arm tightly as they walked to their seats at the long, formal dinner table.

Chapter Seven

That same Saturday evening that Jed Bradburn made his splash into La Grande society, Lee Morgan settled down in his hotel room with a copy of the *New York Times* and read it front to back. He found it helped now and again to find out what was going on outside the confines of the small town he currently lived in. Not often, but once in a purple moon, something happened in the nation or the world that was interesting enough to read about.

This issue of the newspaper did not furnish him with such an occasion. He cleaned his weapons, both .45's, the one in his holster and the spare in the bottom of his carpetbag, and got to sleep early. Sunday he would ride out to the Circle B ranch and position himself in a spot where he could spot and follow anyone who might rustle cattle from the ranch that night.

While Morgan snored in the hotel, Nancy held

sway over her domain in the Wildcat Saloon from her barstool where she perched with a cold beer in one hand and a wary eye on the night's gathering.

The girls had been busy upstairs, as they usually were Saturday nights. She watched Zack run the bar with his usual casual efficiency. Zack had dropped in one day and stepped behind the bar when the barman she had inherited with the place fell and broke his leg and never made it back to work. Zack had worked the bar ever since.

Zack was a runaway husband, she was sure, but he never talked about it, and she never asked. She had done him a time or two as a favor when she thought he was going to explode. Since then he'd built up a sleeping arrangement with one of the widows in town, and he even hinted they might get married. She hadn't the heart to remind him about the family he left back east somewhere.

The night rolled along about as usual. One small fight started, but a deputy sheriff defused it before it got out of hand. There were the usual arguments over card games, but no gunplay.

She had seen a big man come in and noticed his size and the rugged looks that some women liked. He was nearly six feet, with wide shoulders narrowing to a small waist and arms like oak branches. He looked like a man used to hard work but not liking it.

He bought six beers and settled down to a game of cards. The first four hands he played he won. He had dealt the first hand, asked for a new deck and then started winning. Nancy figured he had palmed at least four aces from the first deck, maybe a king or two as well.

By the time the six beers were gone, the man waved at Zack and demanded a bottle of his best whiskey and a shot glass. Zack looked at Nancy for a go ahead and she nodded.

She watched the big man. He was loud now, boisterous, and a continual bother to other poker players.

Walt Flowers sat at the table just behind the big man, and he scowled at him often, stood once and almost said something when the man won a large pot and roared with approval.

When the others at the table voiced their disapproval, the big man said, "Hey, you wanta goddamn play poker, we goddamn play poker. You run outa money—tough shit. You go get some more or go home and screw your old lady. Me, I'm playing some more goddamn poker."

Walt Flowers groused and went back to his game. Ten minutes later the big man roared in anger when he lost a pot. He jumped up and sent his chair crashing over behind him. It hit Flowers in the side of the head and spilled him out of his chair onto the floor.

The big man saw it and guffawed in delight. He made as if to help pick up Flowers and tipped over the poker table, spilling cards and chips all over the floor.

Flowers came to his knees roaring in fury. He got to his feet slowly, stared at the big man and waved some others aside. He planted his feet and feathered his hand just below his six-gun.

"You big bastard!" Flowers roared. "You get outta this saloon or you go for your iron. No other goddamn way!"

Flowers grabbed at the handle of his six-gun and started it out of leather.

The big man laughed, waited, then just as the other man's weapon was almost free of its holster, the big man drew and fired. Flowers never got his weapon cocked. The round hit him in the chest, drove him back two steps then dumped him on the floor, blood gushing from the chest wound that had missed his heart but had smashed a rib halfway through his lung.

Flowers coughed up blood, his eyes went glassy, and he struggled for breath. Blood seeped from his nose as he tried to breathe. He gasped for air again and again, then he took one last look at the big man and tried to say something.

The words never came out. Flowers slumped over sideways and died.

The big man looked around the saloon. "Okay, so I killed him. The bastard drew on me first, right? Half you men in here saw him draw. I didn't want to kill him but I had to. He was about ready to kill me. Somebody go get the sheriff so I can get this over with."

He sat back down at the table, reloaded the spent round in his .44 with powder, lead and cap on the nipple of his percussion revolver and pushed it back into leather.

"Now, we were playing some poker here. Do we have a game, or don't we?"

Two men dropped out. Four others shrugged and took their chairs again. New dealer, new hand.

It was ten minutes before Sheriff Larson came in and looked at the dead man. The saloon quieted. The big man didn't seem to notice.

"I see your five dollars and raise you ten," he said pushing chips into the pot.

"Who shot this man?" Sheriff Larson said in the quiet.

The killer heard him and laid his cards face down in front of him. He stood and turned, his hand wavering near his right thigh where his iron rested.

"I shot the man in self-defense," the big man said.

Sheriff Larson came over and looked up at the man.

"You new in town?"

"Came in this afternoon."

"What's your name?"

"Dub Devilin. You the sheriff?"

"That I am." The sheriff looked around. "Anybody see what happened here? Milt, you're level-headed. Tell it to me."

"Devilin here knocked over Walt's chair, then the table. First one an accident, the table on purpose. Walt got up and yelled at Devilin, then started his draw first. Devilin was faster and killed him with one shot."

Sheriff looked around. "That the way you other men see it?" A dozen heads nodded. "Damn, Walt was a good man." He turned back to Devilin. "Where you from?"

"Down the road a spell."

"Gonna be in town long?"

"Ain't decided."

"Walt has friends around here. Might be best if you hit the road."

"You ordering me out of town, Sheriff?"

"Can't do that, Devilin, but I can suggest. That's

what I'm doing, suggesting that you ride on down the trail."

"Or what, Sheriff?"

"No threats, just a suggestion."

Devilin laughed. "What a piss poor sheriff. No balls. Won't even tell me to get out of town. Damn, but I like this place. About the right size."

Nancy slid off her stool, walked up beside Devilin and picked up the whiskey bottle.

"Sheriff Larson might not tell you to get out of town, but I can tell you to get out of my saloon. Get out—right now. Your money is no good in here anymore. Walt was a friend of mine."

Devilin forget the sheriff and grinned. "Missy whore, you own this scum-filled establishment?"

Nancy picked up his half-filled glass from the table and threw the whiskey in his face. He gasped.

"I own it, and I want you out on the boardwalk, right damn now!"

Devilin grabbed her forearm with his bear paw of a hand and pulled her toward him.

Somebody behind him growled. He drew his six-gun and spun around. "Who the fuck did that? You man enough to complain to my face? You do and you can join old Walt over there for a double funeral." He grinned, looked back at Nancy and nodded.

"Oh, damn, this is gonna be good. My own fucking county. Like the place, like the saloon, even like the hot pussy owner here. Yeah, wet and wild, that's how I like my women."

He looked at the steps that led up to the cribs and the office. "You must have a dandy spot upstairs there, Missy. Let's just go up and see."

He pushed his six-gun into leather, grabbed the bottle of whiskey from Nancy's hand and pushed her toward the stairs. She caught a chair, then dug in both feet.

Two men moved between the pair and the stairs. Both were big and heavy, neither wore a gun.

Devilin dropped Nancy's hand and slugged one of the men before he could get his fists up. He jolted to the side, fell over a poker table and crashed to the floor. He didn't get up. Devilin moved in on the second man with a series of fast blows to the head and chin, one final punch to the man's jaw sending him sprawling onto the floor.

Devilin turned and found Nancy standing there with one hand over her mouth, too surprised to run. He caught her hand again, picked up the bottle of whiskey and continued toward the stairs.

No one else tried to stop him.

Devilin roared in laughter, picked up Nancy with one hand and carried her up the stairs. At the top he turned. "What the hell, is this some kind of a freak show or something? Get back to drinking and gambling. Ain't that what you come in here for? I don't need no help with this hot little pussy here. No goddamned help at all."

He had carried her up the stairs by one arm, roaring and laughing all the way. Zack came around the bar holding a sawed-off shotgun and with fire in his eyes. Sheriff Larson caught his arm.

"Better not go up there, Zack. You do and both you and Nancy probably would die. Just slow down and let's think what we can do. One more poking won't hurt Nancy none. She'd be the first to tell you that. Let's just play this slow and steady and see what happens."

"We can't just leave her up there."

"This Devilin ain't really done nothing against the law yet, not unless Nancy wants to call this rape. Then we'd have a case. Don't know how we could try it."

Zack still held the shotgun. "Just one round. Nobody would blame me. Splatter him all over the hallway up there."

"No, Zack. Now settle down. Let's wait and see what happens."

Somebody yelled for a beer at the bar, and Zack went behind it and started working again. Sheriff Larson sat at the far end next to the door and watched and waited.

A half hour later, Devilin marched out to the top of the stairs and looked down over the saloon.

"Shut up, you assholes down there, and listen to me. My name is Dub Devilin, and I'm now owner of this dump. Nancy sold me sixty percent of it, so what I say goes. Gonna be some changes around here. I'm boss, not Nancy, understand?"

He marched down the stairs. Above him Nancy came out in a dressing robe. Her hair was mussed, a bruise beginning to show on her cheek and eye. She came halfway down the steps and paused.

Devilin didn't notice her. "Yeah, some big changes around here. First off, the whores are gonna parade around in their birthday suits, stark naked. That's right, pussy and tits out there for all to see. Why should they care?

"Gonna cost every man who comes through

the door a dollar. I call it a door fee. To see the pretties in their nothings costs you a dollar. Upstairs is three dollars now. So get your money ready. You men in here tonight don't have to pay the dollar fee.

"Hey, you two whores, strip it off and get to work. Got to pay the rent here."

Nancy came down the rest of the way on the stairs and sat on her stool at the end of the bar. She looked shaken and afraid. She motioned to Zack. When he went down the bar to her, she whispered.

"Get word to Lee Morgan. I think this guy is Chance Rivers. Find him tonight!"

While Nancy slid off the stool and went back up the stairs, Devilin was in back helping the two whores there strip off their clothes.

Zack told the sheriff what Nancy had said, and Sheriff Larson slipped out of the saloon without Devilin noticing him. The sheriff tried the hotel first, pounding on Morgan's second floor hotel room door until he got results.

Morgan had fallen asleep reading the paper and went to the door, bleary-eyed and groggy.

"Yeah?"

"Morgan, open up. Sheriff Larson."

The door opened and Morgan waved the lawman inside. "What's so damn important?"

"Some crazy man just killed a man in the Wildcat, then took Nancy upstairs and bedded her and claims he owns the saloon. Nancy said she thinks he's Chance Rivers going by another name."

Morgan pulled on his boots as the lawman talked. He caught his gunbelt off the bedpost and buckled it on and tied down the holster. He put on his Stetson and motioned the sheriff out the door.

"He still there?"

"Was when I left."

"What name is he using?"

"Says he's Dub Devilin."

"More likely the devil himself. Lots of people in the Wildcat?

"Yep, and bound to be more. Devilin has the whores walking around naked until they get taken upstairs. Charging a dollar a head as an entry fee."

Morgan chuckled. "The gent has an imagination to go with his gall. I'll find out if he's Rivers soon enough."

"How?"

"I don't know. Figure it out as I go along."

The two checked the Wildcat Saloon door and found it open and most of the attention at the back tables where one of the whores put on a little dance on the tabletop. Devilin cheered her on.

Morgan slipped into the saloon and joined the back of the crowd now staring at the naked whore and her dance. A moment later a cowboy jumped on the table, grabbed her and carried her toward the stairs. Everyone cheered.

When the clapping stopped, Devilin took over.

"Girls will be back down in about twenty minutes, so drink up and play some poker. Have a good time."

In the silence after the big man spoke, Morgan bellowed.

"Hey, Rivers, Chance Rivers, want a word with you."

Morgan watched the Devilin man but he never

blinked, never looked over, just went on talking to one of the men at a poker table. Maybe this big take-over guy wasn't Chance Rivers after all.

Morgan bought a beer at the bar and worked his way near Devilin. He came closer and caught the man's attention. Morgan waved his beer and grinned.

"Be damned, Devilin, ain't you from Portland? Swear I saw you a couple of times at a saloon down on Front Street."

Devilin stared at Morgan and shook his head. "I been through there, but only once. Mostly I'm from Idaho and points in Montana, if'n it's any business of yours."

Morgan shrugged. "Don't matter. No business of mine nohow." Morgan sipped his beer, edged away and worked his way into the crowd.

If this guy was Chance Rivers he was one cool cowboy. He never winced and was in charge all the time. Morgan had to talk to Nancy. How? She said something about a back stairs. Morgan pushed through the crowd to the back door. The outhouse behind most saloons got a good workout. He went into the alley and saw the narrow stairs up the side of the two story Wildcat Saloon to a door.

Morgan went up the steps two at a time and prayed the door on top would be open. It was. He slipped inside, hurried down to Nancy's room and knocked.

"Go away," her voice said.

"Morgan here," he said loud enough so she could hear him but low enough so no one else did. He heard a bolt slide and then the door opened.

She grabbed him and pulled him inside, then

slid two heavy bolts in place and fell into his arms.

"Damn, I don't know how this all happened. Is that bastard down there Chance Rivers?"

Morgan kissed the bruised cheek and smoothed the hair out of her eyes. "Nancy, I don't know. He might not be. I tried out his name but he never blinked. I asked him if he was from Portland and he said he was from Montana. It may be an act. I just don't know."

"You've got to run him out of town, Morgan. He killed one man. He pushed around Sheriff Larson. He said he wants to take over the whole county. Isn't that what Chance Rivers does?"

"Yes, but others have done the same thing. We have to be certain it's Rivers before I can move."

She hugged him tightly. "I wish you could stay here tonight, but he'll be back."

"Tomorrow night I have to be out in the country. We think there might be some rustling and I need to watch for them."

"You can't leave me here with this . . . this killer. He took my .38 six-gun, but I've still got that little .45 hideout. Where did I put it? In my top drawer. I may have to kill this bastard myself."

Someone pounded hard on the door.

"Nancy, you dressed yet? Hurry up and get down here. We got more business than your whores can handle. You want to go back to work?"

"Fuck no! And I ain't dressed yet. Hold onto your balls a minute."

She had bellowed the words at the door. There was a moment of silence, then laughter came through the door.

"Damn, you may be all right. Get your ass downstairs as soon as you can."

"Yeah, yeah."

Nancy found the derringer in the top drawer. Morgan broke it open, made sure it had two rounds in it and that they were fairly fresh. They were solid rounds. He handed the weapon to her.

She finished dressing, then unbolted the door and looked out. One of her naked whores walked past with a cowboy in tow.

Nancy motioned to Morgan. "You better go down the back stairs. Safer that way."

Nancy stepped out into the hallway with Morgan right behind her. A roar came from in back of Morgan. He turned around and saw Devilin standing there fondling one of the whores.

"Nancy, what the hell is this wiseacre doing in your bedroom?" Devilin thundered.

Chapter Eight

Morgan stared down the bully outside Nancy's bedroom.

"I'm an old friend of Nancy's, and I'll be in her bedroom any time I damn please." The words came out so hard and deadly that Devilin frowned and took a step back.

"Yeah, maybe so, but I own this place now, so watch your damned step." Devilin turned and stormed down the hall, banging into one of the naked whores who came out of her room leading a spent cowboy to the back stairs.

"Outa my way, whore!" he barked as he rushed past them.

Nancy looked at Morgan. "Thanks for standing up for me. Do you think he's really Chance Rivers?"

"I don't know. I'm not sure that Rivers would have backed down so easy just now. We'll just have to wait and see. Are you going to be all right here for the next two days?"

"I'll manage. I'll let him think he's running things. I'm worried about Zack. He's got a temper, and I saw him behind the bar with the shotgun. It's sawed-off and with double aught buck rounds. He could kill three or four people gunning down Devilin."

"I'll try to talk with him. I've still got a hunch that Chance Rivers is cooling off his hot streak out at the Running R ranch playing at gunman. Tomorrow night might help me find out for sure. Can you handle Devilin?"

"I can. I've done wild men before. Devilin calms down after a good poking. I'll do him four or five times and he'll be exhausted and sleep tonight and half through Sunday."

"Be careful. This might be the kind of animal who enjoys killing people." He reached in and kissed her cheek. "Now, I'll go down the back stairs and inside and try to talk to Zack."

Nancy nodded and closed the door. He heard the bolts slide home as he moved away. One naked woman stood at the door of a crib. Inside the small room a cowboy was pulling up his pants. The woman was slender with a little pot stomach, small breasts and only the hint of pubic hair at her crotch.

"Want a quick one?" she asked spreading her knees and pumping her hips toward him. He saw a flash of pink.

"Busy right now," Morgan said. "Maybe later."

Two minutes later he slid up to the bar in the Wildcat Saloon and waved for Zack to come down. No one was near them at the bar. Devilin wandered around the poker tables, announcing there would be a big money game at a back table in an hour. Cost a hundred dollars to buy in.

"Fat chance any takers around here," Zack said. He polished a whiskey glass with a cloth. "Nancy all right? He didn't hurt her, did he?"

"Slapped her a bit, but otherwise she's fine. She's worried about you."

"Me?"

"Afraid you're going to use the shotgun. She says she doesn't want you to. Too many people could get hurt. Just let it rest a while. He'll get tired and move on or he'll make a big mistake. Then I'll help and we'll take care of Dub Devilin."

Zack's eyes shone. "Oh, yeah, I can wait. Just don't want him to get away scott free. I got a score to settle with that big bastard for the way he treated Nancy."

"Don't worry, he won't walk out of here without a walloping memory of La Grande. Now, I'm going to leave it in your hands. Keep it calm and collected. Don't do anything stupid tonight, and we'll take care of him soon."

"Can't wait," Zack said moving down the bar to take an order for some cold beer.

Morgan watched Devilin who was playing the big owner. Soon he'd make a big mistake. Morgan tried to fit him into the Chance Rivers' mold. He was right-handed—at least his six-gun was on his right hip. The size could be right. He couldn't tell yet. Just have to wait and see. If it was Chance and he was just now getting to La Grande, where had he been for the past two or three weeks?

Morgan pondered it as he went back to the hotel and dropped on the blanket. He figured it should be safe now to pull off his boots and get some sleep. He wouldn't get any tomorrow night, not if the rustlers came on schedule.

In the shadows beyond the hotel where Morgan slept, a lean tall man waited beside the Two Aces Gambling Hall and Saloon. He had been there 15 minutes and the long cigar had burned down almost to a stub. He took one more drag, blew out the smoke, dropped the butt on the ground and crushed it with one of his fancy $20 shoes.

Another shadow came out of the back of the alley, weaving just enough to be noticed. The boots scraping on the ground brought the tall man around quickly, his hand reaching for the hideout in his jacket pocket.

"Me, Percival," the shadow said. The man came closer and the tall one relaxed.

"You're late. What the hell's going on?"

"Got a little drunk, had a little woman. What the fuck you expect after we been out in that damned valley for two solid weeks?"

"Tough, Percival. You're getting paid right well, ain't you?"

"Yeah, sure, but the guys—"

"Your job is to keep them happy. Once every two weeks they come to town. Now how is the total steer count coming along?"

"We got two hundred and forty way I tally. Damn, five or six or even ten at a time don't count up fast. Why don't we just take out a couple of hundred and be done?"

"Because then some real experts would come in and do some fancy tracking and your neck would be stretching at the end of some store-bought hemp, that's why. We do it my way and we all make some money and you don't get hung."

"Yeah, okay. I see. Guys are getting a little bit jittery. Long time to be in the same spot."

"Let me worry about that. You left one man with the herd?"

"Sure, like usual."

"You get everyone wrung out tonight and get back out there tomorrow, and tomorrow night you do it again. In another two weeks we'll have enough for a drive. Then it's payday and a bonus for every steer we sell over two hundred. Remember that."

"Yeah, we remember."

"You got enough cash for a good time in town tonight?"

"Could use another twenty. Bert done gambled before he whored so he went broke and had no fancy woman money."

The tall man handed over $20 from his purse and frowned. "This comes out of Bert's pay, you tell him that. No more mistakes, and don't get thrown in jail. If you get jailed get word to me and I'll get you out somehow, but I can't show up down there."

"Yeah, yeah, we been here before, remember."

"Just because it worked well once is no reason for us to get sloppy. We do it the right way, the way I told you. The big outfits never miss ten head, and the little ranchers don't have the men to track down the critters."

Percival nodded in the dark. "Yes sir," he said knowing how far he could push. "I best be finding Bert before he explodes or something."

"Just be careful and then get back to the herd."

The tall man turned and walked away like he always did. Another small dig to let Percival know who was in charge.

Percival held the $20 in his fist and walked out the alley and moved the other way toward the saloon where he left Bert watching a poker game. Bert would be glad for the extra cash, but he'd only get five dollars.

Ten minutes later Percival had given Bert his fiver and the kid had lunged for the first whore he found and ran up the stairs with her. She was a two dollar lay, and Bert would do her, then have a beer and do another whore.

Percival went to another saloon and watched the fancy women. One was better than the rest. The next time she came down the steps he was right there to grab her hand.

"You look like you're ready, cowboy," she said.

He caught one of her breasts and rubbed it, then tried to get his hand down the front of her robe. She slapped his hand away, grabbed it and led him up the steps.

"Oh, yeah, you're ready. You want the two dollar regular or the three dollar special I have. It's so fancy you'll fucking near pass out."

Percival grinned. He handed the woman six dollars. "Damn, I want the special twice. Yeah, do me the special twice, and make sure I don't pass out so I can enjoy it twice as much!"

Lee Morgan wore his fringed buckskin shirt and jeans as he rode toward the Circle B ranch Sunday afternoon. He'd taken a nap in the morning and then another one after eating his noon meal, waking about four in the afternoon. He felt fit and ready. He'd get supper at the ranch house, then take some food along in a sack to help him stay awake.

He wished there was some way to keep coffee hot without a fire. He'd seen one man boil coffee, put it in a fruit jar and wrap it in a blanket. Two hours later it was still warm, but not what he'd call hot. Maybe someday someone would invent something like that.

At the ranch, Jed met him and fed him.

"Haven't had any more rustling that we know of," Jed told him. "We been watching along the northeast side of our range, but nothing's been happening last couple of nights."

"Tonight must be the night," Morgan said. He ate beans and a slice of ham and a pot full of early garden vegetables, then took the sack of sandwiches Biscuits had fixed and headed for the northeast end of the ranch, just beyond where the majority of the cattle were grazing now.

He found a little green blush of trees near a tiny stream that fed into Catherine Creek and tied his mount's muzzle shut with a kerchief. The animal could still breathe. She just couldn't drink or make horse talk. She had to open her mouth to vocalize. He didn't want her smelling out the smuggler's horses and chattering with them, giving away his presence.

He settled down, had one of the sandwiches and a tin cup of cold water from the little stream. Then he waited.

It was nearly midnight, and nothing had happened. He stood up and stretched, walking up and back a cleared space inside the grove of trees and brush.

It was an hour later, after another sandwich and a cup of water, when Morgan heard some horse talk. He edged up to his lookout spot he'd cut in the brush and watched. Two horsemen went by 30 yards in front of him. They walked their mounts, moving at a deliberate speed, knowing where they were heading.

Morgan followed them on foot. He took advantage of the soft moonlight coming through thin clouds and melted in with every bush and tree. He knew the cattle were less than a quarter of a mile away.

Morgan watched as the two men systematically picked out the oldest steers and drove eight of them back the way the riders had come. He let them get 100 yards ahead of him, then jogged back to the grove, untied his mount and stepped into the saddle.

Now all he had to do was follow them. They used a different track this time, a longer route, but stopped about two miles away to do the single trail trick with the steers.

Morgan wanted to charge up and collar the two rustlers and take them back to hang, but that wouldn't get at the root of the problem. Who hired them, and more important, where did they hide the herd they had rustled?

The lead rustler had just returned to the six steers left. Morgan had hidden behind a pair of small pine at the edge of the open space and 50 yards from the cattle. He didn't want to get too close.

When the cowboy cut out a steer and started driving it along the trail north and east, the critter suddenly bolted and raced straight at the trees where Morgan hid. There was nothing he could do but hold his position and hope that the steer turned, leading the cowboy away from Morgan.

It didn't. It aimed for the trees like a telescope on a rifle sight, passed by and was ten yards beyond before the cowboy rode up to the trees.

When the rustler saw Morgan's horse, then Morgan on it, he cut left sharply, bellowed a warning and rode straight into the hills and the cover of the pines.

Morgan was sure the steer would veer off and was caught not ready for a confrontation. He pulled out his six-gun, but by that time the cowboy was out of range.

Morgan kicked his gray into motion but when he got the animal up to a gallop he could see only a faint shadow of the rustler heading into the trees. He had no chance at all of catching him.

The other rustler never showed up where the five steers were left. After an hour waiting, Morgan kicked the steers into motion and drove them back the two miles to their home range. Then he headed for the Circle B ranch house to tell Jed what had happened.

It was after four A.M. when Morgan rode into the ranch yard. He unsaddled his horse and put her in the small corral, then angled for the ranch house.

Jed met him at the kitchen door.

"Heard you ride in. What happened?"

Jed started a fire going in the kitchen range and put on water to boil for coffee.

By the time the coffee was ready, Morgan had recounted his tale and Jed pounded his fist on the table.

"Damn, what rotten luck. That wouldn't happen one time in a thousand and it has to be just when we don't want it." He lifted his brows in the light of the kitchen lamp and shrugged. "What the hell, we'll just have to try again.

"Maybe the next time farther down the trail," Morgan said. "Down there where we lost the tracks on that sheetrock. I've got a hunch the holding pen must be up in there somewhere."

Morgan told Jed about the man he hunted.

"I figured maybe he was the gunman they hired at the Running R. Thought if I shut down this rustling, Johnson would decide he didn't need a gunman and cut him loose, then I could track him again. Now I'm not so sure. My man could be the one in town messing up the Wildcat Saloon and Nancy. Calls himself Devilin and he nigh on to fits the spelling of his name."

"How you going to smoke him out?"

"Don't have the slightest idea right now. I've got to think about it and find these damn rustlers. How did your dinner party go Saturday night?"

"Wish you hadn't asked. Kind of made a fool of myself a time or two, but I waded through it. Got to set beside Priscilla which made it worthwhile."

"Sounds like you're getting sweet on that little gal."

"A man could do worse. But then, I don't know what her father would say. He's a man of means. I got a scallywag little scrabble of a ranch."

"Can't know until you asked him."

Jed grinned. "Yep, and by then it'd be too late if he gave me the go ahead."

They both laughed.

Then they both went to bed. Morgan figured

he'd sleep until noon and get to town about two
in the afternoon.

That's the way it worked out.

The first thing Morgan did was go to the Wildcat Saloon. He paid his dollar at the door to some
cowhand serving as collection agent.

Inside he found four naked whores making the
rounds. That meant one new one. He didn't see
Nancy on her stool. At the bar he ordered a cold
beer and watched Zack who motioned with his
head. Morgan saw Devilin come down the steps.
He went directly to the bar and held up two fingers, and Zack poured him two fingers of whiskey
in a beer mug.

Devilin downed it in one pull, put the mug
down and turned around. Morgan decided the
big man was sizing up everyone in the saloon.
His glance washed over Morgan and came back.
He snorted and looked back at the patrons.

Five minutes later, Morgan decided Devilin had
picked out his victim. For what purpose, Morgan
didn't know. Devilin walked past a man at a card
table, then came back and looked at his hand.
Devilin made elaborate and meaningless hand
signals to the other players.

The target, a tall man with blonde hair and
a fairly heavy build, saw the shenanigans and
flushed. When he saw who was doing it, it looked
like he tried to control his temper.

The second time Devilin did the same thing, the
man stood and turned to face Devilin.

"Would you mind playing your kid games somewhere else? We're trying to play grown-up poker
here."

"You sure as shit ain't trying very hard, asshole. Otherwise you wouldn't even notice me. You want to play poker, sit down and play."

The tall man sighed. He put his hand of cards down on the table and turned slowly.

"I would play if some asshole wasn't looking over my shoulder."

Devilin charged as the other man knew he would. The shorter man ducked low, bending his knees, hitting Devilin at his waist, then lifting up quickly levering Devilin off his feet, flipping him over his shoulder and dumping him on his back on top of a poker table.

Devilin rolled off clawing for his six-gun. He got it out, cocked and aimed at the tall man.

"You kill me, asshole, and you'll hang for murder. I don't have a weapon." A dozen men around the room yelled out in agreement. He heard a few six-gun hammers cock back in the sudden silence.

Slowly, Devilin pushed his Colt back in leather and walked around the broken table. His first punch went wide and the other man, somebody called Fritz, slashed out with a left-hand jab that caught Devilin on the nose, flattened it and brought a gush of blood.

Devilin saw the blood on his hand and roared in fury. He charged forward, took two stinging punches but caught Fritz around the back with his thick arms and lifted him off the floor. He kept driving forward until Fritz's head slammed against the wall.

Devilin dropped Fritz then drove in, kicking him twice in the stomach. The third time he kicked, Fritz came alive enough to grab the boot and twist it, bringing a scream of pain from Devilin, who twisted to the side and slammed into a poker table before crashing to the floor.

Fritz gained his feet, shaking his head to clear it, as he waited for Devilin to get up.

"Fucking bastard!" Devilin screamed. "For that you die!"

He rushed at Fritz who sidestepped and let Devilin come up with empty hands. Devilin came in slower the next time, taking a swing that Fritz saw coming, stepped inside and slammed two hard punches to Devilin's face. Then Fritz danced back.

"A fancy Dan," Devilin mumbled. He feinted one way, then another and caught Fritz around the chest and backed him into the edge of the bar. Devilin tried to knee Fritz in the crotch, but the smaller man covered himself with his leg.

Devilin whirled Fritz away from the bar, got one hand free and slammed a haymaker punch into Fritz's jaw. The thinner man sagged and fell to the floor.

Devilin, now breathing hard, looked at Fritz for a moment. Then he bent, picked up Fritz and slammed him down across the top of the bar. Fritz lay where he had been hurled. He never moved. His head hung over the inside of the bar.

Zack came up slowly and touched the man's temple, then the usually surging carotid artery at the side of his neck.

Zack looked up, his face painted with fury. "You done it this time, Devilin. This man is dead. Somebody go get the sheriff."

Devilin started for Zack but he lifted the double-barreled shotgun.

"Please give me just one excuse, Devilin, and you'll get both barrels of double aught buck. Come on, Devilin, give me an excuse to blow you straight into hell."

Chapter Nine

Morgan had his six-gun out as well, trained on Devilin. Now he was sure the man wasn't Chance Rivers.

"Hold it, Zack. Keep him covered but don't fire. Too many men behind him. On the other hand, if he moves more than his lungs to breathe, I can blast him into hell with one head shot and not hurt anyone else."

"Did somebody go for the sheriff?" Zack called.

Half a dozen voices called out that two men went to find the lawman.

"What the hell can he do?" Devilin sneered.

"Put you in jail until the court convicts you and you get hung by your neck until you are dead, dead, dead," Morgan said. "Nobody deserves it more than you do, Devilin. About goddamn time, I'd say."

"Don't count on it, Morgan. I got me a bone to smash with you, too, once we get this cleared up. That asshole challenged me. He provoked the fight. It was fair. I was in fear of my life. A good lawyer will shoot your plans to hell."

"Might not let it go to trial," Zack said.

The sheriff and two men came running in.

"Zack, tell me what happened here," Sheriff Larson said.

Zack told it the way it played out. Sheriff Larson nodded. "That the way the rest of you saw it?"

A dozen voices yelled in assent.

"Fine, Devilin, or whatever your real name is. You're under arrest for murder. You come along with me peaceable or you could be in a lot more trouble."

Morgan saw it three seconds too late. The sheriff moved quickly toward Devilin blocking Morgan's sight line. He couldn't fire without hitting the lawman.

Devilin sensed it the second it happened. He drew his six-gun in a fraction of a second and shot Sheriff Larson in the heart. As he fell Devilin aimed at Morgan but the man wasn't there. He shifted his aim to Zack and fired a second time, then grabbed a poker player standing nearby to shield himself.

"Nobody move or this Jasper gets his brains blown all over the saloon. You savvy?" He screamed the words. For a moment he scanned the room for Morgan, then jerked the hostage along in front of him as he backed toward the rear door.

"Don't let the bastard get away," somebody yelled.

"Yeah, you go after him," another voice sang out.

Morgan had seen the shooting coming. A second before it happened he dove over the bar and landed behind it. He saw Zack take the round in his shoulder and crash to the floor with the shotgun held carefully so it wouldn't fire.

Morgan crawled to the far end of the bar and from the floor level looked out to see Devilin make the last few feet to the back door. He opened it, stepped outside, then pushed his shield back inside.

Morgan came around the end of the bar racing for the back door. He bumped men aside to reach it and motioned the gawkers back from the door.

He pushed it open and felt more than heard a six-gun round come slamming through the air space and hit somewhere over the bar. He looked out at knee level and spotted Devilin running down the alley.

Morgan held his fire, darted out the door and took off at a run after the killer. Pure rage pushed him on. The bastard had shot down the sheriff with no cause, then wounded Zack. The man had to be eliminated from society one way or the other.

Devilin dodged behind some wooden crates in back of the general store and fired one round at Morgan from 40 feet. He missed. Devilin was down to one round left unless he had primed all six rounds which wasn't likely.

Morgan surged ahead to some metal barrels and watched Devilin move again to where the alley met the street. The killer vanished around the corner of a brick building, and Morgan raced to the same corner and peered around.

The brick side of the store extended 60 feet

to the cross street ahead with no door. Morgan darted around the corner and sprinted for the next corner. Devilin must be on Second Street somewhere.

The first business was a general store. Morgan ran in the front door and stared around. Two clerks stood at the back counter acting not at all like they should. Morgan slipped along the wooden floor soundlessly as he moved toward the back, holding his .45 aimed at the ceiling.

The two clerks stared at him in fear and wonder. One looked at the back room, then leaned against the counter so he wouldn't fall.

Morgan darted to the side of the partition and worked up to the door into the back half of the building without a sound. He bent and looked into the room from waist height.

A door slammed in back, and Morgan ran full tilt through boxes and stacks of goods and hardware to the back door. He peered out and found Devilin sprinting down the alley.

Morgan saved his rounds. Devilin must have only one left, while he had all five of his. Devilin probably had a hideout which would account for two more rounds.

Morgan ran after the killer who continued to the corner and rounded it. This time Morgan came up to the same corner but at the far side of the alley, not next to the building.

"Damn!" Devilin brayed. He had been standing flat against the wall waiting for Morgan to rush around the corner so he could shoot him at point-blank range. Devilin ran on again.

Now Morgan was within 20 feet of him. He could kill him with one shot, but he wanted this one alive. He fired once at the running man's legs, but missed. It was a low percentage shot and usually he didn't try it.

Devilin caught up with a light buggy rolling along the street and jumped inside. A moment later a small bald-headed man bellowed in anger and leaped out the far side. Devilin whipped the horse and surged down the street.

Morgan looked for a horse, but none were on the street. Then a cowboy came in from an alley, riding a roan.

Morgan ran up beside him. "I'm chasing a killer in that buggy. I need to borrow your horse."

The cowboy stared at him a minute, then shrugged. "Belongs to the ranch, anyway," he said and slid off. Morgan swung on and kicked the roan into a gallop after the buggy which had turned the first corner to the left, heading out of town.

Morgan knew he could catch the buggy any time he wanted to. A horse can easily outrun a buggy. He waited until Devilin was past the last house at the edge of town, then galloped up from the left and leveled his weapon at Devilin from ten feet away.

"Hold it, Devilin!" Morgan shouted. The surprised man looked over his left shoulder in surprise, yanked hard on the reins and sent the buggy shooting to the left directly in front of Morgan. He had to turn the horse to prevent a collision.

Morgan pulled back, letting Devilin take a little-used trail that wound out of town toward the river. A half mile later, the trail ended abruptly at a green field, where he saw someone had laid out a baseball diamond. Morgan sat on his horse as Devilin pulled the rig to a halt. They were

40 yards apart. There was nowhere for Devilin to drive except through open country along the Grande Ronde River.

They stared at each other for a minute or two.

"Morgan, what do you want?"

"I want you in jail on murder charges."

"You some kind of a lawman?"

"Nope, I just don't like to see people get away with murder. Shouldn't be too hard. You only have one round left in that iron."

"I have solid cartridges, now loaded with six fresh ones."

"No chance, Devilin. I saw your piece back in the saloon. It's a percussion just like mine. Only I have four rounds left in mine. Ready to go back to jail?"

In reply, Devilin slapped the reins on the horse and jolted the buggy directly at Morgan. It was a tactic he'd seen before. He rode hard right at the buggy, then jerked his mount to the right too far for Devilin to turn into him without tipping over, but Devilin tried it anyway.

The buggy tipped up on the two outer wheels, then the near wheels lifted a little more and more until the rig tipped over on its side and snapped the tongue and the traces. The horse stayed on her feet as the buggy dragged through the grassy field to a stop.

Morgan held 30 yards away from the crash, watching for Devilin. He didn't surface. Morgan rode around the rig once, then saw Devilin sprawled over the buggy's seat half-covered by the torn black canvas of the top.

Morgan stepped down from the horse and advanced cautiously. Morgan couldn't see Devilin's head, which meant the killer couldn't see him. If he were alive and this was a ploy for a sure killing shot, Devilin would be working strictly by his hearing.

Morgan picked up two rocks from the ground and threw one at the side of the buggy. It missed and hit the ground but made little noise. He tried with the second one and this time hit the frame of the rig with a loud thunk.

Devilin came up quickly, his right hand extended at the sound, and he fired. Morgan had his weapon out as well and tried for a shoulder shot on the killer, but the round missed on the outside.

Devilin roared in anger, threw his six-gun at Morgan, kicked out of the tangle of the buggy and ran for the woods that lined the river.

Morgan ran after him, not wanting to take the time to mount up. It would be a foot game now. He got into the brush shortly after Devilin did but somehow the big man had vanished.

As he had done so often in woodsy chases, Morgan stopped and listened. He heard the gurgling of the stream as it came down gentle rapids. Then a new sound, the swish of a branch and the small crack of a stick underfoot to the left.

Morgan started that way and glimpsed Devilin's brown jacket as he slid behind a cottonwood tree. A gentle wind whipped the cottony seeds toward Morgan until they nearly blinded him. He moved toward the big tree and saw Devilin bolt away from it and run for another tree along the side of the stream.

"No good, Devilin. You're on foot and not a

good woodsman. You might as well give up and face the music."

"Rather let you put a bullet through my brain than face a trial in this fucking town. They'll hang me after a two hour trial, and you know it."

"You murdered three men including the sheriff. What's to like about you?"

As they talked they worked their way along the river bank. Morgan never had a clear shot. Too many small trees and willow shoots confused and shaded the target.

At least they were headed back toward town, Morgan decided. Ahead he saw where the river swept in a wide curve, and no trees grew along the bank there. They probably had been uprooted when the river dug out the bend over the years.

Devilin hesitated at the open space. Here he must know that he would be a perfect target.

"Three more rounds, killer. What are you going to do now?"

Devilin looked at him through 20 yards of willow, then ran and jumped as far into the Grand Ronde river as he could. It was just downstream from the bend, and the river had still dug out a deep trench. Devilin went underwater, surfaced and swept toward Morgan who had hurried to the bank.

Morgan had no safe target, only the man's head and flailing arms. Another ten yards downstream Devilin came to shallow water and soon was only in the river up to his waist. He struck out for the far shore another 20 feet away.

Morgan knew he had to cross. He ran to the shallow part, waded in and fell. He had held the six-gun high but water splashed on it and he scowled, hoping he hadn't wet the caps on the nipples so much they wouldn't fire.

He kept his footing then and waded through the water to the far shore where he saw Devilin stepping out of the stream to the bank, then running again toward town.

Morgan closed the distance. The killer was getting tired. At 20 feet, Morgan brought up the six-gun and pulled the trigger. The hammer hit on a soaked cap on the nipple and the round didn't fire. He cocked the weapon and pulled the trigger again, aiming for Devilin's legs.

The round fired and Devilin bellowed in pain, turned and stared a moment over his shoulder, then kept on running. When another shot proved to be wet as well Morgan pushed the weapon back in his holster and ran harder.

Ahead Morgan saw a small cabin. A woman with a child were outside where she hung wash on a clothesline.

"Get inside!" Morgan shouted, but the woman couldn't hear him. By the time she could, she saw Devilin charging down on her. He caught her by the waist and pulled her against him. A knife blade glittered in the sunlight as he held it to her throat.

Morgan stopped well away from the man.

"Come closer, Morgan. I want you to see this woman die when I slit her throat. Come on."

Morgan moved up to within ten feet of him and stopped.

"You kill her and you have no protection," Morgan said. "Then I'll strangle you to death and dump your body on the courthouse steps."

"No chance, big talker." He shook the woman. "You got a horse here, girl?"

"No, my husband has the mare. He's at work."

"Damn. Where's the closest riding horse?"

"About a mile downstream, out of town."

"The other direction."

"Don't rightly know."

The knife moved slightly and blood appeared on her throat. The woman screamed, and Devilin laughed.

"Now, tell me or I'll slit your throat ear to ear. You understand?"

"Mrs. Jensen, two houses down, has a riding horse in a little shed out back of her house."

"Good girl. Now you and me are walking down there, hear?"

"What about my baby?"

"Morgan can take care of him. Move."

The child looked four or five to Morgan and could take care of himself. Morgan walked 20 feet behind the other two as they worked down a lane toward the next house. They passed it, and apparently no one was home. The next house was a little larger than the other two. It had a shed in back and an outhouse, and there was smoke coming from a kitchen chimney.

"Good, the lady is home. Back door. Quickly." Devilin looked at Morgan. "You interfere in any way and I'll kill both women. You can count on it. They can hang me only once. I can kill a dozen times getting away if I have to."

Morgan edged toward the back of the house beyond the rear kitchen door. When Devilin looked at the door, Morgan rushed around him and to the back of the shed.

The horse, a dapple gray, watched him come. The mare didn't have on a saddle, only a bridle where she munched on hay at the small manger. Morgan untied the lead line and backed her out of the shed, dropped the line and whacked her on the rump. She stood there. He slapped her again, then twice more before she stepped forward, then took off at a trot toward the flatlands beyond the house.

Devilin came around the shed a moment later with the woman still in his grasp. The horse had moved 50 yards into the open field and kept going.

"You did it. Damn you."

Morgan lifted the six-gun and turned the cylinder back to the unfired, wet cap. He'd heard that those caps on the nipples could dry out in time and fire just like new. He had a shoulder in plain view and aimed the weapon at Devilin and pulled the trigger.

The weapon fired and Devilin took the round in his right shoulder, slamming backward and losing his grasp on the woman, but the knife made a slash through her blouse on her shoulder as he went down.

Morgan leaped toward the man and got there in time to kick the knife from his right hand and pin his arm to the ground with his boot.

Morgan talked to the woman as he watched Devilin. "Ma'am, are you cut bad on your shoulder?"

"No, not bad. I can tend to it, or Mrs. Tarnell can. First I want to go and get my little Bobby."

"Sorry about this, ma'am. You were brave through it all. He truly might have hurt you bad, but no more. Oh, could I bother you to ask the lady for a piece of twine or rope. This one needs his hands tied behind his back so he's up to no more mischief."

A half hour later, Morgan marched Devilin up to the courthouse and to the jail.

"Who's the senior ranking man here?" Morgan asked the two deputies who stared at him. One of them held up his hand. "Got a prisoner for you. As of now you're the acting sheriff. It's your duty to keep this man under lock and key for his trial. Make damn sure he doesn't get away. You should call a doctor and have him treat the patient in the cell, but keep him handcuffed while the doctor is with him. You understand all this?"

"He the bastard who killed Sheriff Larson?" the deputy asked.

"That's the man. So take special care of him. Oh, this man must not die of his wounds or die while trying to escape. If he doesn't stand trial, I'll hold you personally responsible. Do I make myself clear?"

The deputy nodded, caught hold of Devilin and shoved him toward the row of six cells.

Morgan gave a small sigh of relief as he stepped back to the street and hurried over to the Wildcat Saloon.

It was starting to get dark as he walked in. The place was almost back to normal. The blood had been scrubbed off the wooden floor and bar where the two men had died. Nancy sat on her stool at the end of the bar.

The collection man was gone from the door and the whores in the back all had at least some clothing on.

"You get him?"

Morgan nodded.

"Good, about time. You decided if he's the real Chance Rivers or not?"

"He's not Rivers. Just another overbearing maniac who soon will feel the bite of a hemp noose. He's in jail. Who can get the legal machinery rolling?"

"Loophole Larson will do it. He'll get the charges spelled out and filed so he can defend Devilin. He often does that. I'll see him as soon as he comes in."

"How's Zack?"

"He'll live. He took a round in the shoulder. Doc fixed him up. Missed the bone. I told him to take a few days off and rest up. He earned it."

"What about you?"

"Hell, I earned it, too. I got my saloon back. I got the girls acting like real whores again instead of show-off sex kittens. We even figured out who Devilin wasn't. Now how do you find Rivers?"

"Find him by finding the damn rustlers. I got to thinking that there could be somebody on the Running R who is doing the rustling and old man Johnson don't know nothing about it. Seen it happen more than once. Big spread has lots of places to lose a few hundred head so nobody knows about them. Another couple hundred with strange brands on them can get lost out there, too."

"So you riding back to the Running R?"

"Nope. Going to rest up tonight, and tomorrow I'll try and find where them rustlers are holding the herd. If I can find that, I'll get a quick line on who the boss is and then we'll see which way the damn fur flies."

"Still think it might be somebody on the Running R?"

"Still a damn fine possibility. I know for sure that Jed Bradburn isn't rustling his own cattle."

Nancy nodded. She waved for her new barman to bring Morgan a beer. "You want to stay with me tonight?" she asked softly.

Morgan grinned. "Not tonight. I need to get some real sleep, but I'll take up your offer later."

"Deal. Finish your beer. Have some supper and get some sleep. You'll probably need it chasing rustlers tomorrow."

Morgan agreed with her.

Chapter Ten

That same afternoon the sheriff died, Jed Bradburn came to town to talk to the banker, H. Justin Parmley. He had a sound business proposition. Jed needed six or eight good blooded bulls to run with his herd to produce better quality, stockier and heavier steers. He'd seen it done at other ranches.

He sat in the chair beside Mr. Parmley's desk in the bank, well aware that Priscilla watched him from her desk on the other side of the room. Parmley had looked over the sheet of estimates that Jed had drawn up.

"Mr. Parmley, my four year plan is working out well. Next spring I'll have near a hundred head of steers to sell, and the price is around forty dollars a head right now. That's four thousand dollars cash money. All I need to get some good breeding bulls is two thousand. I've got a seller and a good price, and I need them now so we'll have a better drop next spring."

Parmley looked up, his face serious. He pointed at the set of figures on the paper. "Mr. Bradburn, from the looks of your plan it does seem possible, but won't you have a lot of expenses between now and next spring when you get that bank draft for your market-ready steers?"

"Yes sir, I will. My crew said they can wait a bit for all of their pay, and I'm keeping them on over the winter months. I can run a tab at the general store, and I've got a backer who will stake me to what else I need before the money comes in. That's why it's such a good deal."

"Yes, I see what you mean. Let me think it over for a couple of days. You come in on Friday and I'll have a decision for you." Both men stood up, realizing that the interview was over. He'd done the best he could. If the bank wouldn't loan him the money, he might talk to Nancy.

"Now, young man, I figure if I don't let you go in another minute or two, I'm going to have some real trouble on my hands. That young lady over at the far desk has been shooting angry glances at me for the last five minutes. If I'm not mistaken, she wants to talk to you.

"Oh, it was good to have you to our house for dinner the other night. It turned out to be a most enjoyable evening. I especially liked the way you made the *New York Times* story seem not quite so important as the price of beef in Portland." He held out his hand.

"Well, I'll see you Friday, then."

Jed shook the banker's hand and and walked over to where Priscilla sat at her desk, tapping a pencil on a notepad.

She looked up, her pretty face clouded with a frown. "That certainly took long enough. What did Father say? Did he approve of your loan?"

Jed slumped in a chair beside her desk. "Not exactly. He said to come in Friday for his decision. So, looks like I got to wait until Friday."

"Oh, that makes me just furious. I told him you had an excellent set of figures and a fine ranch and that he should loan you the money. Now I'll just have to start all over again on him."

She reached out her hand and touched the back of his. "Well, it will work out all right. I assure you. Now, enough of the banking business. It's after four o'clock. I was hoping that you might want to take me to supper at one of the restaurants."

Jed looked at her in surprise. He only had a five dollar gold piece in his pocket and hadn't planned on anything like this.

"Well, sure, I'd like that."

"It doesn't have to be an expensive place. I just want to have supper with you and talk. Then you can walk me home. Maybe we could ride in the backyard swing like we did the other night."

He remembered kissing her that night and he nearly blushed, but just grinned. "Yeah, that would be great.

"I have to check at the general store for mail, then I'll be back and we'll go get an early supper. That be all right?"

She shook her pretty head. "Not in the least, Jed Bradburn. I'm through here for today. I'll go with you to the store and save you that long walk back here." She grinned, and her dimples popped into place.

They left the bank after she talked a moment with her father who looked at Jed and nodded.

Once outside the bank, Priscilla caught his arm and walked close beside him. For a moment she pressed his arm against her breast, then she eased up and they walked side by side.

She looked up at him and smiled. "Jed Bradburn, I do enjoy walking down the street like this beside you. It seems so natural. I want everyone to see us walking this way."

For a moment Jed knew he couldn't say a word. He looked down and grinned at her and wanted to kiss her, but that was impossible right here on Main Street.

They went in the front of the general store to the post office, but there was no mail for Jed.

"Where should we have our supper?" he asked wondering if he would have to steer her to a more moderate priced place.

"The Ochoco Café has good food. It's nice there without being expensive. I always try to watch not to spend too much on things like this." She looked up at him and smiled that secret way she had lately.

The roast beef dinner and desert cost only 60 cents each, and Jed was greatly relieved. By the time they finished it was a little after six and not nearly dark yet.

"Let's walk down by the river," she said. "I like to throw rocks in the water. Do you ever try that?"

"Like skip a flat rock across the water?"

"My record is six skips," Priscilla said.

"Six? You'll have to show me."

They walked down three blocks to the Grande Ronde river and looked for rocks.

"I've got a good flat one," Priscilla said. She bent and threw the rock low and hard at the water to skip it. It slanted out in one huge jump and then made one more skip before it sank.

Jed found a round rock and showed it to her, then he bent low so his hand was just over the water and threw. The round rock skipped four times.

"Jed Bradburn, you cheated. You threw it too hard."

They both laughed and walked farther along the stream behind some trees. There was no one else around and no one could see them.

Priscilla stood in front of Jed and looked up at him. Slowly their faces came together, and then his arms came around her and he held her close as he kissed her lips. Her arms went around him and they made the kiss last for a moment, then came apart but still held each other.

"Such a beautiful lady," Jed said. It was the first thing that popped into his head.

Priscilla smiled and reached up to kiss him again. She kept her lips tightly closed and his tongue touched them, then pulled back. When their lips parted this time, she sighed and lay her head against his shoulder.

"Wishing all day I could do that," Priscilla said. "Even right there in the bank and then in the café. Jed Bradburn, you are such a fine man! I might just kiss you again."

When they parted this time, she swayed in his arms.

"Oh, I'm a little dizzy. I think I better sit down a minute."

There was a clearing near the bank where they

were still closed off from any prying eyes. They sat down, and she leaned against him.

"Jed Bradburn, there is nothing that I'd rather be doing right now than being here with you. It just feels so wonderful." She laughed softly. "Of course you being a fine kisser doesn't hurt either."

"Priscilla, I don't want to get in bad with your father. If he knew we were down here . . ."

She put a finger over his lips, then kissed them quickly and pulled away.

"Jedediah, you let me worry about my parents. I get along fine with both of them, especially Daddy. Let's just enjoy the afternoon. I love to sit here and watch the water."

She lay back in his arms and he held her. They talked about the town, their schooling, a dozen things. Then she turned and Jed reached down and kissed her. When his tongue touched her lips this time, she opened them and sighed and hugged him tighter.

His tongue explored her mouth and then withdrew, and she edged her tongue into his mouth a moment, then came out and broke off the kiss.

"Oh, my!" she said. "That just makes me feel all warm and happy and contented." She looked up at him. "You know, sort of hot and wondering about . . ."

She stopped and ducked her head against his shoulder. He moved his legs. He had had a full blown erection the first time he kissed her and now it was throbbing. He caught her chin and turned her head and kissed her cheek, then her nose and lastly her lips again.

"Oh damn!" she whispered just as his lips closed

over hers. As he kissed her his hand came between them and lay on her breast. He knew she would yell at him and move his hand, maybe even get up and run home, but she didn't.

The kiss continued and she sighed again and he rubbed her breast through her dress. When the kiss ended her hand came up and covered his on her hot breast, but she didn't move his hand.

She looked up at him and sighed again. Her face was so open and vulnerable that he wanted to kiss her again.

"Jed Bradburn, I hope that I can trust you. I simply will not be one of these girls who gets married when she's three months pregnant. You will respect me, won't you?"

He started to move his hand but she held it there. "No, you don't have to move it. Your hand there makes me feel just wonderful. What I'm saying is that I don't want to feel so great that I get carried away and rip my clothes off. You know. I can't do that—not yet."

She kissed him on the lips quickly. "Jed Bradburn, I'm in love with you. Everyone but you knows it. I love you so much it hurts. We can kiss and, you know, feel around a little, but I absolutely won't go all the way."

Jed tried to say something, but his voice was ragged and she smiled and kissed his lips quickly again.

"I know, Jed. I know how excited you men can get. But I know I can trust you so we won't do anything we'd be ashamed of tomorrow."

She moved his hand and unbuttoned the three fasteners in the middle of her dress and put his hand back at the opening. Jed looked at her and she nodded. His hand stole through the opening, moved away the soft chemise and closed around her bare breast.

Priscilla gasped when he touched her bare flesh. "Oh, my! Oh, Jed, darling! Oh, my!" He left his hand still for a moment, then began caressing her.

When Jed bent and kissed her, this time her mouth came open and his tongue darted inside. When they parted she sighed again and looked up at him, a tear in one eye.

"Jed, it's so glorious!"

He moved her hand down to where his erection bulged in his pants. She felt him, then stared at him wide-eyed and he nodded. Slowly she rubbed him. Inside her dress top, his hand fondled one breast, then moved to the other one and rubbed it, feeling the heat. He found her nipple and tweaked it and pushed it side to side.

She clung to him. "Oh, Jed, I've never been so happy, so ecstatic in my life. No one has ever touched me that way before. Not anyone. I'm so thrilled that it's you."

Jed moved his hand, unbuttoned the top two fasteners on her dress and another one below, then spread the fabric apart. He looked around. It was starting to get dusk. No one was anywhere around. He kissed her lips gently, then caught hold of her chemise which covered her breasts. He looked at her.

Slowly Priscilla nodded.

Jed lifted her chemise to her throat and stared at her perfect breasts. They were larger than he had guessed. Bright pink areolas an inch wide circled each breast and the nipples now filled with hot blood stood tall and a deeper shade of red. When he bent and kissed her breast, Priscilla yelped.

Then her eyes went wide and she shivered. Her breath came in panting gasps and she pushed her hips against him as the first of the tremors crashed through her. Her whole body shook, and she moaned and cried out in relief and joy as the climaxes powered through her young body again and again. He held her breast as she jolted and shivered and then finally relaxed and looked up at him as if he were a miracle man.

When she could breathe again, she reached up and kissed his lips softly, then hugged him. "I've heard a girl talk about doing that, but I never had before. It was . . . it was just so exciting, so thrilling, so perfect!"

She looked at him. His hips moved under her hand. "You, too?" she asked.

He nodded since by then he couldn't stop. He pushed against her, and she leaned back in the grass. He moved half on top of her, his hips pounding against hers, his fires building. He shoved his hips at her again and again until he was spent and felt the wetness inside his underwear.

Oh, damn, she probably would never speak to him again. His breath came in sobbing gasps for another minute and then he pushed back from her. Her face had a wide-eyed stare for a moment, then she smiled.

"Did I . . . did I frighten you, Priscilla?"

"No, of course not. I'm so thrilled that I excited you, that you did it right here with me. It's the first time I've ever seen a man, you know, climax that way. So powerful! I thought mine was great, but you were so domineering, so insistent, so wild to get it done, even all by yourself."

"Good, good. I was afraid that I'd lost you, that you'd be angry with me for not being able to stop."

"Darling, how could I be angry with you? I didn't stop either. You're the man I love and someday we can be together, inside me the way it's supposed to be. But not now. Not until . . ."

"Priscilla, will you marry me?"

She threw her arms around him, her breasts crushing against his chest. She kissed him so hard he thought his lips might be bruised.

"Yes, my darling. Of course I'll be your wife. It's what I've been dreaming of for over a year now, and you never even knew."

She pulled her chemise down, then buttoned her dress. "I think it's time we get home, before it gets completely dark. I want you to ask Daddy if you can come courting. He won't have any objections, I know. Then after a few weeks, we can make the announcement and set a date. I want so terribly much to be married to you, Jed Bradburn."

They walked home, arriving at the fancy three-story house just before dark.

Afterwards on the ride home, Jed couldn't remember what had happened, but he did know that Mr. Parmley had said he could come courting if it was all right with Priscilla. Right then she burst through the door into the library and caught Jed's hand and told her father indeed it was more than all right.

Somehow the ride back to the Circle B was

shorter tonight. Jed even sang some old herding
songs he had learned years ago. Jed laughed. He'd
never felt this way before. He'd had lots of wom-
en, some wild, some for the first time, but not
a one of them had ever made him feel the way
Priscilla did. What a day! What a wonderful girl!

Early the next morning, Morgan mounted the
same gray he had rented before and made the ten
mile ride to Jed's Circle B ranch. He would have
to go farther on to the east to find the sheetrock
where they had lost the rustlers. However he
wanted to be sure that Jed knew he was out
there and figured he could pick up a quick lunch
from Biscuits. The man made a great roast beef
sandwich.

An hour after he left the Circle B ranch, Morgan
found the sheetrock again. He worked both sides
critically, then began to challenge every tree and
bush that lay next to the side of the canyon wall.
He was in for a long haul, had even brought a
pair of blankets in case he had to stay overnight,
and had some tins of food in his saddlebags for
an emergency meal.

Morgan worked the rest of the morning checking the sides of the valley. At noon he dropped
down near a small stream and had one of the
sandwiches and a cup of water. He didn't want to
start a fire and boil coffee. Smoke up here would
travel miles and give him away.

It was well after two o'clock that afternoon
when he worked around a small pine tree, brushed
back some branches and found what had eluded
him. Through the scattering of brush and some
pines, he saw an opening in the rock wall no more

than ten feet high. The shifted slabs of rock over it seemed to close off the whole area, but they left a small passage from this valley down into another valley over a gentle ridge.

He left his horse, walked through and saw tracks, both horse and cattle. He had found the route again. He followed the tracks to where they came out of the timber into the valley that extended to his left a mile or two.

The tracks were there and then suddenly gone. Ahead he saw a small stream, no more than a foot deep and five yards wide, that chattered down from its birthplace high above in the ridges and peaks.

Brush out all traces of the tracks from the rock to the stream, then drive the cattle up the creek for a mile or so to discourage any tracking.

Morgan brought his gray through the passage and rode upstream. He kept a wary eye out for any sign of cattle leaving the creek. He found evidences of it in two places, the last one producing tracks on the opposite bank that he could follow.

A mile upstream the stream slanted to the left and around a bend in the valley. As he worked to the bend he smelled wood smoke, and then saw a thin stream of smoke coming from a patch of timber near the end of the valley.

Spotted over the green grass in the high valley were dozens of cattle. He had found the rustled herd.

Morgan rode into the edge of the timber and moved upstream. After almost a mile, he dismounted and worked over to the edge of the timber to check on the smoke. It was still there, stronger now, and he could see the edge of a tent through a break in the brush.

Morgan worked forward now on foot, keeping sight of the camp, making sure he was well in cover, and watching and listening for any sign of humans. No rider worked the cattle in the valley. They all might be out setting up another rustling job on one of the ranches.

The closer he came to the tent, the slower he moved, making certain his cover was complete.

Another ten minutes and he crawled on his belly to a point he had picked for observation. He was 30 yards from the camp, which he now saw had two tents that would hold four or five men each. A cooking fire held a metal grill and a steel rod set on forked sticks for hanging pots.

The creek ran by the side of the tents for drinking and washing. He had seen no one at the camp so far. To one side, two saddle horses twitched at flies. Both had their saddles off.

Morgan waited.

Ten minutes later a man came out of the nearest tent, stretching. He went to one side, urinated, came back and put a pot of water on the grill for coffee.

Just one man? The coffee maker called out and someone else in the same tent answered.

"What time?" the outside man asked.

A head poked from the tent. "Said sometime about four. That's all he told me."

The man by the fire wore a six-gun on his hip. Morgan had never seen him before.

Morgan decided it was better to take the one man now and get the other one later. He circled the camp in the brush, came up behind the tent, drew his six-gun, checked the five loads, and then ran lightly toward the man squatting by the fire. The rustler whirled but was too late to miss the revolver that hit the side of his head and made him unconscious in a second.

Morgan took the man's weapon and tied his hands behind him with some leather boot lacing. Morgan walked quietly to the tent, flipped up the flap and stood in the door, his weapon covering the man in blankets on the floor.

"Up and easy," Morgan said.

"Who the hell are you?" the cowboy asked.

"I'm your new pard in the rustling business. Up and out and no problems, or you're dead where you sit."

The cowboy got outside and Morgan tied his hands behind his back. The first man came around groaning, then shouting before he saw Morgan.

"What have we here?" the older man who had been unconscious asked.

"I'd say we have two candidates for a walk to their own hanging. Rustlers who get caught red-handed don't live long in this part of Oregon."

"Ain't no rustlers. We work for the Running R."

"Then you're about ten miles off their property. I figured there would be six or seven of you considering the two tents."

"Just us two."

"What's your name?" Morgan demanded.

"Percival," one said.

"I'm Tom," the other one admitted.

"Well, Percival, shall we ride now or wait for your other mates to arrive?"

"Just the bloody two of us!"

"A bit Englisher, ain't you, Percival? Don't know as we've ever hung an Englisher around here."

"You a lawman?"

"Nope, just an interested citizen."

"How the hell you find us?"

"Percival, you know that two hundred head leaves tracks, even when you drive them up a stream. Smart, but not smart enough."

"We strike a bargain?"

"Not likely."

"Like trading us for the mastermind of the affair. I can give him to you on a platter with kidney pie and plum pudding for desert."

"Somebody from the Running R?"

"I don't play games, laddie. If you want him, the two of us get to ride out of here for California."

"Interesting, but I'll get him anyway. Looks like you're about ready to drive this herd to market."

"No such thing!" the younger man said.

"Shut up, Tom." Percival scowled at the younger man, then looked back at Morgan. "If you're not a lawman, what's your interest?"

"Personal. Friend of mine lost a lot of beef."

"So take back the beef, and get the head man at the same time. You'll be a hero, and you'll still have somebody for the gallows."

Tom stood and looked down the valley through the trees. "He's a coming, Percival."

"Quick now, man. You get the boss and the cattle and every penny I got to me name, almost fifty dollars. Is it a deal? How can you go wrong? No man should hang for snipping a couple of beef. Have a heart, man. Look at the lad there, not over twenty he ain't. You want him never to see twenty-one? Make up your mind, man. He'll be here in five minutes."

Morgan looked at the kid and saw a lot of himself in the young man when he was that age. He drew his knife and cut the rawhide.

"Get on your horse and get out of here, Tom, and never get tied into a rustling job again or I'll find you and hang you myself. Git!"

Morgan looked at Percival. "Work a deal with you. I need one rustler to testify against the big boss. You testify, and I guarantee you that you won't be prosecuted. You'll walk free as soon as you testify and the trial is over."

"I'd rather ride out now."

"Then I might not be able to convict the boss man riding up. You've got two minutes to decide. Yes or no?"

Percival stared at the rider and chuckled. "Hell, why not. Never did like that son-of-a-bitch anyway. Serve the big bastard right."

Morgan hid in the tent as the rider came closer.

"Cut me free so he won't suspect," Percival said.

When Morgan cut the leather thong, Percival rubbed his wrists and waved at the rider.

"A bargain is a bargain, mate. I won't douse you. He's meat in your skillet. Here he is."

The rider charged in the last few yards, skidded to a stop and jumped off the horse.

"Percival, you old skinflint, we're going to move out the herd tonight."

Morgan stared at the boss of the rustling operation from inside the tent, and his jaw dropped in surprise.

Chapter Eleven

The boss swung down off his horse and confronted Percival.

"Wasn't that Tom I saw riding out? Where the hell is he going?"

Percival shrugged.

Morgan stepped out of the tent and grinned. "Well, if it isn't Loophole Sheeler, the fast talking lawyer and top hand on the rustling game. Good to see you."

"What the hell?"

"About the size of it. Going to be your address for the rest of eternity, I'd say. Don't try for that hideout. Ease it out of your pocket and drop it on the ground. Now, Loophole!"

The lawyer shrugged and pulled a small hideout pistol from his jacket pocket and let it fall to the ground.

"Now, put your hands behind you."

"You expect to get me back to La Grande? I've

got five more men coming who can shoot and don't mind a body or two."

"We'll be gone by the time they get here. Tie his hands behind him, Percival. You know how."

"Don't do it, Percival," Loophole said. "The two of us can take him right now."

Loophole lunged toward Morgan, but the barrel of the six-gun slammed downward and hit Loophole on the side of the head. He grunted and dropped to the ground, not out but groggy.

"Get his hands tied and he won't cause us so much trouble," Morgan said. "Let's move out before those other men show up. I like the package we've got right now. The others won't move the herd without word from Loophole, will they?"

"Not a chance, Mr. Morgan. They just follow orders. They ain't due back until about dark tonight with some more stock."

"Be a good time for us to get away and arrange to come back later."

Together they got Loophole on his horse, untied his hands and retied them to the saddle horn. Then Morgan headed back toward town.

"You lead the way, Percival. No surprises and no mistakes. We made a bargain and I expect you to keep your word."

"No doubt about it, Mr. Morgan. I might have nipped a few cattle, but when I give my word, I stand by it."

When Loophole started yelling, Morgan put a round over his head, and the sound of the gunfire brought the lawyer back to his senses. He rode on silently. He'd lost his hat and his hair was tousled and windblown.

It took them three hours to ride back to town. Morgan told Percival that they would keep him in jail until the trial in what they called protective custody. He wouldn't be charged and could go out for his meals.

They rode up to the courthouse and caused a stir when the people saw Loophole with his hands tied.

"What did he do?" a stranger asked.

"Broke the law," Morgan said, leading Loophole into the jail. It took Morgan a few minutes to explain what had happened to the deputy now acting as sheriff.

"So we charge Loophole with rustling, but Mr. Percival is here in protective custody. I understand, Mr. Morgan. I got both him and Devilin in jail. Getting to be a busy place."

"It could get busier," Morgan said and headed for the Wildcat Saloon. He told Nancy what had happened and asked if she could point out a pair of reliable riders who could deliver some messages. She called up two men.

"Now, how many cattle ranches are there around here and where are they?"

Nancy drew him a rough map of the Grande Ronde and Catherine Creek valleys and marked the ranches. There were six, two up Catherine and the others on the bigger stream.

"Looks like the Running R would be a good place to meet. I'll write out six letters and you two men deliver them. They have to get to the ranches before dark. Jed is out ten miles. Go out there first, then come back to the other Catherine Creek ranch. The other man will head out the Grande Ronde."

Nancy brought him paper, pen and ink, and he began to write the notices.

"Cattle rustlers discovered. Loophole Sheeler is the ringleader. Secret holding spot for herd found. Send two or three hands to the Running R ranch by midnight tonight. We'll move in on the culprits at daylight, capture those still alive and sort out the stock so it can be driven back to its home range."

After Nancy looked at the letter, they both copied it and sent one rider off for Jed Bradburn's place and the other Catherine Creek ranch.

They wrote out the note three more times, then got the second rider off for the other ranches along the Grande Ronde.

"Will they come?" Nancy asked.

"Do bears like honey? A rancher will do most anything to even the score with a rustler. We've got Loophole dead to rights and a man to testify against him. Oh, does the county have a district attorney?"

Nancy said they did. George Howard had been elected two years ago and was as honest as they come.

Morgan found Howard, who had heard about the rustlers and listened to the full story.

"I promised Percival complete immunity from prosecution if he testifies against Loophole. That way we have an airtight case against him for rustling. I know I didn't have the authority to do that, but I hoped that you would go along with me. This has been a big problem, and the ranchers will really give you a boost if you get this settled."

Howard eased back in his chair and nodded. "Looks like you've done the most work here. I think we can go along with the immunity deal for Percival. I'll make it clear to him that he must testify and Loophole must be convicted or it's no deal. I'll talk to him and get the criminal complaint filed at once and notify the circuit court we have two cases to try. Old Judge Noonan might skip a spot or two and come to town early. He does that for big cases now and then."

Morgan was feeling tired and remembered he hadn't had much to eat since noon. It was close to dinner time by then. He thanked the D.A. and went to find an eatery.

A big steak with all the trimmings made him feel better. He went back to see Nancy. Word was out about the rustlers, and everyone was surprised about Loophole.

Morgan had a cold beer at the bar and asked Nancy how long it would take him to ride to the Running R.

"About an hour and a half. You've been out there before."

"True, and I don't have to be there until midnight. Mind if I have a nap on your big soft bed?"

"You want company or you want to sleep."

"Tough decision, but this time I better get some sleep. Wake me up at ten o'clock."

Upstairs, Morgan fell on the soft featherbed and went to sleep almost before he got his eyes shut.

He woke up by himself at nine o'clock, shook his head to rattle his brains around in the right spot and hurried downstairs. He waved at Nancy, traded horses at the livery and rode for the Running R ranch.

No guard met him at the ranch's big gate. When he rode into the ranch yard a dozen lanterns lit the area near the bunk house. A big jug of applejack had been uncorked and it flowed into all sorts of glasses and mugs and cups.

Morgan found the elder Johnson who stared at him in the lantern light a minute, then let out a screech and rushed toward him.

"Don't know how you nailed him, Morgan, but we all owe you a big vote of thanks. Might even scrape up a small reward. The guys have been talking about it. How in hell did you find them bastards?"

Morgan told them a little about it. There were 15 men in the group. Each had a rifle and a six-gun and plenty of loads and rounds. Only the riders from the Block WW hadn't arrived yet, since they were the farthest out on the Grande Ronde.

The Running R cook worked up a midnight supper for the men, and they ate steak and potatoes and a mess of vegetables, lots of coffee and applejack chasers.

The Block WW riders came in about 12:30 and had a quick bite, then Morgan figured they should be heading out.

"It's a four hour ride and not easy. When we get close, the key word is quiet. If we go in there talking and laughing, we won't have no rustlers at all come daylight. Anybody in the army?"

Two hands went up. "We've got to have no talking or singing or whistling, no noise at all when I pass the word. Won't be for some time. But when I say quiet, that's what it means if you men want any rustlers to hang next week."

They rode out with Morgan in the lead followed
by Johnson and Jed. Jed pulled up beside Morgan.
"How the hell did you find them? I thought we
worked them tracks to a stand-off?"

Morgan told him about the last valley near the
sheetrock.

"Took some closer looking than we did that
day," Morgan said. "Should get some stock back
for you tomorrow."

It was a long, hard ride, and they took their
time. Even when they got there and in position,
they would have an hour or two to wait for dawn.

Three hours later they stopped for a break. By
then any effect of the applejack had worn off and
half the men took a quick snooze. A half hour of
rest and then the posse was back in the saddle.

When they came into the valley where the herd
had bedded down for the night, Morgan called a
halt. He divided the men into two groups, sending
one across the valley and to come up the other side through the trees until they could smell
the campfire smoke. They would sit there and
wait.

Come dawn, Morgan and his half of the troops
would charge the camp with six-guns blazing,
surprise any rustlers still there and capture them.
If any got away, Johnson and his blocking force
would grab them as they ran through the trees.

"None of these guys will have time to saddle
a horse, so they'll be on foot. Don't let them get
past you."

Morgan moved them up the valley to the bend,
then sent Johnson and his crew to the other side
of the valley.

"Work around just inside the timber line until you see the campfire or smell the smoke. Stay a couple of hundred yards back, then none of our stray rounds will hit you."

Johnson nodded. He'd done some time in the Union army in the Civil War and knew what he was doing.

Morgan moved his men up another half mile, then they dismounted, tied their horses and hiked forward cautiously. They smelled the wood smoke at once, but Morgan moved them closer. When he figured they were 200 yards from the end of the valley, he took Jed ahead and scouted it out. They were only 100 yards from the camp. He saw the glow of a campfire, so somebody was still there. He counted four horses tied to a line but there could be more.

Dawn was another hour away.

Morgan went back and brought up his nine men. He positioned them beside trees and behind fallen logs 30 yards from the tent. They would fire their rifles just over the tents, with three rounds each, then stop firing and see what the rustlers did. If they chose to fight, they would pick them off with rifles as they came out of the tents. No sense getting within pistol range unless they had to.

"Now we wait for dawn," Morgan told them. He talked softly to each man, then went to the middle of the line and waited.

Dawn came slowly, a hint of light to the east, then a burst of brightness against a cloudy sky, followed by a gradual lightening that showed the tent and five horses.

One cowboy lifted up and waved at Morgan,

holding out both hands in frustration, asking "When?"

Morgan told them he'd fire the first shot, then they should join in for three rounds. When he could see the coffeepot sitting on the burned-out fire, he decided it was light enough. He shouldered his borrowed rifle and sent a round into the coffeepot, slamming it off the fire with a surprisingly loud clatter.

Two dozen rounds peppered into the top of the tent and into the trees. He had explained they didn't want to kill the men inside, just flush them out and capture them.

"Cease fire!" Morgan bellowed, and the firing stopped. The tent flaps flared and two men came out with their fingers laced together on top of their heads.

"Where are the rest of them?" Morgan barked. The men said in the other tent. One more man came out, then one sprinted from the tent, shooting over his shoulder at the line of gunmen. Morgan tracked him with his rifle and fired. The man took the round in the upper left thigh, tumbled into the woods, lost his six-gun and lay there screaming for help.

The last man came out of the tent with his hands over his head and it was all over. Morgan and Jed rushed forward and checked the tents, found them to be empty and waved the two squads into the camp.

The wounded rustler was patched up so he wouldn't bleed to death, then all five men were tied with their hands behind their backs and set on the ground.

Next order of business was breakfast. They

checked over the rustler's supplies and found bacon, eggs, biscuits, strawberry jam and coffee. One man found a fry pan and went to work setting up breakfast for everyone but the rustlers.

An hour later, they sent six men into the meadow to start rounding up the steers. The rest of the men followed shortly with the rustlers tied together with a long lariat.

It took most of the morning to sort out the various brands, with two men cutting and the rest holding their share of the cattle in different sections of the valley.

By noon they were done. Jed had found 18 of his steers, all three year-olds that would be ready for spring market.

"That's seven hundred and fifty dollars you just saved me, Morgan," Jed said.

Morgan grinned. "Consider that my wedding present to you. I hear you're courting Priscilla."

Jed grinned. "Yeah, about time, I reckon. Kit and me are taking off, driving our bunch out of the valley first. We have the smallest herd. Guy from the Running R said they have near sixty head in their batch."

Morgan waved and rode out to check with Johnson. The big man grinned.

"Saved us a batch of steers, Morgan. My thanks. Now I won't need that gunman. He's starting to get on my nerves anyway. I'll send him into town tomorrow and you can have that hi-de-ho shooting contest with him."

"Might just do that," Morgan said. He sat on his mount as the various crews began driving their herds through the one narrow outlet to the next valley.

Morgan turned for town. It was another three hours ride and he wasn't looking forward to it.

Morgan tied his mount to the rail in front of the Wildcat Saloon just after 4 P.M. and made it to the first table. Nancy slid off her stool and brought him a shot of whiskey and a cold beer.

"Done?" she asked.

Morgan looked up and nodded. He grabbed the beer and tipped the bottle, draining it in one long pull. Then he gasped for breath a minute before tossing down the whiskey. He stared at Nancy.

"Nigh near to done."

"Catch any more rustlers?

"Five more. Johnson said three of them were too damned young to know what they were doing. One said he was sixteen, the other two seventeen. He whipped them with a stick and put them on their mounts and yahooed them down the valley. Better than hanging, and they would remember it the rest of their lives. The other two older ones he said he'll bring into town tomorrow. He might and he might not. Nobody cares. They got their steers back, over two hundred and fifty head all tolled. That's ten thousand dollars worth of beef steak."

He looked at Nancy, and his eyes drooped shut. He had to catch himself from falling on the table.

"Upstairs," Nancy said. "You need about thirty-six hours of sleep. When I can't even keep a man's eyes open, he's in a bad way."

She took him up to her bed, pulled his boots and pants off, then rolled him into bed. He was sleeping before she could pull a silk sheet over him.

"Damn," she whispered. "A man in my bed and I'm walking away. But then he's too pooped to pop. Just wait until I get him rested up."

Morgan slept until ten the next morning and woke up furious with himself. He dressed, reloaded his six-gun with fresh charges and hurried downstairs. He waved at Nancy, took his mount back to the livery and took out another one. Morgan rode to the edge of town where the river road came in from the Grande Ronde. It was the way men rode in from the Running R. If he'd slept in and missed Chance Rivers coming to town from the Running R, he'd bash in his own face.

A half hour later he saw two men coming along the trail. He rode out to meet them. One of them was small and weasel-like. The other man sat tall in the saddle with broad shoulders, a gun tied down on his right thigh. He wore a surly expression and only glanced at Morgan as they passed.

Morgan stopped his mount and turned.

"Chance Rivers," he called. The big man spun around, surprise and anger on his face. He dug his spurs into the horse's flanks and charged ahead toward town.

Morgan slammed after him. Morgan wondered if Rivers knew where he was heading. It looked like he was simply running. At least Morgan knew he had the right man this time. Now all he had to do was capture him without killing him.

Chapter Twelve

Even though Morgan's horse was fresh, he couldn't catch Chance Rivers before the man reached town. He darted past a team of six pulling a heavy freight wagon, and by the time Morgan got around them at the intersection, Rivers had dropped off his mount and vanished inside a store.

Morgan rode up in front, leaped off his horse and ran for the door. It was a saddle shop and leather goods store. He hesitated at the door, then ducked low and charged inside. The overpoweringly pleasant smell of the leather hit him like the smell of his mother's kitchen. It took him back to his father's leather shop in Idaho.

As he slid through the door a shot slammed through the air above him. When the sound of the exploding powder in the weapon faded, he heard footsteps on the stairs toward the back of the establishment.

Morgan waved at a man poised over a half-done saddle and dashed for the steps which led to a second floor with a closed door.

Morgan went up the steps close to the wall and saw that the door was not latched. He crouched low, then edged the door open slowly. It was a small sleeping room, but no one was in it. An open window showed why.

He charged to the window but saw only the top of River's head vanishing down the side of the building.

When Morgan sped across the flat roof to the far side, he found a ladder and Rivers jumping off the last rung.

Morgan went down the ladder quickly and followed the big man down the alley to the street. For a moment he lost Rivers when he vanished around the corner. Morgan ran around the building and stood panting on Main Street, looking for Chance Rivers.

A scream came from the second store down, a women's wear store. Morgan charged toward it and saw three women inside, all near hysterics. He stepped inside. One of them pointed to the door that led to the back. He had out his six-gun and walked silently to the panel. He slammed it open hard, standing beside the wall out of any line of fire from the backroom. One shot smashed through the opening and buried itself in the wall.

Morgan dove through the door, hit the floor, rolled and stopped behind a screen. A woman stood there bare to the waist with a new chemise in her hands. She smiled at him but made no move to cover her breasts. She pointed toward the back.

"Hold it, whoever you are," Rivers' voice boomed from the other side of the room. Now Morgan saw that it was divided into three dressing rooms for ladies to try on garments.

"You back off, laddie. I've got my hog leg nuzzled up to this woman's head, and she's a bloody corpse in about five seconds if you don't turn around and walk out the front door. I can see you, so don't do nothing stupid or this woman dies."

Morgan moved closer to the topless woman. "Is there a back door?" he asked in a whisper.

She shook her head.

"Okay, Rivers, you hold the high cards. I'm going." He pulled a blouse around the woman and then whispered, "Walk out the door and close it behind you. I'll stay here." She nodded and slipped into the blouse. Morgan made footsteps on the boards with his boots as the woman walked to the door, went out and closed it behind her.

Morgan held his six-gun under his shirt and cocked the hammer without making any sound. He waited behind the screen. For a moment nothing happened. Then a woman in the rear gave a sharp cry of pain.

"No, don't."

"We've got some time to wait, so what's it going to hurt?"

"My husband will kill you, that's what."

"He'd have to find me first."

Morgan looked around the screen and saw where he figured Rivers must be. There was no cover between his position and Rivers.

"You can't touch me as long as you hold that gun," the woman said.

"I can lay it down easy, but close to hand."

"I still don't think so. All the women out front know I'm here and that you're here. They'll talk, I'll get punished, and you'll get shot dead. My husband is the district attorney."

"Where's the back door?"

"There isn't one."

"Not even a window?"

"It's a small shop."

"He'll be waiting for me out front, but I've still got you as a hostage. I walk out with my gun to your head. First, you get into some clothes."

"You don't like me almost naked?"

"Sure, but you said I couldn't fuck you. Grabbing tits isn't enough."

"I'll dress. Just don't hurt me."

Morgan waited behind his screen. He moved one end of it soundlessly so it was closer to the path the two would take to the door. Rivers would have to come within two feet of this screen. That's when Morgan would have his chance.

"No, don't do that!"

"Just a few more feels of your tits isn't going to hurt you, is it? Damn, wish I had time to poke you. Bet you like to get fucked, right?"

"Really, that's no way to talk. Now let me get dressed."

It seemed to Morgan like an hour, but he knew it was little more than five minutes before he heard them moving forward.

"Now, I'll let you put that gun to my head, but don't you dare hurt me."

"You're not giving the orders, lady. Now move."

He saw a woman's shoe come around the screen. A few seconds later she took another

step, and then he could see Rivers' boots and
pants legs. Rivers was on the other side of her,
his right hand holding the gun to the right side
of her head. A quick slash with his revolver barrel
was Morgan's only hope.

They moved forward again and he could see
Rivers. Now! He jumped out, slashed down with
his weapon, felt the metal slam into metal and
saw the six-gun spin out of Rivers' hand and fall
to the floor. The weapon went off when it hit the
planks, but the round thudded into the wall.

Rivers spun the woman around, his forearm
around her throat, her body protecting him.

"Put down the gun or I strangle her right here,"
Rivers shouted. "I'll do it. I got nothing to lose."

Morgan knew he was right. Slowly, Morgan
lowered the gun.

"Now drop it. No—put it down soft and easy
on the floor, then lay down on your back, fingers
laced under your head." Morgan saw the terror
in the woman's eyes. The earlier flirtation had
degenerated into a private battle for her life. Her
eyes pleaded with him.

Morgan eased to the floor and laced his fingers.

"Damn good. Now stay there for ten minutes
or this pretty little filly gets her brains spread all
over Main Street."

Morgan saw the pair move to the door and
open it.

"Ladies, don't nobody move or you've got a
dead customer here. Sit down somewhere, all of
you."

As soon as the big man went through the door,
Morgan eased to his feet, grabbed his six-gun off

the floor and crept to the door. Rivers stood sideways to him, almost at the front door. The woman was still bound tightly to him by his forearm.

Then he pushed her aside and lunged for the front door. Morgan fired. He heard a roar of anger, then Rivers was out and into the street. Morgan raced to the front door and slid to the floor, looking out at the street. Rivers ran down the middle of the street, somewhat limping.

Morgan came up and raced after him. Morgan had four shots left, Rivers just two. Rivers darted into a saloon. Morgan was close behind him now, making up time on the limping man.

The saloon was dank and dark, and Morgan crouched inside the front door letting his eyes adjust. He spotted Rivers across the room and dove for the bar, wedging behind it. Rivers didn't shoot, realizing how short on rounds he was.

"Shut up, everybody!" Rivers bellowed. When the sounds of the voices inside died, Rivers yelled in rage.

"What the hell you chasing me for, damnit?"

"That little girl in Portland you raped, Rivers. Her pa don't like you. The Portland police are looking for you. That enough reason?"

"Who the hell are you? Like to know who the bastard is who I'm gonna kill."

"I'm Lee Morgan, Rivers. You'll remember that name right up to the time you drop through the trap on the scaffold with that noose around your neck."

Morgan edged around the end of the bar and saw Rivers running for the back door. Too many people in the way for a shot. Rivers only had two rounds left.

Morgan waited for the killer to get out the back door, then he followed him.

Chance Rivers stood 30 feet in back of the door with no protection.

Morgan edged out the door and dove behind a heavy wooden crate.

"I'm tired of running, Morgan. Go ahead, gun me down."

"Can't do that, Rivers. A jury's got to give you that sentence, not me. Hell, you might get a good lawyer and win your case."

"Not a chance in hell. You gun me or I'm gonna kill you. Take your choice." Rivers took one step forward, then another. He still had two rounds.

Morgan used up one of his four rounds. He aimed at the big man's right knee and fired around the edge of the box. The round drove home, shattered Rivers' knee and dropped him into the alley dirt.

"Damn you, Morgan!" He blasted a round into the edge of the wooden box, sending splinters at Morgan but no lead.

"Toss your iron to the side, well out of reach," Morgan ordered.

"Damn no, not until you kill me. Too damn tired of running, just too damn tired."

"You'll feel different tomorrow. You'll want a good woman and some whiskey and a poker game where you can cheat and get away with it. It's all a big thrill, isn't it?"

"Yeah, for as long as it lasts. For me, it's over. Never figured on living this long. So put me out of it, Morgan."

"Can't do that. I'm no lawman. I'd hang for gunning you."

"Tough luck." Rivers writhed in pain as he crawled forward, pushing with his good leg. Six more feet and he'd have an open shot at Morgan. Lee Morgan edged around the box, aimed and fired at Rivers' good leg. The round struck home, and the outlaw bellowed with rage and pain.

"Broke my goddamn leg, you bastard!"

"Throw out the gun and we'll get you to a doctor. He can give you something for the pain."

"Bastard!"

"Tough luck, as you said. Pitch out the weapon and your hideout. Never knew a gambler not to carry one."

"Fucking bastard! Maybe I'll just lay here and bleed to death."

"You're not bleeding that much. All you'll do is pass out from the pain. Make it easy on yourself."

"Morgan, I hope you rot in hell right beside me."

He threw his six-gun to one side, then worked a hideout pistol from a pocket and pitched it out as well.

Morgan came out from behind the box and ran to the saloon door. A dozen men crouched there, watching. "Somebody find a big wheelbarrow and somebody else go get the doctor."

An hour later, Morgan had Chance Rivers booked into the county jail on a Portland murder charge. The doctor confirmed that Rivers' right leg was broken. He put it in a heavy plaster cast and told him not to walk on it for a month. The doctor said there wasn't much he could do about the knee. When it healed it probably would be stiff. Maybe some doctors in Portland could paste his knee back together again.

Morgan figured he'd done a good day's work so he left for the closest restaurant and ordered two bowls of the beef stew, a pot of coffee and all the rye bread they had.

After he ate, he wandered down the street. He would be taking the afternoon stage tomorrow. The doctor said that would give Rivers' leg and knee a chance to settle down a little. He prescribed a moderate dose of laudanum for the pain but cautioned that the deputies should administer only a teaspoonful twice a day, so Rivers didn't get addicted to it.

Morgan went into the Wildcat Saloon and stepped up beside the high stool at the end of the bar where Nancy sat.

"So, I hear you nailed Chance Rivers."

"True. How about a beer, Zack? That is, if you can tend bar with one good wing."

"Easy." Zack flipped up a beer and unsnapped the cap.

Morgan took a long pull from the beer.

"Jed Bradburn is in town looking for you," Nancy said. "He should be out ranching, but he's courting the Parmley girl. You know about that?"

"Some."

"He said he got that loan from the bank to buy his new bulls. If that kid don't watch it, he's gonna be a big important rancher around this end of the woods one of these days."

"Wouldn't at all surprise me."

"What would?"

Morgan grinned. "Maybe you running for mayor of La Grande. Hell, you'd win in a walk. Might be good for the town."

"Her honor, the fucking mayor," Nancy said and laughed.

Jed came in the door, saw Morgan and hurried over. "Hey, big man with a gun, I've got a bone to pick with you," Jed said.

Chapter Thirteen

Lee Morgan looked up from his beer at Jed Bradburn with a curious frown.

"You've got a bone to pick with me? What about?"

"Hear you nailed that Chance Rivers killer and you never even asked me for a hand. Hey, I owe you a favor. Little miffed you didn't ask for some help."

Morgan grinned and signaled Zack for a cold beer for Jed. "From what I hear you been too busy courting a certain young lady to have any time left for anything else, even ranching."

"Now, Morgan, Jed was just working on his future brood stock. Can't blame a man for that," Nancy said.

"Man's got to strike while the bird is still in the bush, so to speak," Jed said with a grin.

"Congratulations, Jed." Morgan held out his hand and took Jed's. "Figure a good woman might just straighten you out so you can amount to something."

"Ain't that the truth. Fact is, I'm about ten years late now getting hitched to a single plow, so I figure it's about time." He pulled at the beer and put it down on the bar. "Also that same woman is outside waiting. She wants to talk to you about something and wouldn't tell me what."

Morgan finished his beer, put the bottle on the bar and turned. "No sense in keeping the lady waiting." He looked at Nancy. "Don't you go running off. I've got some business to talk to you about as well."

Outside, Priscilla walked up and down in front of the hardware store next to the saloon. She looked up as the two men came out.

"Mr. Morgan, I just wanted to thank you myself for all you've done for this town in the few days you've been here. You solved a rustling problem that we've had for over a year now. Loophole Sheeler had been stealing cattle from these ranches since way last spring. It's high time he was stopped. My special thanks." She reached up and kissed his cheek. "Now that's done. I don't like my debts to go unpaid. Will you be around for our wedding?"

"I figured you might be my best man," Jed said.

"Thanks for the invite, but I'm afraid I'm leaving town tomorrow on the afternoon stage. I have a date in Portland with the chief of police and a cell for Chance Rivers."

"Oh, well, we'll miss you," Priscilla said. She rummaged in her reticule and came out with an envelope. "Mr. Johnson was in this morning and said the ranch owners had taken up a collection to reward you for locating their cattle. More than ten thousand dollars worth of rustled stock, he said. He gave me this envelope to give to you."

She handed it to Morgan. "Didn't ask for any reward," he said. He opened the envelope and inside found six $50 bills. "I can do with this what I want?"

"Certainly," Priscilla said.

Morgan handed it to Jed. "Use this to buy another blooded range bull for your herd. You'll probably need another one."

"I can't take it, Morgan. It's yours."

"I'd just lose it in a poker game. Besides, I'm getting paid by the man in Portland. Keep it. Now, whatever happened to that wanted poster on you from Califonria?"

"You knew about that?"

"Everyone in town knows about it."

"Well, the acting sheriff said he had a letter from them just yesterday. The sheriff in Hangtown is new and said that old wanted was never authorized and ain't legal. He's sending out a hundred letters to sheriffs all up and down the coast telling them that the paper on me is no good at all."

"So, you won't have to worry about that any more."

Jed tapped the envelope in his hand, then folded it and pushed it in his shirt pocket.

"You come by this way, you stop and look us up," Jed said. Priscilla touched his shoulders and then they were gone, holding hands and chattering.

Morgan went back in the Wildcat Saloon. Nancy still sat on the stool.

"It work out all right?" she asked.

"Good as rain. Almost time for my afternoon nap."

"I've got a convenient spot upstairs."

"Sounds reasonable."

A few minutes later, Nancy locked her door and turned around.

"Hear you're heading out tomorrow on the afternoon stage. That don't leave us long for me to say thank you. You just gave me back my saloon. You realize that, don't you?"

"He wouldn't have lasted a week before somebody put a bullet in the back of his head."

"Glad it was you who put him in jail. The good folks of La Grande will do with him what should be done." She grinned at him. "Since you're leaving tomorrow, I was hoping that you didn't have any plans for tonight—actually the rest of the afternoon and tonight. We might spend it testing out my new featherbed."

Morgan nodded. "Might be able to work out something along those lines. What in the world would we do for such a long time?"

"We could make up some games, something you're usually in too much of a rush to try. Something soft and gentle and then wild and strange, just so nobody gets hurt."

Morgan pushed one hand down the loose top of her dress and closed around one of her breasts.

"Figure we might be able to do that. Could even start now."

They did. After three quick ones, Nancy dressed and went downstairs and had Zack go to the café up the street and bring back two of their best steak dinners with all the side dishes. They ate naked, sitting on the big bed with a small table between them.

When the food was gone they lay on the feather-bed, resting and making up new games.

"I figure I'm good for about six more, so get your favorites up early on the dance card," Morgan said.

For them the dance didn't end until nearly three A.M. when they finished a bottle of wine and then went to sleep.

It was ten o'clock the next morning before Morgan woke up. He was alone in the big bed. He dressed and waved at Nancy as he hurried through the saloon.

"I'll be back. Got to make sure my prisoner is ready to go."

At the sheriff's office, they had the paperwork transferring the prisoner from the Union County jurisdiction to that of Multnomah County where Portland sprawled.

Morgan checked with the stage company. Their rig should roll in just after noon, would make a 20 minute food stop for passengers and be ready to roll again at 12:30. Morgan bought two tickets and said he'd have one prisoner with a broken leg who might take up some extra room.

"No worry. We only got one man continuing through, and three more tickets sold counting yours," the station agent said. "Plenty of room. Will he be handcuffed?"

Morgan said that he would.

He cleaned out his hotel room, packed his bag and then had a short good-bye with Nancy. She said she didn't like long ones unless they were in bed.

"You take care of Jed. He might need some more financing before that spring cattle drive. He's going to make it big out there. I just got me a feeling."

She agreed with him, let a tear slip out of her eye and turned away. "I don't let nobody see me cry," she said. "Now get out of here. Just be sure to stop in the next time you're through this way."

Morgan grinned, patted her on the shoulder and walked out of the saloon.

The trip back to Portland was long and tedious. They arrived a day and a half later after one breakdown, a near runaway and a brand new driver.

Morgan got the prisoner in a cab and took him to the new Portland police station where they met him with grunts of approval.

"Especially like the broken leg and shot-up knee," the sergeant in charge of the booking said. A captain of police came out and signed off the transfer orders and ushered Rivers into a cell. The big bad outlaw had been meek as a mocking bird the whole trip. He might have been contemplating his survival chances.

Morgan took a hotel room and the next morning stepped into the office of Kiel Rothmore, the Portland merchant who had hired him to find Rivers.

"He's in the custody of the Portland police," Morgan said.

"Some things that money can buy are valuable after all," Rothmore said. "My daughter won't know he's in jail, but I will and that will help everyone. I expect that he'll be convicted and hung for the death of the man in the saloon. I'll make it a special point to be there for the hanging."

Rothmore paused. "Is he injured?"

Morgan told him about the physical damage to Rivers.

"Good. The man will now understand pain for longer than the few seconds it takes him to fall through the trap."

He took out a pad of bank drafts. "Do you want cash or a draft on my bank?"

"I'm sure your draft is good, Mr. Rothmore. That would be the safest. I hear there are still some ruffians around the gentle streets of Portland even in these modern times."

Rothmore wrote out the draft, signed it and handed it to Morgan.

"What are your plans now, Mr. Morgan?"

"A few days rest perhaps in your pleasant city, then a visit to Alaska. I understand the ice has broken and the interior cities are now reachable by steamer. I might make a tour."

"You do good work, Morgan." A man came in a side door and whispered something to Rothmore who nodded. The messenger went out.

"Excellent work. I've just confirmed that Chance Rivers is indeed in the custody of the city police and has injuries of which you recounted." He stood. "Now I have other concerns. Thank you for your services."

Lee Morgan left the office checking the draft. It was for the stipulated $5,000, and there would be no trouble cashing it.

What did he want most now? A long hot bath, then a fine dinner, followed by a bit of amusement, perhaps a play by a roving band of thespians or a long game at the quarter limit poker table.

He was rich for the moment. He had just made as much money in two weeks as most working men earn in ten years. He deserved a little holiday.

He grinned. Nobody knew where he was. Nobody knew what he was doing. He could even sweep back into Idaho and find out what was happening at the old home ranch.

Morgan shook his head. That part of his life was finished. The sheriff there would never leave him in peace. He'd go his own way, find his own work, and take pleasures where he found them.

First the bath. Who knows? The girl who brings the hot water might just want to take an early bath herself. Such things had happened before.

Morgan picked up his pace as he headed for his hotel and his bath and who knew what else. That was half of the enjoyment of going whichever way the wind blew him, making friends and defeating enemies as they arose.

Watch out, Portland! Here comes Lee Buckskin Morgan. You better be ready for him!

DIRK FLETCHER

*The pistol-hot Western series filled with
more brawls and beauties than a frontier saloon
on a Saturday night!*

Spur #37: Missouri Mama. When a master forgert starts spreading enough funny money to dam up the mighty Mississippi, Spur discovers the counterfeiter has a taste for the town's trollops. And the only way McCoy can catch the bastard is by making pleasure his business.
_3341-0 $3.50 US/$4.50 CAN

Spur #38: Free Press Filly. Sent to investigate the murder of a small-town newspaper editor, McCoy is surprised to discover his contact is the man's busty daughter, who believes in a free press and free love.
_3394-1 $3.99 US/$4.99 CAN

Spur #39: Minetown Mistress. While tracking down a missing colonel in Idaho Territory, Spur runs into a luscious blonde and a randy redhead who appoint themselves his personal greeters. Now he'll waste no time finding the lost man—because only then can he take a long, hard ride with the fillies who drive his private welcome wagon.
_3448-4 $3.99 US/$4.99 CAN

LEISURE BOOKS
ATTN: Order Department
276 5th Avenue, New York, NY 10001

Please add $1.50 for shipping and handling for the first book and $.35 for each book thereafter. PA., N.Y.S. and N.Y.C. residents, please add appropriate sales tax. No cash, stamps, or C.O.D.s. All orders shipped within 6 weeks via postal service book rate. Canadian orders require $2.00 extra postage and must be paid in U.S. dollars through a U.S. banking facility.

Name _____

Address _____

City _____ State _____ Zip _____

I have enclosed $_____in payment for the checked book(s).
Payment <u>must</u> accompany all orders.☐ Please send a free catalog.

Keep it mutual!

Bri-

&

"Marriage books written by people who aren't therapists or marriage researchers are usually full of 'common nonsense' that has little bearing upon marital success. *Choosing Us* is the exception. It is the long-awaited resource for couples committed to building progressive, equitable relationships where both partners have highly demanding careers. It is not a how-to guide to replicating Gail and Brian's relationship. It is a source of wisdom for creating your own."

—**Chanequa Walker-Barnes**, clinical psychologist and author of *I Bring the Voices of My People*

"How can we flourish together? What does mutual submission really entail? Why must I look inward before casting blame on my partner? When there are no models, how do we build something healthy together? While there are countless marriage books, few focus on cultivating egalitarian unions where couples grow together and individually fulfill their created purpose. *Choosing Us* achieves this and equips readers to love selflessly, even when it's counterintuitive and inconvenient. This book will bless your marriage and empower you to love your partner more authentically. It illuminates how couples can thrive beyond the honeymoon phase and go the distance together."

—**Dominique DuBois Gilliard**, author of *Subversive Witness: Scripture's Call to Leverage Privilege* and *Rethinking Incarceration: Advocating for Justice That Restores*

"Marriage is a journey, and no matter where you and your spouse are in it, *Choosing Us* is an important guide. The Bantums share with tender honesty, inviting us into their past, and offer incisive questions, encouraging us in our present. They do not shy away from pointing out how gender, racial, and ethnic identity and cultural norms can shape faith and marriage, inviting all readers to consider the assumptions and expectations we bring into it. Do yourself and your marriage a favor. Read this book."

—**Kathy Khang**, author of *Raise Your Voice: Why We Stay Silent and How to Speak Up*

"*Choosing Us* arrived on my desk at the right moment in my marriage of thirty years. Without minimizing how hard it is to sustain a marriage, especially when negotiating differences in race and culture, the Bantums demonstrate that marriage is difficult but worth it. They open the inner sanctum of their trials and growth as a couple struggling to fight their own demons and those inherited from family and culture, letting the light in and the wisdom born out of their faith and struggle to come through. *Choosing Us* speaks transparently to readers of our naive assumptions about love and lopsided gender roles that we bring into marriage. Gail and Brian bring their full selves to this book, two strong-minded people willing to listen, negotiate, forgive, and grow. *Choosing Us* offers readers invaluable lessons on how to use natural differences and conflicts to work toward a loving relationship that is built on the strength of one's differences, creating a healthy marriage as the first step in building a just world."

—**Renita J. Weems**, minister, biblical scholar, and author of *What Matters Most: Ten Passionate Lessons on the Song of Solomon*

Choosing US

US
Choosing

Marriage and
Mutual Flourishing
in a World of
Difference

Gail Song Bantum and Brian Bantum

BrazosPress
a division of Baker Publishing Group
Grand Rapids, Michigan

© 2022 by Gail Song Bantum and Brian Bantum

Published by Brazos Press
a division of Baker Publishing Group
PO Box 6287, Grand Rapids, MI 49516-6287
www.brazospress.com

Printed in the United States of America
Library of Congress Cataloging-in-Publication Data
Names: Bantum, Gail Song, 1975– author. | Bantum, Brian, 1975– author.
Title: Choosing us : marriage and mutual flourishing in a world of difference / Gail Song Bantum and Brian Bantum.
Description: Grand Rapids, Michigan : Brazos Press, a division of Baker Publishing Group, [2022]
Identifiers: LCCN 2021033317 | ISBN 9781587435379 (cloth) | ISBN 9781493435227 (ebook) | ISBN 9781493435234 (pdf)
Subjects: LCSH: Interracial marriage—Religious aspects—Christianity.
Classification: LCC BT707.3 .B36 2022 | DDC 261.8/358—dc23
LC record available at https://lccn.loc.gov/2021033317
Baker Publishing Group publications use paper produced from sustainable forestry practices and post-consumer waste whenever possible.

22 23 24 25 26 27 28   7 6 5 4 3 2 1

To our Regroup squad:

Beth and Justin
Carrie and Jeff
Michelle and Jeremy
Liz and Kevin
Kenneth (and Kathleen)
Marshaé (and Liz)

for the gift of letting us
journey with you

Contents

Prologue

Our Why

In some ways, our marriage and relationship has had a certain storybook feel. Two young college students, at schools three hundred miles apart, are introduced by Jeannette, a mutual friend. A first letter. A first call that lasts two and a half hours. She calls him back, and they talk for another two and a half hours. More letters. More long-distance calls (between 11 p.m. and 5 a.m., when it's ten cents a minute). They fall in love. *Then* they meet in person. They share a first awkward car ride, neither of them looking at the other because voices were all they knew. A year later, he proposes. Another year later, they're married. It's practically a movie.

But a lot can happen in twenty-seven years. A mutual friend of ours set me (Gail) up with Brian because she had heard that my mom had just died and knew that his dad had recently died as well. Unexpectedly, a serious long-distance relationship emerged. But when I told my dad I wanted to marry Brian, I was confronted with a heartbreaking choice: either obey him

1

and not marry Brian because he was a Black man, or disobey my dad and potentially lose years of relationship with him. He asked me to leave the house when I chose Brian. As a result, I had to navigate life in close quarters with Brian's family for every school break thereafter. We decided to get married while we were still in college, grieving the fact that my dad wouldn't be at our wedding. Upon graduating, we quickly had to figure out how to pursue each of our calls to ministry. A year later, we were figuring out life with a newborn while Brian headed back to school for seminary. Two years later, we had our second child and grieved the loss of Brian's mom to cancer. As if those losses weren't enough, during those years we also endured three miscarriages.

But in fits and starts we made our way. Brian graduated from seminary as I scrappily worked part time, then full time, as a worship minister. We were unexpectedly pregnant with our third child, trying desperately to figure out how to raise three young kids while completing school and pursuing our vocations. Eventually, and years later, I would heed the call to seminary while Brian pursued his doctorate. Both of us still working on the side, the baby tagged along with us to classes, lectures, and music practices like a boss! A few years later, we moved to Seattle, where Brian landed his first job in the field he had worked so hard for, while my gifts would also be fully received and realized in this new season. My dad and I were finally able to reconcile twenty-one years later as I heard him earnestly say to me, "Brian is a good man." While pointing to a Korean-Black, mixed pop artist on the television, a woman named Insooni, he also said, "She's my favorite artist. If you'd had a daughter, I bet she would've looked like her." Tears! That's my Korean father's way of saying, "I'm sorry." He died one year later, in 2017, after battling cancer.

This journey was anything but a straight line for us. We both had a sense of call. We both wanted kids. But what that looked like, when to have kids, who would work, who would stay home, how to balance it all, and how to build a life together was a work in progress. Without a plan, our home life fell into the common tropes: Gail at home with the kids, me at school. I (Brian) got into Duke for a master's program. It seemed easier (to me) to keep picking up side jobs to make ends meet, but this also meant more hours of Gail at home with little ones. Sometimes it meant tense conversations because Gail's dream was drifting further away while I was on a path toward mine. And sometimes it was hard for me to hear, if I heard at all, because I felt like I was working all the time. I was reading just enough, or maybe just a few pages, and felt like I wasn't measuring up. The journey involved watching as Gail got passed over at our church because she's a woman. It was years and years of taking turns while other people seemed to be on a fast track or enjoying their twenties while we plodded along, just trying to get through. It included watching as my (Brian's) mother endured and ultimately died from lung cancer.

As we raised our kids, questions of race and ethnicity and belonging continued to press. How do we instill in them a sense of being Korean? Of being Black? Of navigating racial ambiguity and not quite fitting in? And in the midst of it all, it was discovering ways to love and be present for each other, trying to create a new culture in our life together. Along the way, we've come to realize that everything goes in the pot, so to speak. Being committed to each other's flourishing in a world of racism and sexism means we need each other to become our whole selves.

Now we've begun to reflect on our journey more intentionally, as well as the journey we've shared with other couples trying to find their way in a world of difference. This book has been tugging at us for a few years. Having been married for twenty-five years, working as a pastor (Gail) and a professor (Brian), we've walked with many couples who are asking questions about marriage, balancing careers, and navigating race in a world where the violence of white supremacy only increases.

When we got married at twenty-one in a little church in Maryland, there was nothing elaborate—a church that neither of us were members of, a small reception at Brian's mom's house with his family, a few of Brian's church folk, some random neighbors, and a handful of Gail's friends. We had no idea what we were in for or where we were going. We had talked about going into ministry together, about *maybe* planting a church, but we were certain that whatever we did, we would be in it together. Those senses of call took us on some winding paths. For me (Gail), it started as a part-time music director, then volunteer choir director, then worship leader, then seminarian, to associate pastor to executive pastor to lead pastor. The path for me (Brian) was just as circuitous: high school history teacher, educational specialist, seminarian, full-time TA and any other part-time job I could muster, doctoral student, then professor.

It's easy to imagine that where we are now was the plan all along, but in actuality, it's all been about listening and making mistakes, then trying to listen some more. There was never a plan, only an intention to do whatever we could together, to make room for the other, and to avoid some of the pain we experienced in our own homes growing up. While we did not end up planting a church together or working together in ministry, our work and vocations dovetail. We still work out of a deep sense of call to the church and to serve as witnesses to God's presence and work in the world. But we have also found our own unique ways of living into those calls, and it was only together that we actually found how those calls rang most truly in each of us.

In the midst of creating a home and family together, we were also navigating realities of gender and race. As a Korean

American woman and a Black, mixed man, we were both learning ourselves and the way legacies of race and patriarchy had shaped our world. We do our work in a world where our bodies matter, where we are created to enjoy and be enjoyed, and yet the fallenness and pain of this world afflict us in real, concrete ways. What does it mean to be a couple, to be for one another in this kind of world? This has been our question and our journey. It's what we teach, preach, and try to live every day. Along the way, we have been surprised to see how some of our mistakes and forging through the bush have resonated with people we've walked with and taught. What we offer isn't necessarily the wisdom of experts but simply the journey of two people who have been wandering these woods called marriage for a good bit of time.

Little did we know that an idea for a book would mean writing it in the midst of a pandemic, confined to work and live in the same space for a year. We could not have imagined the sudden shift from being on the verge of living as empty nesters to living in a full house of five people again. (And of course, *this* was the time to get a puppy.) In many ways it has been a gift to be together. But being confined to life with one another, trying to live and work in the same space with the same people all day, every day, as many of us have had to learn, can also accentuate fissures, pull up long-buried tensions, and remind us of difficult questions we sometimes avoid about ourselves and the people we live with.

Early on in the writing process, we took a walk to discuss the project and ideas for chapters. It began excitedly. *We are actually doing this! Writing a book together!* But soon, uneven silences crept in, frustrated responses bubbled up, and clarifying questions (laced with the residue of past arguments) finally spilled over, until I (Brian) blurted out, "I don't work for you! I'm not on your staff!" The rest of the walk home was filled with awkward silence.

Worn down, tired because of our new puppy, and our working rhythms undone, little silences became little snips that would take a few days to smooth out. In truth, we haven't fought more than we did while writing this book.

The frustrations were never about one individual thing. They were about trying to navigate expectations, opportunities, and the oftentimes unspoken dance of trying to support the other person while also pursuing what each of us is called to do. As with most marriages, it's the same argument over and over, just in different keys.

Eventually, we found some patterns that worked (apparently puppies need a lot of time in their crates). Slowly, we found our way to an equilibrium, like we always have.

Neither of us comes from ideal, stable families. We didn't know what a healthy marriage looked like. When we met at nineteen, we had very different ideas of what marriage was, when was an ideal time to marry, and what we thought our lives would look like in twenty years. By the time we were twenty, we couldn't imagine life without each other. By twenty-one, we were married. And we were making it all up as we went along. There were no married couples in our lives to ask us probing questions or for us to pattern our lives after. There were certainly no interracial couples who could help us sort out our racial journeys and histories or how they were shaping our newly formed family. And in our evangelical and Pentecostal churches, there was no pattern for two people with gifts and callings where the woman didn't have to put her calling aside for the sake of the family.

So we started with some simple questions. What were things from our childhood that we most wanted to avoid? Where were the patterns of violence or distrust that we wanted to end with us? In this time, we also arrived at our golden rule: We don't do anything big until we both feel total peace in the decision (more about that in chap. 6).

But everything else was trial and error, trust and commitment to being for the other, and more trial, and more error. We had to navigate difficult questions of race in the Korean community. We had to mine formations of masculinity. We had to figure out questions of life together as settled answers got tossed around with each new child or new city or new vocational opportunity or shift. And here we are, twenty-plus years later, still learning, still growing.

While we share a lot of our own story here, this book also reflects our experience of mentoring many couples over the years whose stories are similar to ours. Many of these couples were looking for a different model of marriage than one in which the man intentionally or unintentionally "leads" the family. Others were interracial, while still others had less than ideal family histories. We've wanted to offer not *the* way marriages or relationships ought to be; rather we've offered *a* way—a way that opens up possibilities for both people to discover what flourishing might look like for them and what flourishing life together might offer to the world.

We say "*a* way" because we are sure we have made mistakes. We have done the best we could with what we had. But the possibilities we imagined and the options we refused also grew out of our unique stories. As an interracial couple, we are aware that our life can't always be reproduced in our mentees, students, or children. Traditions and legacies are gifts that are offered so that our children might create their own traditions. We only hope they see the people and the histories that shaped us and how those stories continue to live in them.

Similarly, couples we walk with carry their own histories, scars, joys, and ways of navigating the world. A marriage is not a sourdough recipe that can be perfected with just enough time. Part of our joy is watching our mentees, students, and children create new ways of living, loving, and creating community in their midst in ways we could not have imagined.

We offer our story and hope you can find something of yourself in it. And whether there are places of resonance or difference, we hope this book sparks a conversation about who you are, who the person you're with is, and what you are creating together. Whether you are an interracial couple, or a couple with shared racial and ethnic stories, or a couple within the LGBTQ+ community, your story is not ours, and our story is not the totality of all marriages or relationships. Rather, we hope this book can be an invitation to discover your own story.

We are also aware that a book on marriage and relationships can be difficult in the midst of relationships that are struggling through pain. Too many marriages are spaces of violence, manipulation, and abuse. As you read these pages, hear us in saying that the calls to covenant and to commitment are calls that assume reciprocity and love as the basic shape of marital life. Violence, abuse, and manipulation are acts of dehumanization and violations of covenantal commitments, and God wants more than that for all of us.

We also want to offer a quick note on sex. If you bought this book and began eagerly looking for the chapter on sexual intimacy, you may be disappointed. It may seem unusual to have a book on marriage and relationships and not talk about sex. But marriage is more than who you have sex with. We also recognize that how couples think about sex and sexual intimacy is unique to each couple and tied to the ways they were formed, including experiences of violence and abuse, harmful associations of sex with shame, and the many, varied ways couples can enjoy each other.

While we both believe that the greatest intimacy and power of sex comes in monogamous, covenanted relationships, we also know that just because sex happens in those relationships doesn't mean that the act is holy or beautiful or mutual. We also acknowledge that people have sex outside the confines of marriage. When it comes down to it, vows and a ceremony are not what make the act holy or unholy. Sex is a beautiful aspect of being human and an expression of what it means to enjoy and be enjoyed, one way of seeing and feeling what it means to experience joy and ecstasy.

In a real way, sex is an aspect of the relating that we'll describe throughout this book. Sex is an act of mutual listening, a desire for the other to experience bliss and joy in trust that your partner wants the same for you. Sex in a covenanted relationship is discovering the depths of this one person and sometimes going through seasons that seem slow, dry, or mundane but never resting in those deserts. It is the discovery of new ways of enjoying and the recognition of how new seasons of life invigorate the intimacy of sharing your body with the other. Whether this looks like sex all the time in all kinds of places or sex in regular, scheduled intervals or sex on seemingly rare occasions, it is never simply release or consumption. Rather, it is an act that lives and expresses your journey together, and that requires discovery of yourself, learning the other, a willingness to grow and adapt, trust in the other, and patience.

We hope that not only couples will read this book but also anyone who is hoping for a sojourner in navigating the world shaped by ideas of race and gender and sexuality that have boxed us in and seemed to determine who to be with, and how to be with them, in this world.

Marriage is not an institution separate from race and gender. When people get married, questions of masculinity and femininity and of race and racism don't vanish. Marriage has historically been a way for ideas about gender and race to be turned into mechanisms of control and exclusion. There is a reason marriage was forbidden for slaves, that interracial marriage was illegal until 1967, and that same-sex marriage was illegal in many states until 2015. Marriage has been an arena in which some of the most violent and pernicious legacies of racism and sexism persist and are reproduced.

But when we begin to see marriage not as the pinnacle of what it means to be made in the image of God but as just one good relationship of many, we can also begin to see how marriage is connected to dynamics of friendship, sex, gender, race, mundane everydayness, and life-changing transformations. In marriage, all of these dynamics coalesce into a difficult and beautiful creation—a new culture forged in the life of two people joined together. That new creation reverberates beyond those two people, whether it's in their vocation, in the people they mentor or serve, in what they create or build, or in the children they raise.

We've seen the harm wrought by rigid ideas of marriage. We have also seen the ways that this life together can be a space of fullness and purpose and joy. But it might not be everything we'd dreamed it would be (#relationshipgoals #powercouple). It might require spaces of uncertainty, of patience, of one person going slow so the other can go fast and trusting it won't always be that way. It will be seasons of uncertainty where our manna is the other person's wins while we plod along. But part of what makes life together powerful is that it never requires one person alone to sacrifice, to slow down, to wither. If a couple is to flourish, both people will need opportunities to live into their gifts.

And in the end, it might be discovering that flourishing is something quite different from what we had imagined at the beginning. To live into this, we have had to ask questions about how our bodies do work in the world. We've had to become students of one another, even when it feels like the tests keep changing. We've had to take steps back and ask what hasn't been working and trust that the other person wants to find out too. The story keeps unfolding.

This is our story—the story of a Korean American woman and a Black, mixed man trying to discover what it means to make a life together. To become *we*.

10

ONE

The Plan

People change. Maybe you should give this some time to figure out who you are before you get married," she said. We had flown to California for me (Gail) to introduce Brian to a few of my aunts and extended family. Sitting in the dining room with them, Brian and I tried to listen as best we could. They clearly loved us and wanted the best for us. Brian and I were in love, and after ten months of dating and thousands of dollars spent on phone calls, stamps, and plane and bus tickets, we knew we wanted to spend the rest of our lives together.

We were also twenty years old, and a young twenty at that. My aunts knew that we would change over time, and they were worried for us.

We replied, "Yes, we are going to change. But we are going to grow toward each other." We were *so* smart. Of course we were going to change, we thought to ourselves. We even knew

11

how we were going to change. We had a plan for our lives, a calling even.

Now, with our own children nearly grown, we see what they saw. We had no idea what was in store for us or who we were.

But part of what changed us wasn't just graduating from college or the first job or clarifying vocational goals. Our life together was a journey of discovering the questions we didn't realize we were asking, the histories and the stories that kept pulling and tugging and shaping us under the surface of our lives.

While we weren't wrong to believe we'd grow toward one another, there was a fundamental misconception: we thought we knew who we were to begin with. In our young minds and hearts, we looked at one another and thought growing toward one another was simply a matter of loving the other person. But we didn't understand that we were trees that had been planted in very different orchards and nurtured in different soils. Just as a tree has little understanding of itself as it grows, we had so much to learn about ourselves and our own stories, even while we were trying to grow toward this new person in our lives.

Self-discovery is an ongoing process because we are never finished becoming. As each year passes, as we enter into periods of lack or plenty, hardship or joy, and loss or abundance, the light of who we are refracts a little differently in new moments. The growth we experienced in ourselves and toward one another was sometimes a series of conscious decisions and explicit conversations. At other times, the growth was stopping and breathing for a moment, taking stock of what was underneath the frustration or the boredom or the work of just getting through each day, to ask ourselves who we were and who we were becoming, for ourselves and for the other person, in that moment.

As we begin to think about relationships, even before we can begin to talk about what it means to join our lives together, we need to first ask who we think we are. There are plenty of personality types and gift assessments and premarital work-shops on family systems, but part of the question of knowing ourselves is beginning to recognize that we cannot know the totality of who we are in that moment or who we are going to be. And yet, in the midst of this unknowing, there are tributaries and rivers and lakes of history, dynamics of power and oppression, formations of masculinity and femininity, structures of race and ethnic identity, all working in the midst of the stream that is our life.

The work of charting the rivers of history that live in us and have shaped us never ends. Learners of a way, be it an instrument or a life of faith or an art, are always learning and discovering something new about themselves and how they've changed over the years. This is no less true of ourselves as individuals. But when we bind our lives to another and live in daily intimacy and closeness, these transformations are even more pronounced.

When two people choose to become a "we," they begin to discover more of who each person is. In our own experience, and in counseling couples navigating relationships, preparing for marriage, or working through years of marriage, we have seen how the illusion of certainty and assumptions become this extra baggage that fills the rooms of their lives until they have no room to move or to even see the other person. But the biggest assumptions that rarely emerge in these conversations are the ones people make about themselves. Usually, people think they know themselves. That's why they can be so sure they are right and the other person is wrong. Not only do they know themselves, but they also know their own history, the way they are navigating their community, and the questions or discomfort of being different.

This certainty might be about issues of character or person-ality traits. But maybe they haven't asked how, as a Black man, for example, they have navigated predominately white spaces and how that experience has shaped or is shaping them. Maybe as a man, they haven't asked how dynamics of gender are moving under the surface of the frustrations at home and the ease they feel at work. Even while we are discovering who we are, we are also navigating a world shaped by race, gender, and sexuality. And none of these are realities that we fully understand in ourselves at any given time.

We want to begin this book by reflecting on personhood. We are being intentional in avoiding the word "individual," because no one exists apart from communities and families and stories. A person is always a patchwork. But a person is also a point where all of those stories and people and communities coalesce into one beautiful, unique burst of light. What happens when two bursts of light join?

To understand this, we need to think about the ones who are being joined.

We Both Had Plans

As teenagers, each of us had a plan for our lives, of who we thought we were and how we thought our lives would go. Here were our respective plans:

Gail's Plan	Brian's Plan
• Become the first Asian American female conductor of the New York Philharmonic • Produce albums on the side for artists like Mary J. Blige, in my "free time" • Live in a cute condo in NYC • *Consider* getting married when I turn thirty • Marry an athlete • No kids • Livin' the life!	• Get married • Have three to four kids • Become a pastor or a teacher • Coach soccer • Live in my hometown near my mom

14

Clearly, we were a match made in heaven! And plans change. We lose people we love. Small and not-so-small knocks change the trajectory of our lives, and sometimes we wake up realizing the life we had imagined for ourselves did not materialize. But we also can't quite imagine wanting a life that could have been either.

For us those losses and those meetings all seemed to ping "just so," bringing us together during our sophomore year of college. And that meeting would wreck our plans, at least in the ways we had imagined them.

Gail

My plans were upended when my mother suddenly died of cancer after my first year of college. I met Brian through a mutual friend not too long after I returned to school. He was an athlete, but a nerdy one. I started to reconsider my calling in life. We married while we were both still in college. At age twenty-one, I decided to enter vocational ministry and got a job as a musical worship leader. By age twenty-three, we had our first child, and six years later, we had two more. At age thirty-one, I entered seminary with three kids in tow between the ages of two and seven.

I'm a pastor. He's a professor. And I think: *I've become my mother.*

There is always more to the story than lists. In reality, I've always been told that I have big dreams, sometimes seemingly impossible dreams. My dad made me learn the violin from the time I was three years old, which later evolved into learning many instruments toward the goal of becoming a conductor. Looking back, I'm not sure I ever knew a life apart from learning, honing, crafting, and perfecting something with the intensity they say being a professional musician or athlete cultivates. Music was what I gave my life to—hours upon hours nearly every day—working to get into one of the few elite music conservatories in the world. By the time I started my senior year of high school, I had already participated in major summer music festivals and received acceptance letters from The Juilliard School in New York City and the Eastman School of Music in Rochester. I'm sure there was a bit of talent mixed in with the hard work to get to where I was, but I valued my determination and laser focus more than anything. I had a plan. And everything was coming together just as I had planned, or so I thought.

Two years later, I found myself home after my first year of college on summer break, caring for my mother. She had been diagnosed with stage four lung cancer out of the blue. After she fought for life for over seven weeks, my brother and I sat with her in the hospital room as she labored for her final breath. Those weeks simultaneously felt like forever and not enough. That summer changed everything.

Death, sudden loss, and suffering shift perspective. My mother's death, and pondering a life that seemed too short, made "my plan" seem ridiculous. I found myself questioning everything. My mom wanted to be a pastor, struggled through seminary at age forty with English as a second language, and was barely able to see it through to fruition before she died. "Who cares if I became the first this or the first that if I could literally die tomorrow. What am I doing with my life?" I asked myself.

It was one month after she died that I had my first conversation with Brian over the phone. It was only about six months after she died that I sensed a strong and unrelenting call to ministry—a vision and a remembrance of a prophetic word I'd received when I was eight years old at my parents' Pentecostal church in Chicago.

I believe God used that time, when my heart was especially tender, attentive, and desperate, to speak truths into my life and to remind me of the promise spoken over me years prior. They were truths about my vocation and the people I would need to thrive, whether I realized it or not. At the time, Brian was not like *anything* I had imagined in a partner. He had dreams of being a suburban dad with four children (four!) living the cul-de-sac life. He liked music I had never really heard of. When I first talked to him, the only reference I had of how he might be was Carlton from *The Fresh Prince of Bel-Air*. In the end, I didn't imagine having kids initially and wanted to live a career-driven life in New York City, the city where my parents had immigrated. None of what Brian represented and wanted was in my plan.

Brian

Reading Gail's account of how her life plans changed, I am reminded of just how little I had to give up. For me, the risk was hoping for something more, not letting go of big dreams.

My plans before meeting Gail were pretty ordinary: to marry, have kids, have a steady job as a teacher or coach, and live in the suburbs near my mom. But everything changed one night my sophomore year of college. A mutual friend told me about Gail. "She loves soccer," she said. Apparently, that was enough. I learned that Gail went to music school and that her mom had recently passed away from cancer (my dad had died the previous year too). In hindsight, I'm not sure what I was thinking. I am sure that it came off a little strange and desperate when I wrote her a letter introducing myself. Then I called her, before the letter had even arrived.

I was just hoping to make a good impression, but we talked for two and a half hours, then hung up, and she called me back, and we talked for two and a half more hours. That's how it started.

I don't think I would call it "love at first hearing" or say that I knew this was the person I was going to marry. But I knew there was something there, even if I couldn't describe what. When I picked up the phone, I didn't know I'd find someone to navigate this in-between life with. I didn't know my understanding of Scripture or theology or life would get flipped inside out. I didn't know I could be so afraid of losing someone. I didn't know I'd be a person who would write books or even expect to be listened to. But in the hours of conversations, the heated conversations about women in ministry or the Bible, in laughing and writing letters, my plans were not so much being thrown out but hollowed out and filled in with a richer and more expansive vision. I had plans to be a pastor of a Southern Baptist church, the "head of the household," and a teacher in a Christian high school. But the containers I had been given were too small for the world that I met in Gail. With each of our conversations, the world I knew was being poured out to make space for a bigger world.

In some ways the plans weren't too far off. In other ways, today I am living a life I could not have dreamed of—as a pastor's spouse, a professor, and a father of three amazing boys. But it was completely unexpected and seemed beyond the realm of possibility. Some of the impossibility was just in the narrow world I lived within, theologically and socially. Part of it was realizing that I was incredibly change-averse (and still am). And part of it was just the fact that Gail is someone I would have never had the courage to meet in person. I would have noticed her and probably had a crush from a distance. To be honest, when I first started talking with her, I thought she was "Blacker" than me, which struck me as odd since she is Korean. And I didn't know what I thought about that, about meeting this Asian American woman who seemed to have a soulful way about her. Truthfully, though, it was my own blackness and disconnection from Black life that I saw in her and that created questions in me. And that was all going to be part of the journey, a journey that began with a phone call.

Embracing Change

When we first met, I (Brian) cautiously smelled my food before I ate it. I turned up my nose at sushi, ginger, and Japanese curry. But one day, I ordered a tuna sandwich, not realizing that it was raw. And to my amazement, I liked it. Loved it actually. That was my gateway to sushi. But I drew the line at ginger. Then I tried a bit again eight years later, only to find that I also loved it. Food is one small way that I came to realize that who I am is always changing. And these new things that I was encountering were also opening up places for us to eat, foods we could order together, creating new possibilities and new connections.

It feels like something you'd read in a Hallmark card, but it's true: everyone changes. Everything changed for us the day we first spoke on the phone, even if we didn't realize it at the time. We took a step onto a new road, with no map other than a sense that where we'd been in life wasn't where we wanted to go.

It hasn't been easy. There have been moments and periods of time when we wondered if the marriage would last or if we could endure lying next to someone from whom we felt painfully distant—a pain that could only come from tearing. We've had to figure out who we are, as individuals and as a "we," and how our individual stories shape our shared everyday life. Life together has been both a settling and a stirring. Whether asking questions about who God is and who God called us to be, or navigating the racial and ethnic communities that we felt both connected to and distant from, we've had to ask ourselves who we were in the midst of these shifts and discoveries and who we would be to each other. We continually find ourselves, only to find that we've become something new as well—and that we have to learn each other all over again with each new bend in the road.

But in the midst of this, we had no models, no people to journey with or other families that we really saw ourselves in, especially who we were becoming together. In truth, we were *so* different. While we connected quickly, it was clear early on that our plans were very different, as were our stories, our likes and dislikes, and our formations.

I (Gail) am a Korean American whose faith was deeply formed in Black and Korean Pentecostal traditions. I love R&B, soul, and Brazilian music and was shaped in predominantly Korean and Black cultures, and ultimately saw myself living single in New York City.

I (Brian) came to Christ in a Southern Baptist church, didn't believe women could be in ministry, liked alternative rock and country music (it's a long story), grew up in predominantly white spaces with my white family, and hoped to eventually live in a nice little house in suburban Maryland with a wife and four kids.

These differences never defined us, and by the time we met we were already undergoing all the changes that young adulthood brings. But initially these differences were reminders that in every situation we had very different frames of reference for how to think about what to do on a Saturday, or where to eat, or what to work toward. It wasn't always the specific differences that mattered but recognizing that there were differences that needed to be discovered.

In varied ways, those early senses of call and vocation never left us. I (Gail) shifted from classical music performance and dreams of conducting orchestras to leading worship, leading leaders, and eventually leading a church. I was conducting in ways I could not have imagined as the dream manifested in unexpected ways. I (Brian) had thought about ministry but was always drawn to teaching and coaching. I only had a vague sense of what professors did. My only strong models of a teacher were my high school history teacher and soccer coach. Twenty years later, I find myself teaching in seminary and "coaching" doctoral students.

We had dreams and calls and hopes, but we also had few models of what it looked like to get there. And when we began our life together, those dreams shifted and expanded and twisted along the way. In the midst of what we knew, and especially everything we didn't know, the path was hard and beautiful and surprising.

Stretch Marks

What happens when one or both people in a marriage begin to change? It's rare that we feel the change and say to ourselves, "This is amazing! Look how much I'm growing!" More often, unexpected circumstances lay things bare in our lives, showing us something about ourselves that we didn't know was there or that we thought we had dealt with. Maybe something is grinding in the relationship that we can't quite put our finger on. Or maybe something is binding us together, like decisions to blend or compromise, but we're not fully conscious of these changes. Sometimes it is the tensions that feel pronounced, while the signs of intimacy and connectedness can be taken for granted. Because it can seem so natural, we don't account for the growth that was happening through our small glances or touches or observations.

And although we are both in the same relationship, these changes are never experienced in the same way. We are like instruments, one made of oak and another of birch. As the humidity and temperature shift, we adapt and bend in unique ways. The wood of our lives is our respective stories, the joys we've seen, the insecurities we've harbored, or the obstacles we've had to overcome. With each passing season, we carry what we were and what we had become, whether successful or dysfunctional, into the next season.

When things begin to shift and we start to feel the stretching—which sometimes feels like tearing—it is never an easy process. Sometimes it might feel like it's the person you're with who

21

doesn't seem to fit or who seems to irritate. Sometimes it might feel like the job isn't right or we're in the wrong town or our family is either too close or too far away.

And often it isn't just our own inner world or familial circles that press us. The way the world renders some bodies invisible in one moment and hypervisible in another, ways that we see privilege boost up some people while we scrape and claw for every inch—systems of oppression and silencing are always pressing in. As we have gotten older, we have discovered the power and insidiousness of these systems.

We are navigating all of it, the individual, the interpersonal, and the social. It's in those moments of stretching that the sinews of ourselves stretch in ways we do not expect. Part of building a life together is acknowledging that we do not know the ways we are growing or the forces that are pulling or pushing us. But when we recognize that change is inevitable, we can begin to look for the signs or opportunities to stretch—or to at least warm up before something gets torn.

While there's a healthy market full of self-help books and personality tests to help us "get to know ourselves," part of the challenge in a relationship is learning who you are *with the other person*. It's like the difference between trying to do a squat on solid ground and trying to do a squat on a balance board. On solid ground the motion seems straightforward. But on the balance board you have to engage your stomach muscles and your back, and there is the definite possibility of falling. But being committed in a relationship is also being committed and open to self-reflection about who you are, and who you are with this person, and opening up to the possibilities and acknowledging the strains those discoveries will reveal.

We've seen a lot of people, especially a lot of young couples, hope for a plan. Especially for couples who are married after living on their own for a good part of their life, we hear again and again about having to manage and negotiate expectations.

We are inundated with tools for evaluating ourselves and how-to manuals for just about anything we can imagine.

To be sure, there is a place for plans and preparation. But part of adequately planning is also recognizing the limitations of any given circumstance. When we begin to think about the persons who enter into a relationship, we begin to see just how little we know about ourselves. Ironically, learning one's self is also about embracing what can't be known—the uncertainty of changes before us, of what we might discover as we explore how our past or our social space or our bodies shape the way we experience the world. Learning one's self is embracing the mystery and depth we each hold within us—a process that continues throughout our lives.

No Model to Follow

There aren't many advantages to having no money, no long-standing family traditions, and no fundamental stability in the home. In a way, these all were connected to one another and to the difficult relationships our parents had while we were growing up.

My (Gail's) parents struggled to assimilate. My father spent most of his time and energy at home (outside of his job and ministry), staying safe within the local Korean community. My mom, on the other hand, almost feverishly tried to embrace what "American life" (read: proximate to middle-class white people) meant to her. She had an incredible imagination for greater opportunities and a degree of freedom to pursue her call. But my parents were eleven years apart in age as well, which my mom often suggested felt like a generational difference.

Their marriage had unstable and challenging moments for much of my childhood. So when my mom packed up her things and left for seminary in another state when I was eleven, the news wasn't surprising. Was it hard and sad? Did I cry myself to sleep often? Did I think I was dying when I got my period at school that semester she was gone? Of course. I was eleven. Life in my home rarely felt predictable, much less filled with traditions I looked forward to. This left little room for instilling in me what a thriving married life looked like, or at least an image of something I would want for myself.

Traditions were faint and inconsistent in my (Brian's) childhood. My mom and dad were divorced by the time I was eight. My dad was in and out of our lives depending on his state of sobriety and financial security. But somehow they were always friends. Maybe that's what made it all so strange. Within any given year we might go from my dad visiting on Thursday nights so that he could watch *Knots Landing* and *Dallas* with my mom to then not seeing him for months and only knowing the state of things because of my mom's increased stress over money.

For both of us, the only tradition was the uncertainty that seemed to fill our childhood. New houses, new living situations, schools, maybe a vacation, but more than likely time away was visiting a relative for a week or two. This is not to say that our parents didn't instill some beautiful things in our lives. But those lessons or strengths or inclinations weren't really a result of how they lived together for our sake. In a way, our parents were trying their best, seeming to fight their own demons while also trying to show us love in the best way they could.

We have always been looking for those models, to see some semblance of what life together might look like. More than likely the ideal was never really there in the first place. So we had to make our own image, cobble together the little pieces of what we glimpsed or what we wanted to avoid, and patch it together until it fit us.

The Certainty of Change

As we finish chapter 1, we invite you to self-reflection and, more important, to reimagining who you are even as you discover the person you're with. This process begins by flipping one's perspective about certainty, resisting the lure of the static, and embracing ourselves and each other as dynamic creatures.

Because we were married so young with no models of "success," we didn't have much of a plan. For us, the plan was simply to get to the next thing and figure it out from there. The clearest part of the plan was to not recreate the pain of our childhood homes, while holding on to the small joys or patterns of love that were present.

Part of what gave us the freedom to live with that posture was recognizing the changes that had already happened in each of us, even in the few years of knowing one another. We might have had some semblance of a plan when we were nineteen, but in our first few conversations, we could see we were changing and that there was so much life in what was growing within us and between us. The possibility of ongoing change felt more hopeful than scary. Whether jumping from a lifetime of training to follow a call, or accepting an invitation to a fish fry, or deciding to have children, we had not only seen the scary uncertainty but also the harvest of what that change made possible in our lives and in our relationships.

Most of all, by accepting the flip from the certainty of a plan or a prescribed goal to the certainty of change, we could recognize that the other person was going to change. We knew we were not going to be the same people we talked to on the phone in those early days. And we couldn't control who the other person was going to be. There was no plan for personal growth any more than there was a plan for familial life or vocation. There was only a direction, toward and with one another.

The power of the flip allows us to see the possibilities in the shifts and tensions that emerge. Rather than the tensions being a deviation from or an obstacle to the plan, they become moments to sound one another out, to take stock, and to see how our lives together might open to new possibilities.

Discussion Questions

- What have you discovered about yourself because of the person you're with?
- Has anything you've discovered scared you?
- What's been enriching?
- What have the unplanned parts of your life taught you about yourself?

The static holds on to whatever makes us feel safe or seen or comfortable or unchallenged. Sometimes we need these responses simply to get through difficult times. But what happens when we grow accustomed to the terror or the discomfort and live feeling afraid to let that go for something more?

A static personhood tries to maintain the tethers of its personhood because it only knows itself in relationship to those connections. But sometimes those tethers also preclude or block the possibilities of new connections and new experiences that allow us to discover new aspects of who we are or who we might become.

Discussion Questions

- In what areas of your life do you feel like it's safer to stay the same rather than risk something new?

A dynamic view of personhood (and relationships) sees the possibility of relationships, experiences, stretches, and shifts as an opportunity to live in the fullness of the world and contribute to it. But it never happens without some pain. And while this idea might seem like it is simply resisting the lure of the static, it's slightly different because it asks us to make a fundamentally different assumption about who we are and who we are going to be. When we feel ourselves beginning to change, we might experience this initially as loss, especially in a relationship. But what if we assume that change is a part of who we are?

Discussion Questions

- In what areas of your life have you sensed change?
- What have these changes added to your life?
- What have these changes added to your relationship?

TWO

Learning
the Other

Self-reflection might seem like an odd place to open a chapter on learning another person. But self-reflection is tied to learning the person you share life with because we can never take for granted that we know ourselves fully, either who we were, who we are, or who we will be.

I (Brian) always thought of myself as a sensitive guy. I was raised by a single mother and lived large chunks of my childhood in a house full of women. I heard all their stories of comments they'd received and of the ways my mom and aunts had been treated at work. My mom encouraged us to go to therapy when we were teenagers. I was always talking about my feelings and reflecting on why I had done or not done something. And yet, so often my self-reflection tilts toward self-rationalization. Insecurity or uncertainty can awaken curiosity and humility, but it can also harden the walls that protect the ideas we have about ourselves. Self-reflection is a risky act that asks us to wrestle with the possibility that we did not handle a situation perfectly and that we could stand to grow in the way we respond to situations and people.

Self-reflection is akin to the Christian idea of confession. We don't mean confession in the sense of creating a laundry list of the ways we have failed. Rather, we mean it in the sense of Augustine's work by the same name. There, confession has two meanings. The first is confessing who God is, the one Augustine's heart restlessly seeks. Confession is to say, "God, you are . . ." The second meaning is confessing who we are: "God, I am . . ." These two statements are related to one another, calling and responding, shaping how we imagine God and how we imagine ourselves.

Confession in this way doesn't have to be, "You, God, are so amazing, and I am dirt." But even in this distorted sense of confession, we see the relational aspect of identifying our short-comings, because there is always a relationship that we have violated. The negative claim we are making also reflects a hope, something that we aspire to be in relation to God and others.

When we connect this to confession in the Christian life as the combination of the "We believe" of the creeds and of "God forgive me, for I have sinned," we see the reciprocal nature of confession as both self-reflection and relationality. We consider who we are, and we consider the one we are with.

Confession also allows us to enter difficult conversations as moments of discovery rather than a battle to be won. One of the biggest challenges in relational conflict is to acknowledge the complexity of the other person and ourselves. We are frustrated or tired or hurt, and it is easy to ask why the other person cannot see what we see, or why they are not doing what we would like to be done. When we see disagreements as a tug-of-war where we cannot give ground, we also lose the opportunity to discover something of the person we share life with.

In a relationship where two people share the mundane and the life-changing, learning the other person is always going to be a process of recalibrating the tools we use to see and under-stand who this person is. But in this case, *we* are the tool, and like trying to observe the stars in the sky, we always have to adjust for the fact that we sit on a spinning marble of rock and are constantly moving. The seasons shift, the weather changes, and through it all, we are trying to discern the same stars. If we are to learn the other person, we must also account for the ways we are changing. We must confess the ways we ourselves are moving.

Gail

Our life together has been a continual learning process.

During our first five-hour phone call, connecting with Brian felt easy. When we finally met in person two months later, after dozens of letters and even more hours on the phone, it seemed odd to speak to each other in the flesh. At that time, things like video apps and social media weren't available to help me figure out his vibe before meeting in person.

After taking a thirteen-hour bus ride from Rochester to Har-risburg, Pennsylvania, I was picked up by Brian and our mutual friend, and we headed off to visit Brian's family for Thanks-giving. Throughout that awkward first meeting and car ride, it seemed more natural for both of us to look straight ahead while catching up. As soon as one of us looked over and saw that the voice wasn't coming through the phone, we'd sense the strangeness and stop talking.

Later, when I moved in with Brian's family during the sum-mer of 1995, I discovered who he was around his family. And the learning didn't stop there but continued as we navigated our first post-marriage living situation, as we had to make our first big decision about career choices, and as we found out we were having our first child. The learning continued as we made a decision about grad school, as I saw who Brian was *in* grad school, and then as I learned who he was in a steady job and career after more than a decade of juggling multiple jobs while living the in-between life of a grad student.

It's one thing to figure out your own likes and dislikes, to grasp who you are and who you want to be. But the dynamics change when you're in a relationship. The arc of an intention or a frustration begins to slide in unexpected ways when you're with the other person day in and day out. As we begin to learn who we are, we are also learning who we are *with* this other person. On this journey together, we are rediscovering our own stories and histories and tendencies, and we are also learning about this person with us, in their unfolding and discovery.

Learning about one another is one of the most foundational parts of a relationship. It doesn't make much sense to even talk about this as a "step." "Of course we have to learn about one another!" you might think. But there's a difference between learning about a static and unchanging topic and learning about *someone* who is dynamic and shifting. The person we are with is not a table that can be disassembled to see how it's put together. He or she is not a tree with a prescribed amount of light and nutrients that are optimal for growth and that simply need to be memorized and applied.

Instead, people are both static and dynamic. There are aspects of who we are that will remain, while parts of who we are will change or adapt to the pressures of life. For example, I have always been uber-social, but having three kids and leading in ministry for more than two decades have allowed me to appreciate and even crave time to myself. What I need has changed over time, especially as I grew deeper into the work of full-time ministry. And as I have changed in my social needs and wants, Brian has also had to learn the person I have become as a pastor.

The people we journey with, especially in committed, intimate relationships, are not who they are always going to be. As much as personality tests like Myers-Briggs and the Enneagram reveal underlying qualities, bents, or preferences, how we inhabit those preferences and tendencies will shift over time.

To learn one another is to recognize that we all change, including the person we are with. Learning one another is an ongoing process of reflection, conversation, taking stock, being patient, stretching, and asking the one we are with to stretch with us. This process can sometimes be painful; sometimes it feels like the other person is stretching away from us. There may be less to talk about or fewer shared hobbies. Or maybe you'll find that the way you each approach uncertainty has shifted because one person got burned or hurt and now is nervous or cautious, while the other is still willing to take chances.

Learning the other can feel unnerving because it means having to admit there are things you don't know. And even when you think you know them, sometimes they surprise you with how they've changed.

When we were barely older than teenagers, the idea of change and learning one another wasn't a shock. We hadn't lived on our own, and we were still figuring out our sense of call and vocation. Living on shoestring budgets meant very little freedom to discover new things beyond a different kind of snack at the grocery store or the new clothing store at the mall. Early on, our world was very small. But because we met so young, there were also lots of changes to come and a lot to learn, and twenty-five years later, there's a lot that we are still learning about this person we've chosen to share our lives with.

Early on, we each knew we needed to be attentive to who this other person was, learning their story and how they were wired, but also figuring out how the other's who-ness mingled with the other's own. Neither of us had many reference points because we had never really known life without the other.

Seeing the other person can be hard, especially as we get older. Our stories and patterns become deeply grooved in how we walk in the world. Becoming a student of the one we are with means seeing who they are and who they might become and all the changes along the way.

Who Are You?

Before we think about the other person, it's important to note how our own history and identity shape how we perceive him or her. It's all fine and good to talk about "learning" the other person, but if we don't have the language to describe what we're seeing, or if a part of our own history shapes how we interpret someone else's behavior, we will tend to pass over a detail or a story or a pattern and assume we know the cause. We have to sit with ourselves and our stories before we can begin the work of learning the other.

In premarital meetings with couples, I (Gail) often use an exercise called "Who Are You?" The exercise not only helps people tease out why they do the things they do, but in their recalling and telling, it also allows the other person to hear the *why* behind what that person does and the deeper history they carry. It goes something like this:

- Recall a memory that typifies your *relationships* growing up. How did you engage with parents, siblings, extended family, neighbors, and so on? Were the relationships gregarious? Subdued? Tense? Abusive? Fun-loving? Strict?
  a. **Ways of doing**: How or in what ways do you replicate this behavior today? Or how have you been formed?
- Recall a memory that typifies how your family *thought* about things. Were family conversations usually hopeful, pessimistic, positive, judgmental, racist, closed-minded, or generous?
  b. **Ways of thinking**: How or in what ways do you replicate this behavior? Or how have you been formed?

34

People don't just happen. Most of us don't make up how we will respond to the world and each other out of nowhere. We learn how to respond to the world and relate to each other from our environment. We are how we are and who we have become because of many influences and experiences over a lifetime—both in positive ways and through acts of resistance and negation.

Gail

When I think about the decades of peeling back the layers in Brian's story, it not only helps me appreciate who he is now but also allows me greater capacity for more grace, patience, understanding, and advocacy. I remember one particular premarital counseling session when the pastor discussed the results of our Myers-Briggs personality tests to help us better understand each other. This was a few weeks before our wedding.

"Brian, it looks like you're a fairly firm introvert, and Gail . . . well, you're quite the opposite," he noted. Those simple words opened a new chapter in our relationship of assumptions and expectations—you know, the ones where couples tend to project affinities and objections based on personality tests. "Why do you always drag your feet when it's time to go to my staff Christmas party?" I'd ask. Or, "Why do you always fall asleep right before we're about to host our small group at the house? If you don't want to host these gatherings, just say so!" This behavior seemed so ridiculously passive-aggressive. "Just say so!" was what I'd always say, whether out loud or in my head, as I gave him a side-eye and kept it pushing. These moments would be infuriating at times, and quite frankly, from my perspective, it seemed as if it *only* happened when it was for my engagements or for the gatherings I initiated. Isn't that always the way?

As the years passed and these moments layered upon each other, I began to notice patterns. From the moment he and

I started dating, Brian told me about suffering constant ear infections that necessitated surgery when he was eight years old, which left him with significant hearing loss in his left ear. Over time, I would notice moments when we were at a gathering or a restaurant where he seemed to be straining to hear the conversation over the background music or would be frustrated by the hum all around us. When we sat in theaters or went for walks, he always moved to my left side so he could hear me better. When the boys were young and they would whisper in their dad's left ear and stare at him, waiting for a response, I'd often say to them, "Baby, you have to say it louder because Dad can't hear you in that ear."

The summer when I lived with Brian and his family, I had asked Brian if we could go to the Washington Mall for the annual Fourth of July festivities. I had always loved crowded celebratory gatherings like state fairs, amusement parks, and festivals. Little did I know that such gatherings were a *nightmare* for him. Of course, he kindly said, "Yes, I'll take you." But a couple hours before we left the house, he was nowhere to be found. It didn't take long to discover where he was: stuck in the bathroom with anxiety-riddled stomach issues. Mind you, this wasn't the first time our plans had been foiled by a similar situation. The ignorant and ungenerous part of me blurted out, "Why do you always do this?! If you don't want to go, just say so!" Or worse, "Why can't you time this and take care of it earlier?"

Fast-forward, and I've learned that for most of Brian's childhood, living in a loving but constantly shifting environment and reality—eight homes in seventeen years, teased throughout elementary and middle school, parents' divorce, his dad's alcoholism, and his dad's death—took a toll on Brian's body. Stomach issues were his body's way of dealing with stress and anxiety. In learning this about Brian and by growing aware of how his hearing loss could also cause incredible anxiety in public, I've come to see that his social angst isn't necessarily about introversion. Sometimes our story, our experiences, our realities, when pressed over time, cause us to navigate the world in ways we can't quite articulate or express to a loved one. Not only does learning the other mean gaining particular knowledge about that person; it also calls out action and advocacy on our part. Empathy leads to different decisions.

Over the years, I've learned to decline certain joint invitations if it means that Brian will struggle to participate. I've learned to save the seat on my left—always—whenever there's an occasion for saving seats in crowded spaces. I've learned to set him up at a restaurant so that his good ear will face the most people at our table. The beauty in learning the other is that it transforms us. And our transformation is not just for our own sake; it also enables the greater good of the whole.

Having a son who is also physically affected by stress, I have grown aware that one's responses to something in the moment don't always correspond to one's desire for it. Our whole body and being is a product of our story. But we are also more than any single response we can offer in the moment.

This was especially important for me to grasp because, even as I was learning and discovering things about Brian, I was also learning things about myself. I had to confront the fact that I didn't grow up with parents who extended much grace to me. It was a life of hustle, during which we weren't allowed to stay home from school just because we had a 101-degree fever. Mine was a "do it sick anyway" upbringing. In fact, I remember being allowed to stay home from school only when I broke my leg. We didn't have insurance, so I lay on the couch until I could wrap up my leg and put a little pressure on it to make it through a whole day at school. It was brutal. But it was my reality. And in many ways, it led me to harbor an unhealthy expectation of that grit and hustle and to project that expectation onto everyone around me.

Brian has taught me a lot about grace and what it means to be human in all of its beauty, frailties, and imperfections. As much as I thought I needed to be ten times better, stronger, and more resilient than everyone around me (to be seen, to be heard), that kind of facade isn't sustainable. And, by God's grace, I found myself with a partner who never played that game or allowed me to get sucked into it. Brian has taught me that we can be gracious with others only when we are gracious with ourselves.

Discussion Questions

- What are little things about the other person that get under your skin that you haven't asked about?
- That maybe you've made some assumptions about?
- How has your own upbringing shaped those assumptions?

Brian

Every couple is different. And we knew about some of our differences in our first years of dating. But the first twenty-four hours of our married life could not have made these differences more apparent.

We arrived at the door of our new apartment and pulled our few boxes and futon into the 400-square-foot studio. I was ready to lounge and grab some food. Gail was ready to unpack, decorate, and make this home. Little did I know that what she meant was that everything was going to be out of boxes, pictures would be hung, pots and towels and curtains would all be purchased and set up . . . before we slept. "We don't sleep until this is home." And this would be her pattern in every move since.

The next morning after that first move, I heard some soft coughing, a few heavy sighs. I opened my eyes, and there was

Gail, eyes wide open, staring at me. "Are you up? It's soooooooo late!" she said.

"It's 7:30 in the morning, love."

"We need to get up or we're going to waste the day. What should we do?"

"Everything is still closed . . ."

"But still. I'm lonely."

Completion. Anticipation. A plan. Together. These were the first things I learned about Gail as we started to build our life together. She wanted to completely finish one thing before moving on to another. She wanted to enjoy everything she could every day. She wanted to have a plan that she could anticipate and get excited for. And whatever she did, she wanted us to do it together.

I was a bit more "play it by ear"—the kind of person who'd say, "Let's wake up around 11 or 12, eat some brunch, and see what the day brings." You can see the challenge, right?

Every couple has to navigate personality differences like these. Learning Gail meant beginning to attend to the ways she ordered her world and finding ways I could contribute to that order, not just dismantle it.

I came to realize that Gail's planning was never about control or a need to know. She tended to plan because she saw a lot. I mean *a lot*. She was able to see what was happening that week, in the next few months, and far beyond. In the midst of everything she saw, she also saw the opportunities to rest, or to go on vacation, or just to decompress. And she cannot rest if she knows a job isn't finished or there are boxes left to unpack.

As much as I love a spontaneous trip or walk, I know that if Gail hasn't finished the task at hand, the trip or the treat will not be relaxing or fun. In the small things, every day, our life together gave me a chance to learn how she operated so that I could partner with her and help her feel seen and supported. For me, there's nothing better than a distraction while we're unpacking ("Let's go get McDonald's!"); for her, there is joy when the job is done. And in the midst of it all, she wants to be together. Drink coffee. Get a snack. Go to the grocery store . . . together.

Over time, we have both softened our edges. I get up earlier (without her needing to wake me!); she can relax in the midst of a project or leave some boxes unpacked. She can endure a few hours away from me while I'm on a bike ride, even though I know it's still itching her insides a bit. And I know that when she is stressed or feeling like there are too many things to hold, she is going to need help finishing the job before she can rest or take some time off. Learning one another's quirks and tendencies, seeing them as part of how our partner is wired, allows us to value the way their gifts and strengths add to the home, even as those differences can stretch us.

Sometimes the most intense moments of learning come amid conflict. Some of Gail's and my earliest arguments took on a familiar pattern. Gail, usually talkative and eager to share a thought or an idea, would grow quiet. I would find her cleaning something or going on a walk or running errands by herself. Picking up the signal that she was upset, I would badger her to talk about it until she finally did. Then I would turn around and accuse her of some slight, bringing up the ten things I had been sitting on for the last three months that were completely unrelated to what she was upset about. We would be quiet and barely talk for a day (sometimes two if it was bad), and then we'd apologize and talk through what had led up to the argument.

What kept me from hearing Gail was my tendency to feel any criticism as an attack. I had been teased as a kid and tried to be as quiet as possible in classes, trying to follow every rule. As my mom struggled with depression, I operated like a barometer in the house, feeling out any subtle change and trying to clean or help out when I saw she was welling up or getting

40

frustrated. I was the good kid, the one who helped, who saw, who wasn't like the "other" kids. Any type of criticism shattered who I thought I was.

All this meant that I was also very prickly when it came to criticism that I felt was unfounded. So whenever Gail would get upset or frustrated, I would feel like she didn't see all the things I was thinking or doing for her. I was lost in my own interpretation of our lives. And because I was so lost in my insecurities, I never really heard or learned what her worries or frustrations were, or how she was experiencing our relationship in that moment.

As we got older and I began to have a better sense of who I was, I also started to see what was underneath some of Gail's worries or concerns or frustrations. This is not to say that I don't still struggle with insecurities, but I recognize there are some aspects of my story that keep me from seeing and being present to Gail in difficult moments. Learning yourself in order to learn the other person means beginning to ask why certain patterns persist.

Discussion Questions

- What are the moments you got upset when your partner raised an issue or a frustration?
- What kept you from hearing their concern or hurt?

Ways to Learn the Other

There are many ways to become attentive to the one you're with. Using therapy, professional counselors are trained to help you recognize patterns in your life, while couples counselors are trained to wrestle with how each person is seeing and hearing and sensing the other. Personality tests help do much of

41

the same. While not always scientific, personality tests can be great conversation starters. Talking about past events and why a certain conversation keeps arising is a wonderful though often difficult way of seeing how each person experienced a specific moment and what they felt. But how someone navigates their own introversion or extroversion, how they cope with pain and disappointment, or how willing they are to try new things can change over time.

Anyone who has spent a long time with a child knows that change is inevitable. Infants seem to transform even week to week. Just when a sleep schedule's in place and you've gotten the swing of the rocker just right, you figure out they like to be patted on the back instead of rubbed in a circular pattern. Then, seemingly overnight, they don't want to be touched, or they need the rabbit instead of the bear. Raising children is more like tending a garden than building a bookshelf.

Yet in the midst of those changes, we can see certain threads of personality. And we are still those children. As we mature, we have plenty of tools that help us identify our personality types, our work habits, and so on. But we don't have many tools to understand how these aspects of who we are affect living and binding ourselves to someone else—and how the other person inevitably changes us. This cycle continues: as we evolve, the person we are with evolves, and as they change, we adapt and push and pull. This cycle of growth and adaptation is a reality of what it means to live together.

We opened this chapter with stories from our early years, of times when we felt a bit like children, like each year brought new changes and discoveries of ourselves and the other person. But even as we have entered our mid-forties, we continue to discover new facets of the other, and of ourselves. Sometimes these discoveries and changes were beautiful, and our years together allowed us to settle in with one another in a new phase of life or in the midst of upheaval, or even in moments of rest. But

42

other times have found us in the midst of some of the hardest conversations and arguments of our whole marriage. We can tend to get used to the person who has been with us for so long, and then a job change or an emptier house make clear what had been somewhat hidden. Maybe the other person has changed, or maybe I've changed.

Continually choosing each other means relearning the one we've committed to. And this is an ongoing cycle of reflection, observation, and conversation that requires trust and honesty and the courage to ask difficult questions. As you continue to learn about yourself and the person you're with, consider digging deeper in these two areas: (1) observing each other's patterns and (2) learning how the other person has navigated systemic realities, including race, gender, sexuality, ability, and class.

Observing Patterns

Working as an executive pastor for many years, I (Gail) saw it as my primary job to learn how to read the lead pastor so that I could most accurately represent them and their vision for the church and respond to inquiries on their behalf. To read them well was an act of care—to figure out when they would best receive new input or ideas or when it was most helpful to share difficult news. It was important for me to learn their patterns and inclinations during both static and pressed situations, especially when confronted by change. What kinds of scenarios might cause undue stress? When were there opportunities for encouragement? I was constantly reading and learning, not only so that I could do my job well but also for the good and health of the organization.

Learning to notice the patterns of the other, whatever the nature of the relationship, will inevitably help us to look out for the good of the whole—the wider family, the friend circle, the marriage, the staff, the team, and so on. Unfortunately, in dominant white American culture that celebrates rugged individualism, we can too readily undermine the power of learning the other as a communal act. Koreans embrace and value this notion of a sixth sense, called 눈치, or nunchi. Loosely translated, nunchi is the subtle ability to gauge another's mood and feelings, otherwise known as emotional intelligence. Korean culture cultivates, starting at an early age, a heightened sense of situational awareness, or nunchi, a capacity for anticipating another person's needs preemptively, before the need is voiced. In many ways, nunchi exemplifies a culture that deeply values community and the well-being of the whole.

After about ten years of marriage, Gail and I (Brian) had seen our fair share of challenges—not enough money, Gail feeling stretched with kids, worries about our jobs and callings. We began to see a pattern when figuring out how to move forward. Gail's first instinct was always to conquer, make a change, shift the board. For her, circumstances were not going to dictate what our options were. For me, the tendency was to bend and wait, trying to make the best out of what was available and taking advantage of any opportunities that came my way.

Clearly, these were not terribly compatible strategies, but after a while, we started to see a similar conversation emerge, and it trickled into the smaller tasks that any challenge required. Whenever it came time to move to a new apartment or house, Gail was constantly searching ads, noting rents, figuring out timing. Meanwhile, I was sitting back and waiting until it got closer to the move date, feeling a little overwhelmed by all the options and generally settling for what was familiar. But for Gail, the opportunity to move was also the opportunity to improve some aspect of our living situation (usually for the same rent!).

In actuality, both her patterns and mine have positive and negative attributes. Gail's approach meant we had every possible apartment listed and planned for. But part of Gail's approach was also about trying to maintain control in uncertain moments. While my approach allowed for some flexibility, it was also rooted in not working through a certain paralysis I experienced with the prospect of change. So here Gail was, working furiously to find us a new home, and there I was, paralyzed and blankly staring into the distance.

When it came to packing, though, Gail was usually overwhelmed, and suddenly I would spring into action. Eventually, we came to see these tendencies not as inadequacies but as particular ways we each occupy our world. At the same time, recognizing our patterns also helped us see the areas where we needed to put in more effort or needed to contribute more so that the other person didn't bear the entire burden at any given time.

Tensions don't always get figured out so easily, though. We don't always make it to the aha moments, even twenty-five years in. For example, why do we get into our most heated arguments on vacations? We like to call them "intense fellowship" because that sounds softer, but in truth, we argue, and I (Gail) end up spending at least half a day ignoring Brian in what I call "silent fellowship." To this day, we cannot seem to reconcile the fact that I like to see and explore new things and go to new places when I am away from work. And to make things even more complicated, because my everyday job requires me to plan ahead and coordinate and research options and care for lots of people, usually six to twelve months out at a time, I need someone else to coordinate the vacation. (Do you feel me?) Otherwise, it just feels like work in a different setting, with different people.

Brian likes to chill. Like, *chill*. Like, take the first few days to scope everything out and figure out what we could or should do—then chill some more. "I only have seven days, babe!" I'd gently scream through my teeth. "I'm gonna need you to chill on the way there so we can pound the pavement when we arrive!" Vacations to me are maximizing and discovering what is available to us at that particular place, whether it's visiting the local hole-in-the-wall restaurants or shops, kayaking, strolling downtown at night, checking out the scene, or hitting the various beaches if that's where we're at—you know, vacationing! And that is Brian's nightmare. New things and busy social scenes are a literal nightmare for him. I know this. And yet.

For me (Brian), vacations are a chance to get away, to rest and enjoy your people, a time when you shouldn't have to make any decisions or figure out anything new. Just soak in a pool, rest on the beach, read a book, ride a bike. Gail and I have yet to have a vacation like this. After twenty-five years, you would think we would know what the other person wanted and was hoping for. But somehow the first few days always begin with that dreaded question: "So, what are we going to do today?" When Gail asks, I know I'm already too far gone because I haven't figured out somewhere new to go or what the local excitement is. When I scramble for a few ideas that might come to me in that moment, everything goes silent—for a day, or even two. After that, it's a delicate dance. I know it by heart. (I have the conversation practically memorized!) We each enact our respective steps, until it's time to plan the next vacation.

This tension has only gotten more pronounced. We're more financially stable and able to choose our vacations with more freedom. It was easier when the only option was the off-season special at Myrtle Beach. We also know ourselves a bit more now. Gail works hard, grinds day in and day out, and wants to make good use of her few weeks of vacation. She is a play-hard, rest-hard person. But she also spends much of her work time planning, organizing, and being the social woo of her job. Ideally, her vacation would be a place that is new and exciting and planned completely by someone else.

As I've gotten older, I've come to love the woods and nature, bike rides, and hikes. Maybe a bookstore or an art museum. But definitely nothing new. New freaks me out.

You can probably sense the difficulty.

We wrote these accounts of our vacation separately, but it should be pretty clear that we know one another. And in knowing what the other person is going through and needs, you would think we would be able to avoid yearly summer blowouts on vacation, right? As much as we would both love for that to be true, we know that life together is not just solving problems in order to resolve all tension. It is also realizing that some aspects of each person are really incompatible with the other person, and that our needs will shift over time as things change with jobs, kids, and community life. Yet we still have to find a way.

An easy formula for resolving these kinds of conflicts would be ideal, but we don't have one. That said, we are honest about what we need, about what we are willing to do, and what we would really rather not do. We have also been together long enough to know that these tensions may not persist. Gail might come to love bike rides. Brian might come to love new adventures. But until then, we also trust one another to be willing to stretch for the other and find some spaces of respite and joy on the journey.

Discussion Questions

- What are the other person's patterns? When pressed? When confronted by the prospect of change? In times of "plenty"?

Navigating Systemic Realities

All of us live inside vast, complicated social histories. Race, ethnicity, gender, ability, sexuality, and class are all systemic

realities that are lived day-to-day and moment-to-moment. We
live in families and communities that have shaped how we see
who we are and how we ought to recognize and either resist or
accommodate these realities. We'll dive further into the significance of racial and gender formation in the next few chapters.
For now, our focus will be on the ways that learning the other
means entering into that person's deeper social formation.

Gail

I was initially drawn to Brian in part because of our seemingly shared experiences of cultural and racial in-betweenness,
always questioning our sense of belonging wherever we were.
As a child of Korean immigrant parents, I've navigated the
complexities of language and of cultural differences in a vari-
ety of spaces, from home to school to neighborhood. I found
belonging within the Black church as a teenager. Brian would
share his stories with me about being a biracial (Black/white)
child primarily raised by his white mother and her side of the
family, even while learning and becoming aware of the work
his brown body was doing in the world as he grew older. We
shared this in-betweenness from the beginning.

Whenever we find ourselves in public spaces, whether at
church or at the Korean grocery store or while walking down the
street, I find myself noticing other people's stares, glares, fears,
suspicions, or curiosity about Brian. I've also noticed when
we've been in predominantly Black spaces over the years—like
our children's elementary school in North Carolina, or Black
churches, or gatherings within the community—that I see Brian's angst, his questions about whether he'll be welcomed or
seen as "Black enough."

These experiences have opened my eyes to the ways we *all*
have stories and experiences that slowly inform who we are
and how we see ourselves and negotiate our way through the

world. While I've named how learning the particularities of Brian's identity as a Black man is part of my growth in our relationship, there are many aspects of one's story and the often-complicated intersections of gender, culture, sexuality, and ability as well that require attentiveness and care for any relationship to truly flourish.

When our kids were younger and loved playing with LEGO sets, I remember seeing the picture of the Star Wars Millennium Falcon on the cover of the box and having a rough idea of how this thing was going to get built. But if you've ever had the joy of building LEGO sets with your child, you've quickly realized that the beginning stages of the building process are nothing like what you imagined. Why? Because there are pieces you didn't even know existed. Why? Because it's a part of the inside of the spaceship that you'll never see in its finished form. Why? Because it's either part of the fancy detailing of the ship, or it helps create stability for that part of the wing . . . from the inside! If we approach every person and relationship with this kind of "clean slate" mentality, or with an understanding that the internal realities of one's being hold surprising complexity, we'll more readily avoid the temptation to assume "all men" or "all ____ people" should naturally be a particular way or possess certain instincts (e.g., women are nurturing, Asian women are submissive, Black men are dangerous, men can fix cars, women can cook). Start with step one and learn to discover the other person from their beginnings, and how every piece informs their larger story.

Brian

While I grew up in a house of women, I still had so much to learn from life alongside Gail. When we started dating, I happened to be doing a project in a Christian education class that required church visits, and I was visiting a Korean church.

In many ways it was a typical Korean immigrant church with a service in Korean and a service in English, a youth group, and a lunch after the service that had a good number of women cooking during the service. This was part of Gail's upbringing. But I had to learn the history of pale skin to understand why so many Koreans thought she wasn't 100 percent Korean with her slightly darker complexion to see that her experience of the Korean church and the Korean community was a complicated one that had a lot to do with her being a strong woman. And these forms of alienation were a big reason for her finding a sense of place and home in the Black community and the Black church.

She is Korean because . . . she *is* Korean (surprise!). But she also embodies particular markers of Korean culture in small, sometimes imperceptible ways. For example, Gail has a sense of communal responsibility, she values celebration around food (and in abundance), and she has a deep devotion to family. But her life was also about resisting conformity to the ideals Korean culture sometimes asked her to inhabit. Learning Gail also meant learning about the tensions of accommodation and assimilation in immigrant communities, the legacies of patriarchy, and how Black life had been a home for people looking for safe harbor.

I did not sit down with books, reading and studying for hours to learn these lessons. But I did have to learn not to assume that her hesitation about a certain restaurant or refusal to speak Korean to another Korean was just an individual decision. Sometimes we talked about those moments, and other times we were both discovering along the way as we reflected about any given "why" on our journey together.

Discussion Questions

- Think about some of your responses or conversation about the earlier discussion questions. How many of those were shaped by realities of race, ethnicity, gender, ability, or sexuality?
- What are the stories and histories you need to learn in order to understand where the tendencies of your partner might come from?

Learning the other person requires a posture of humility and wonder. In writing this, we realize we may have emphasized how tension or disagreement can sometimes be the way we come to discover who this other person is. But equally beautiful are the moments when we learn how delighted the other person is when we bring home their favorite soda or plan a trip on the weekend. Learning the other means a loving attentiveness that opens us to new wonders and joys, seen through the eyes of the other. It means discovering how they are growing and changing through the years. Life together will always mean a lifelong journey of learning.

THREE

Race and Belonging

Part of what connected us was not only our love of laughter and conversation but also our experience navigating in-between spaces of race. At first glance, the connection between a Black, mixed-race boy from Maryland and a Korean American girl from Illinois and Oklahoma doesn't seem to have much ethnic or racial overlap. But we were both navigating the larger forces and legacies of race in our homes and communities.

Race is not simply a set of biological markers, nor is ethnicity reducible to language or customs or country of origin. Race and ethnicity are laced with complicated threads of belonging and power, exclusion and expectation. As children we don't always see these threads or feel the forces so bluntly. But as we get older, we discover how our bodies are being "read" and all the accompanying expectations or fears.

Learning ourselves and one another means examining how race has shaped us and is continuing to shape us. In some ways, it would have been wonderful if our lives together could be a hermetically sealed chamber where it was "just us." But that is never the case. As an example, it didn't take long for me (Brian) to realize that Gail's connection and sense of belonging in the Black church and community was linked to her struggle with belonging in the Korean community, a community that was working out its own sense of citizenship and loss that stretched between histories of colonization and occupation in Korea and seeking to build new lives in a United States that saw them as foreigners.

This navigation was always present with us, whether in the presence of food, in witnessing questioning looks in Korean restaurants and grocery stores, or in overhearing others' hushed conversations. It was even more present when we began expressing our inner hopes and frustrations, something Gail's home rarely made space for. And it was especially present when we had children and had to wrestle with whether to teach the boys Korean or send them to Korean school.

How does race shape us? Race, in itself, is not real. It is a historical construct invented by European theologians, scientists, philosophers, and colonizers to make sense of themselves. This was not always an explicit exercise but arose from encounters with people and places that were different from them. In their attempt to account for these differences, they used themselves as norms, as ideals, and described others in relationships of inferiority to the ideal of the European man.

Ways of understanding ourselves will always be relational and arise from our encounters with difference. With each new difference and encounter, we develop a sense of ourselves. As groups of people and communities develop a common identity, they share a language around those similarities, and we see the emergence of a culture. But this is never a static, eternal, or natural phenomenon. Cultures and societies are always changing and shifting, many simply becoming notes in the history books or merging with other cultures. Within these societies, individuals are also navigating the norms and expectations of belonging, as well as the limits of belonging.

In this way, identity is an ongoing process, what cultural theorist Stuart Hall calls "identification." Identification is a way of describing how a person or group of people is formed by the histories and language of their society, even as they are navigating those histories in their own unique ways, either pressing against oppressive norms or assimilating to and adopting the norms, or some mixture of the two. What makes this process even more complicated is that people are not simply navigating two clearly defined cultures. These cultural realities are woven into one another, and the process of navigating communities is multifold.

This slightly theoretical framing is important as we think about relationships, because even in our relationships, we continue to negotiate our communities, our broader societies, and their histories. We can never think about relationships without also thinking about the work our bodies are doing in the world and the way our society shapes us.

In-Between Identities

Gail

Identity was complicated for me from an early age. Language was the primary struggle and tether in my in-between journey. For my immigrant parents, a mix of Korean and broken English was commonplace, and it was the primary language spoken in our house. I was protective of my parents when kids would snicker at their accent. But at the same time, I was questioned about my identity as a Korean when I never learned to speak the language fluently or practice some of its cultural traditions.

My mother did everything she could to become "American" (immigrant code for "white"). For her, that meant forsaking some of the traditional practices of her roots: she worked hard

55

to speak as much English as possible; she fought against the patriarchy of Korean culture by trying to keep me out of the kitchen; and we never participated in the traditional New Year's bows that kids perform for their parents and grandparents because radical conversion to white colonial Christianity necessarily erases one's cultural identity and insists that we don't bow to anyone but God. (Sadly, this also meant that I missed out on a lot of New Year's money!) The loss of a particular cultural tether wasn't all bad, but it did leave me vulnerable in some ways. Add to this my slightly darker complexion and the way I looked in general, and the result was that many Koreans at my parents' church would ask them if I was adopted. I never quite fit or felt like I belonged with my people.

Later, when I hit middle school, I found myself surrounded by a diverse group of friends in Tulsa, Oklahoma, where my mother attended seminary. Not long after we settled in, I was invited to attend a prominent Pentecostal Black church with a friend from the neighborhood. And strangely, I found myself feeling at home. My parents had served in Pentecostal Korean immigrant churches back in Chicago, so there was a certain familiarity of language, tarrying, and worshiping with abandon that struck a chord with me in that church. I understood myself in that space, even though I knew I was different. Every week, I stood there on the curb of my apartment building waiting for my friend and her aunt to pick me up. We could count on a couple of the church mothers to look for us, greet us with big suffocating hugs in the lobby, and feed us after service. I felt at home there in a peculiar way.

It wasn't too long after I started high school that I realized there was something deeper I was going to discover about myself and about the racialized formation of my home that I had always known was there but had not yet directly experienced. The guys that I became interested in were mostly the guys I met from the Black Pentecostal church. While my mother generally disapproved of me dating in high school, her disapproval intensified when she saw that the guys I was interested in weren't white (read: "American"). I was pressed to either obey and stop seeing them or be sneaky and go behind her back. Let's just say, I made it work.

Our affections can often speak to where we find belonging and home—people with whom we can be our free and full selves. This isn't always the case, but it bears consideration. In any cross-cultural relationship, we need to ask the hard and honest questions of why: Why am I drawn to this person or these people? Is it the person, or is there something in the idea of what this person represents that adds to my sense of identity or lack thereof? I can't tell you how many interracial couples I've encountered over the years for whom the root of their interest in one another was a sense of wanting to prove that they were "down with brown," or an underlying exotic fetish for submissive Asian women, or the illusion that white is ideal, a prize to be won. Selah.

Brian

For me, race had always been an ambiguous but consistent presence. I am darker than my white mother, but not as dark as the other Black kids in my class. I had straight hair like my mother, but lips like my Black father. The questions of "What are you?" and the subtle glances of strangers from me to my mother and back again were a constant in my childhood. I knew I wasn't white, but I wasn't sure I was Black either.

But by the time I was in junior high and high school, my hair had curled a bit more, and I found that the color lines had been drawn more starkly. While I wasn't sure what it meant to be Black, there were others who drew those lines of difference for me. These small exclusions (a girl's parents would not allow their daughter to date a Black kid) or inclusions (being invited by the Black students' club to help organize the MLK assembly) were all asking something of me. While I may not have felt a sense of belonging, I was part of a larger story and history. My body was seen as Black, in ways that were exclusionary and supposedly dangerous or intimidating, but also in ways that tethered me to a people and a history.

These feelings of belonging and inclusion, or of distance and exclusion, were a journey for me. And the dynamics of race didn't always come out in direct ways that were easy to discern. Those dynamics have proven to be complex and have emerged in specific contexts that Gail and I have wrestled with, like where to go to church, what neighborhood to live in, or even which grocery store one of us preferred.

Gail always teases me that if we are equally distanced from two grocery stores, we will usually choose different stores. I will choose Harris Teeter with its large organic section and free cookies. Gail will choose Kroger where "the people" are. When we first discussed it, it was a seemingly innocuous detail and preference, but as I thought about it more, I was gravitating toward a familiarity and, in all honesty, toward an association that had been instilled in me growing up. Gail gravitated toward Kroger and its resonance with her strongest senses of belonging with people of color. This seemingly small detail was something we talked about, and sometimes even teased the other about. But we also had to recognize how powers of representation crept into our daily lives.

Especially for interracial couples, the process of listening and self-reflection is a necessary part of exploring how race shapes us and our daily lives, even in the smallest ways. Some friends of ours, an interracial couple with a Black, mixed woman and a white man, have a similar conversation about grocery stores, but she goes to the store in the wealthier part of town because she spent much of her childhood in poverty and now chooses stores that reflect a different reality for her.

Part of the process of learning ourselves and learning the other is beginning to question how the realities of race shaped us and them. When I first began dating Gail, I was visiting a Korean church as part of a college project. Gail seemed very different from the people I was meeting there. And while Gail was familiar with the after-church meals, the tensions between the Korean-speaking and English-speaking services, the early morning prayer meetings, and the sense of community, it was only after I began hearing parts of her story that I noticed all the women cooking instead of being in service or saw that the only leaders in the church were men.

Gail's journey in the Korean community is hers to share, but what both of our experiences point to is how the realities of race press on us, even as we navigate those realities in unique and particular ways. I couldn't assume that Gail was Korean American in the ways I had encountered in that church. I would have to allow her the space to offer and discover how she inhabited her Korean American identity.

Navigating Race

Race and ethnicity are not simply about the color of our skin or the features of our face. Race and ethnicity are about identification and finding (or struggling to find) belonging, which we sometimes resist but always have to navigate, whether explicitly or implicitly in our everyday lives.

The three particular areas that we have had to work through, and that we have seen other couples struggle to navigate, are food, church and community, and whiteness. These areas are especially prominent for interracial couples, where the currents of race and the apparent choices to be made are often on the surface of everyday life, where cultural differences or assumptions manifest more acutely.

Food

Food is the flesh of our cultural formation. We gather around food. Certain foods or flavors conjure memories of growing up, make us feel safe, and remind us of a loved one and the way we felt in their company. And because food is such an intimate part of our daily lives, and such a significant thread in the intricate tapestry of our cultural lives, food can also be a place where the different realities of race and ethnicity become apparent.

Food is connected to larger racial and ethnic realities of family gatherings, of economic means or lack of means, to ideas of extended family and friends or nuclear families. Food is family recipes and traditions and flavors of life that give us a sense of who we are. But for many couples, this was not the case. I (Brian) was shocked to hear, for example, that there were Korean women married to white men who never cooked Korean food in the house because their husbands didn't like the smell. Who cooks and what is eaten or not eaten is part of holding the racial and ethnic culture of a home. Dynamics of power and gender are at work in the liturgies of our eating. Who prepares, who cleans, whose palate is attended to, and who has to wait for special occasions or the rare trip home to receive the tastes of their childhood—these are the gates and barriers to the cultural ties that make us who we are. When we foreclose the sharing of our food and the stories of food in our lives, we also miss the opportunities to deepen our understanding of one another's racial and ethnic lives.

Gail

Growing up, I mostly ate Korean food for every meal at home, with some occasional Kentucky Fried Chicken, Little Caesars pizza, or McDonald's when we had something special. My mother would often send rice and kimchi in my lunch, or just a boiled hotdog in a bun, wrapped in foil to keep it warm. Oh, those nasty soggy buns! But mostly, we ate Korean food and shopped at the Korean grocery store that my great-aunt owned in Chicago. As I mentioned before, my mother really loved all the American things, and anytime she would be introduced to different foods, she'd try to buy some (at the "American" store) and have us taste it—like egg salad and Vienna sausages, and even liverwurst spread in a tube! But what she failed to ever buy me were the foods I saw my classmates pull out from their little lunch boxes every day. I wanted to try Chef Boyardee SpaghettiOs, and the yellow potato bread that kids had for their sandwiches, and those pink snowball-looking snacks! Most of the non-Korean food I had as a child was experienced at friends' houses or at church.

I didn't grow up eating much cheese, except on pizza and in the mac and cheese I had at other people's houses. I loved mac and cheese and pizza growing up, and didn't think much about it. It's odd how, as an adult, I'm now obsessed with cheesy meals, especially cheese on noodles or rice. As Brian has been the chef of the house in recent years, he knows to give me the cheesiest parts of the baked spaghetti or the mac and cheese or the chicken noodle casserole. But whenever I find myself in stressful situations or needing a little comfort, if Brian asks what I want for dinner, my answer is *always* "anything Korean or fried chicken." And when I've had too much fried chicken, I have to wash it down with kimchi. It's a thing.

Brian

Gail and I spent the first two months of our relationship talking on the phone and writing letters. We talked about foods we loved and where we liked to eat, but it was always abstract. When we first met, Gail visited my family for Thanksgiving. That's when our abstract conversations suddenly became concrete. We had our traditional meal, complete with turkey, stuffing, green bean casserole, and cranberry sauce that slipped out of a can and still had the ridged form of the can. And rolls. As we began eating, Gail mentioned in passing that she hadn't had butter like this before. The entire table went silent. Gail loved butter. Forget the stuffing, the turkey, the cranberry sauce. Out of all the things she experienced in her first turkey-centered Thanksgiving meal, the lasting memory was butter.

My first experiences with Korean food were a bit more tepid. I remember my first visit to Eastman and eating some 고추장 (gochujang, a red pepper paste) with rice, roasted seaweed, and kimchi in her dorm room. Her grandmother sent it. I smelled it first. Gail laughed and asked why I was smelling it. I put a little bit of the red pepper paste on the rice, wrapped it with a piece of seaweed, and took a hesitant bite. All I could taste at first was the spice, then flavors that were completely foreign to me. The kimchi was almost impossible for me to eat. I just couldn't get past the smell. The next time I visited, I wiped the kimchi on the rice and ate the kimchi juice–flavored rice.

Eventually, after months and months, I found the thicker pieces of cabbage to be a little more tolerable. Then after a few years, it was more interesting. And after still a few more years, I craved it. Part of what kept bringing me back to a food that was so strange to me was Gail's love for it. Obviously, she loved the flavors, and each dish brought back certain memories and comforts. But it was also clear in getting to know her that this food was the center of a larger communal identity and way of being. New Year's, birthdays, Friday nights—for Gail, her food was part of a way of existing and enjoying the world and one another.

If I was going to live with and love Gail, I was going to need to live with and love the food that made her who she was. It meant learning to tolerate kimchi and finding at least a few things on the menu that I could enjoy, since I also knew that

Gail (like many Koreans) would sacrifice her own pleasure if she knew I didn't like the food. She did not want to put me in positions where I felt uncomfortable or didn't like something. But she wouldn't tell me. I needed to learn to like *something* so that Gail could be free to enjoy it fully.

But to my surprise I began not only tolerating kimchi but also craving it. My favorite of all meals (besides cheeseburgers) is soondubu, a soft tofu stew. I never would have imagined loving this meal when Gail and I first met. Food may seem insignificant, but it is one of the daily stitches that bind us together, giving us opportunities to learn one another's stories and discover what the patterns and challenges of each other's lives have been.

Church and Community

Like food, the communities we become a part of, the people and groups that we commit ourselves to and allow ourselves to be seen by, are a significant aspect of our lives together. For us, this community was church. Churches were the central communities that shaped not only our spiritual lives but also our early racial and ethnic identities. These formations were not always positive, but they continued with us. And as we began to walk our lives together, it became clear that we would also need to discover how race was affecting our decisions about which communities we would be a part of, and which ones we could not.

Gail

Even though I complained at times about having to tag along with my parents to church meetings, revival services, and evening prayer meetings, I eventually came to realize how much my imagination and formation were rooted in and cultivated by those seemingly wasteful hours as a child. I remember as if it were yesterday the wailing cries of first-generation Korean immigrant women and men on their knees pleading with God for provision, healing, protection, forgiveness, and mercy for themselves and their loved ones—all at the top of their lungs. Some would be rocking back and forth, others had fists in the air, and still others would be pounding their chests. Our church was Pentecostal in tradition, so there was a lot of talking back to the preacher, and the services were just generally very participatory, engaging, and loud. Not only would I experience this in the church, but I also often heard my parents praying loudly at home in their room. Pentecostals call it "tarrying." It wasn't gentle. It wasn't nicely asking God for anything. No, it was a desperate cry to God, asking that God might intervene and move on their behalf. Desperate!

Little did I know that this kind of desperate expression of faith would translate into a strange familiarity at the church I ended up attending when I moved to Tulsa. It was a Black Pentecostal church—a loud "withholding nothing" church, where there were familiar sounds and similarly desperate expressions of worship. I immediately felt at home. "Oh, I *know* this!" I would often think to myself. The "amens" and "hallelujahs" in response to the preacher or in between songs would easily slip out of my mouth. I would find myself readily "caught up in the Spirit," my feet moving faster than I could keep up. Something about this place, these people, despite the stark differences of how we looked, felt like home, like family, but without the barriers of language. The familiarity of expression, joined to a freedom of language, was what I needed in that moment.

Brian

Growing up in a white neighborhood and becoming a Christian in a white church meant I had to come to terms with my blackness in ways that were often disconnected from the Black community. I didn't feel the deep sense of belonging and joy and creativity that animated Black communities. Rather, the beginning of my racial journey was reckoning with how whiteness had shaped me, realizing that I would be a perpetual outsider in predominantly white institutions. Only later would I come to find belonging in Black spaces.

Early in Gail's and my relationship, I was hesitant about all-Black churches. I was still wrestling with my sense of self, and maybe even the subtle patterns of whiteness that I knew were working in me but didn't know how to make sense of. Growing up, I always knew I wasn't white, but it would be years before I understood how whiteness had formed me. And it wasn't until I saw that formation that I could begin to grasp how it had shaped my desire to be part of certain communities, communities whose approval I sought and who I wanted to be seen by.

For me and Gail, church and neighborhood were where those conversations came to the surface. Would we go to the Full Gospel church in downtown Rochester or the community church in the suburbs? Would we live on the south side of the city or closer to campus? Sometimes our decisions were pragmatic, like choosing to live closer to where we worked. At other times we had options that required us to dig into our racial stories and ask ourselves what we were hoping for, what we were clinging to, or what we were running away from.

These intuitions or hesitations don't always work themselves out in explicit conversations. Sometimes they work themselves out slowly (part of the process of learning ourselves). But the commitment to walking with the other person means being open to stepping into new, different worlds.

For me, this began when we realized the suburban church was not a good fit. Or, to be more precise, when Gail said, "I'm not going to no dead church!" And that was that. So we started to make a home for ourselves at a vibrant, multiethnic Pentecostal church. I spent the first months trying not to stare or seem out of place. But one Sunday, I found myself raising my hands. A few months later, I quietly clapped my hands and closed my eyes. During that year, I came to find that a vital and living faith was slowly being knit into me, something that I would not be able to do without, even if I couldn't name what it was. It was not a Black church, but it was a church that had formations in Black church traditions, where Black, Latino/a, and white folk found a sense of connection with one another and with God. That was a beginning for me. It allowed me to start seeing what my life in white communities had kept from me. It began a transformation, creating a space of common culture in our relationship.

One of the things we had in common as we first started talking was our shared experience of churches having given us a deep sense of purpose and belonging. Even as church and community shaped us, it's also true that communities are bodies of people trying to create a sense of place. Communities always have a larger history. Part of the challenge in being a couple is thinking about not only how you as individuals felt in your communities but also how those communities reflect various ways of being community and navigating a racial world, as well as how those histories shape you and how you live into them or resist them.

We have always been aware that our bodies were doing work in the world. Growing up, both of us commonly heard questions like, "Where are you *really* from?" or "What are you?" From a young age we knew that our bodies were being seen and interpreted and classified, and that people were using a calculus to try to "place" us. This was true for our encounters with white people, but it was also true in the Korean and Black communities we were a part of.

Race is not just about skin tone or facial features. It's also about belonging and being part of a community. Part of the challenge of any relationship is coming to learn and navigate the different ways belonging is expressed within these different racial and ethnic communities. For us, coming to understand how our communities navigated a world of race helped us to also see how we were navigating that world, and how those decisions and inclinations shaped our relationship and the kind of culture we were creating together for each other, our children, and the people we welcomed into our lives.

Discussion Questions

- What were the communities that shaped you?
- Where did you feel the deepest sense of belonging?
- Where did you experience moments of isolation?
- How do those feelings and experiences shape your sense of connection to community now?
- Do those communities and feelings of belonging overlap or differ for each of you?

Facing the Legacy of Whiteness

Part of becoming a couple is understanding how the other person and the communities they've been part of have navigated the work their bodies do in the world, especially in the white world they must step into each day. We should say here that while people of color may feel this tension most profoundly, white couples who we have walked with have also had to navigate newly realized histories of white supremacy or racism, which can create tension within the couple or the broader family. It is not an easy thing to begin to see the world and yourself in a new way.

It's also important to examine the ways the other person and their community have navigated white spaces. Did we come from communities of protest? Did we come from communities that valued assimilation and not making waves? Did our communities ignore the realities of race and injustice in hopes of inclusion in the dominant culture? Did our communities value some combination of these approaches, depending on the issue?

On a more nuclear level, as we grew together and navigated multiple moves and new church communities, and as we had children and began to cultivate a family culture, we had no models of what an interracial couple looked like. We were young and didn't know ourselves. We were too busy trying to survive to think carefully about each step.

But we found along the way that our story wasn't uncommon. There were young men and women in our communities who also felt a bit out of place, in between, or unseen. There were people who were going to school in predominantly white spaces and struggling to make it through. Like we've said, we had no idea what we were doing. All we had was our life and our little apartment. So we invited people in. This might not seem terribly subversive given the violence and terror of white supremacy in the United States. But we were in our young twenties, two kids, and no means. We were not yet in a time of mass protest. All we had was our home.

And in that home, people found people who were wrestling with similar questions, even if they came from different backgrounds. We did not have to speak of being followed in stores, or questioned about our grades, or asked if we "really went to Duke." Those were understood. But in this space, people were also free to be.

The last few years have made clear that racial violence is not a thing of the past. White supremacy and privilege are still present and powerful. Race is not simply about the differences of body or culture or language. Race is an idea that came from somewhere and continues to be reproduced through social systems. It shapes our communities and how we see ourselves, what we see in ourselves and in one another, and what we hope for. These realities do not evaporate when we join ourselves to another, so we have to attend to how race shapes us and our relationships.

It is impossible to talk about the realities of race in a marriage without noting how whiteness shapes communities and the individuals within them. And this is true of everyone. This will look drastically different for every person, regardless of whether they are married to someone of the same race or ethnicity or not. Perhaps one person grew up in a Black church tradition that was always engaged in politics, supporting marches and preaching social justice from the pulpit, while the other person grew up in a Black church that emphasized "middle-class values" and respectability in order to "get a seat at the table." While each person is drawn to the other, they were also formed in ways that shaped how they navigated the world of whiteness, whether in public spaces or at work.

Over and over again these tensions crop up in unexpected ways. "Do we have to go to your company's holiday party again?" "What neighborhood should we live in?" "Are you sure you're going to wear that to the store?" These questions are like a pebble in our shoe: a small irritating discomfort—or they can be like thorns: visceral and ever-present in an era of police violence and racist political machinations. "Why does everything have to be about race?" "If we just work hard, people will see that we deserve the job." "They keep asking me to be the racial-awareness guy." And so on.

Underneath all of these tensions is the ubiquity and unrelenting weight of whiteness in our everyday world. We should be clear here that when we speak of whiteness, we are speaking partially of racial characteristics, and more precisely of the ways that physical characteristics of whiteness are seen as beautiful, intelligent, competent, sympathetic, trustworthy. But we are also speaking of the ways whiteness occupies the world. Whiteness has always been about control and certainty. And

69

part of its power is that the control and certainty it tries to maintain is always hidden. It is not like the power of the sun beating down on us in the summer. No, the power that whiteness tries to produce is more like Earth's gravity, the invisible field of energy that's generated by its mass and causes all things to be drawn toward it. Whiteness cannot be easily seen, but its presence can be felt in our schools, our neighborhoods, our media, our interactions, and even when we look at ourselves. To be born in America is to have to navigate the realities of whiteness.

Race itself is a creation of the white imagination. Non-European peoples did not run around calling themselves "Black" or "Asian" or "Latino." These classifications arose from white colonial imaginations, from the ways that slave traders counted, from how European scientists classified, and from how politicians legislated the people deemed not white throughout the world. In the United States, whiteness was a way of determining citizenship and who belonged and who didn't.

Under the specter of whiteness, Black communities, Indigenous communities, and non-European immigrant communities had to constantly negotiate what to let go of and what to keep in order to be recognized in a society with norms of whiteness (and patriarchy). For some communities, this looked like assimilation and approximating white "normalcy." For others, it meant holding onto traditions and forming new generations in the ways of their elders to allow them to be rooted. At times it has been some combination of these that has ebbed and flowed, pinned together and reconsidered as each new wave of progress or violence moved in, then out.

Whiteness is the presumption to classify, or to turn a lament about a Black man being shot by a police officer into a debate about how all lives should matter. Whiteness is sudden panic when one's whiteness becomes visible and is named and when one's only response is with tears or guilt that a person of color must somehow absolve. It is the everyday questioning or fear of anything or anyone who somehow does not seem to fit or threatens the perceived normalcy of a neighborhood or institution or way of doing things. Whiteness maintains the power of invisibility by cultivating the hypervisibility of blackness. Put differently, whiteness shapes itself through an inherent anti-blackness. And this phenomenon, it is important to say, is not simply an exercise of white people. In a society where whiteness is associated with citizenship and competency and success, anti-blackness is the way to approximate that ideal, and it can be embodied by all people, regardless of skin color.

When two people join their lives, they have to navigate this world together. For Black, brown, and immigrant communities, finding a way through this world of whiteness and anti-blackness might mean an emphasis on maintaining culturally homogenous communities to support and retreat to. For some, it might mean engaging in everyday or public activism, where the focus is on disrupting the circuits of whiteness in one's job or neighborhood. For others, it might mean choosing the paths of least resistance and keeping one's head down, doing what's asked in order to achieve the American Dream.

These tensions have been most pronounced in the interracial couples we have walked with over the years. A common conversation goes something like this: A Black man, Tyson, and his white wife, Melissa, come to us as they are trying to discern a move to a different job. Tyson is working in a company with a diverse staff led by a person of color. He's seen and has been growing in his sense of racial awareness and sense of self. But they're about to have a baby, and his job is only part time. Melissa works for an emerging tech company, which happens to have an open position that could be a good fit for Tyson. The problem is that the company is predominantly white and has little racial awareness. Of course, they hope Tyson can help them change that. He's hesitant. But she reminds us that she has been working full time and carrying the bulk of the financial burden for their family. "As long as he is doing the work he is capable of, does it really matter *where* he does it? Sure, diversity is ideal, but I just don't understand why my sacrifice isn't being seen in this conversation."

In that conversation, it's clear that Melissa has read a few books about race. She's married to a Black man, so she obviously isn't racist, and she's begun to experience the looks on the street. But she also sees the people at her company as people like her. She trusts their intentions the way she trusts her own intentions. Anything that a person might say or do isn't malice or racism, but they are just learning, in the same way she is learning.

But Tyson, a Black man raised in a predominantly white suburb, has begun to discover the depths of his blackness and the histories of Black protest and social critique. He has had enough experiences with well-meaning white folk that he does not completely trust intention anymore and is becoming less sure that predominantly white spaces are safe until proven otherwise. This divergence has created a tension for the couple; what was so certain for Melissa has become a hesitation for Tyson. And the more they talk, the clearer it is that Melissa doesn't understand Tyson's experience in the world.

Couples like Tyson and Melissa are complicated because the questions they're wrestling with are never simply about race; they're also about gender, who's making the sacrifices, and who's following whom. But it's important to begin to see how the dynamics of race and gender (or ability or sexuality) are present in a given relationship over time. It's never about one moment in particular but about wider patterns and how each person is coming to a deeper understanding of the histories, challenges, and power of realities that are different from their own.

The tensions that whiteness creates are always lurking in relationships. Whether in the idealization of beauty or in the ways "safety" or a "good education" are so often associated with particular neighborhoods or people. Some non-white communities might try to approximate these standards or find some sort of access to their benefits. Others might try to create enclaves of pride and isolation, while still others will actively work to overturn systems of oppression and exclusion. Individuals also mirror these tendencies, and in the midst of it all, they must navigate a racial world that whiteness has created.

This is true even for white people who might be reading this. We have seen white students and churchgoers begin to apprehend the history of white violence in their schools or neighborhoods. We have watched the pain that emerges when one person comes to recognize these histories while their partner still wonders what the big deal is.

Whether couples are from the same race or ethnicity or are interracial, we live in a world marked by race. To begin to account for race in your relationship is to also ask how you as a couple will learn, support one another, and grow together as you navigate a world shaped by racism and white supremacy.

These issues become especially prevalent when raising children. The choices before us, and sometimes the choices that are made for us, seem to multiply when we see the ways our children's bodies are read or overlooked or feared, such as when we have to advocate for them to get the resources they need in school, or when the teacher is constantly giving them detention for behavior that other kids (read: white kids) are allowed to get away with. Part of navigating race in a relationship is also exploring how each person is inclined to identify and navigate those challenges. Here are some examples:

- "Keep your head down and ignore them."
- "This is your history."
- "You are beautiful."
- "We need to find a new school."

- "We need to meet with the teacher."
- "Who's his momma?!" (just kidding)

Facing the reality of whiteness in the world is also beginning to account for the ways we have tried to protect ourselves or blend in, or ways we have unwittingly supported the illusions of white supremacy.

Discussion Questions

- What are some ways you have navigated the realities of white supremacy? Maybe through fight or flight? By finding "your people"?
- How do your strategies overlap with or diverge from your partner's strategies?
- What are your conversations about navigating a racial world like? Is there tension? Difficulty understanding? Similarities?

Race and the Interracial "Dream"

To wrap up this chapter, let's talk a bit about interracial marriage. In many ways, it is a sign of how the realities of racism can be challenged and the walls of difference broken down. This is no small thing. But according to the Pew Research Center, only 17 percent of marriages in 2017 were interracial (fifty years after *Loving v. Virginia*).[1] Why is this number not higher? The history runs deep. Each interracial relationship brings with it a unique nest of histories and family dynamics and ways of trying to find a way in a racial world.

But it is also important to note that interracial marriages are not a panacea. They are not a sign of having arrived at a

post-racial, kumbaya-singing community. Even while the percentage of interracial marriages continues to increase, who is
marrying whom is a stark reminder that the realities of whiteness continue to linger. The rates of intermarriage are highest
for Asian American women and Hispanic people. Both of these
groups are most likely to marry a white person.

These statistics don't capture the intimacy, love, and mutual
support each person finds in the other. Each interracial relationship has a reason for existing that is personal and unique.
But we are also creatures of a racial world. And what we love,
what we find beautiful, what we find most comfortable is never
disconnected from patterns of race in the world. We have to ask
questions like these: Why are Black men twice as likely as Black
women to marry outside their race? Why do Asian American
men intermarry at drastically lower rates than Asian American
women? How do standards of beauty rooted in whiteness shape
people's desires?

It would be easy to overlook these questions, these lingering
realities, and to cling to the idea that your interracial marriage
is a sign of reconciliation and getting past race. But in truth we
all carry biases and blind spots, even into our relationships. We
carry tendencies in how we trust or attend to white people in
our midst. We may carry histories of immigrant belonging or
exclusion. These may not have race as the explicit label. They
often take the form of conversations about neighborhoods or
schools, friends, communities, or vacation spots. Race can sit
under the surface of what we'd rather not do or where we'd
rather not go. But it is always there.

Part of what connected the two of us, even with our very
different stories, was a sense of in-betweenness. We were always
creating a culture out of the pieces and strands of our lives, the
people we met, the communities we were a part of. But very
rarely did we ever feel like there was a home for us. It would
have been easy to say that was the goal, to create a new space

of belonging. But this space was always connected to the world. When we walked out of our door in the morning, it was there to meet us. And whether we liked it or not, we carried it with us when we came home. Our bodies were doing work in the world.

Brian

I didn't grow up in a Black community, but my body was read as Black, as brown. In some cases, this meant suspicion or danger. But it also meant recognition and belonging. When I was a teaching assistant at Duke I had to take seriously the fact that I was the only Black TA serving in a class. And when I began my work as a professor, I was the only Black professor most of my students would ever have. My body was doing work in the world, and I was connected to those histories and those realities. For my sake, for my children's sake, I could not pretend I was not a part of that long and beautiful story of Black life in the United States.

This meant beginning to learn my own history, pursuing communities that would help me to understand myself and my history, and my particular place in that constellation of Black life. Part of this was also learning the story of colorism and the ways light-skinned Black bodies were so often privileged for their approximation of white beauty or intelligence. It meant beginning to recognize the small gaps my sometimes racial ambiguity created in encounters with police or teachers or strangers.

While I was discovering my own story, I was also being introduced to Korean American immigrant life, the Asian American experience, and the way Gail lived in between these stories. I had to begin to understand the tensions families held as language or long-held traditions seemed to fall away in their children or their children's children. I had to learn the differences in the stories of Vietnamese, Chinese, and Japanese immigrants.

And I needed to learn why Gail's relationship to her Korean identity and the Korean community was complicated, including why she refused to speak Korean in Korean restaurants and didn't respond to the two Korean people commenting (in Korean) about her being with a Black man, even though she could understand what they were saying. I had to learn that she didn't say "I love you" very often but that when she asked me if I had eaten already, what she meant was "I love you."

Over time, we each began to learn more about the histories and the communities of each other's people. And we began to learn and understand the ways each of us as individuals lived inside of and were formed by or resisted those histories.

Through this kind of learning, we each become part of the other's communities. In a very real way, their people are our people. In our lives together, those histories and those stories become present in our life together and in the lives of our children.

Discussion Questions

- What are the cultural or racial stories that you continue to carry with you?
- What are your partner's stories that you are beginning to learn?
- What stories do you still need to discover?

The enormity of white supremacy, its violence and power, can be overwhelming when we stare at its history too long. When we see the complexity of the problems and the ignorance of too many people, it can feel like nothing will change. And while marriage and intimate relationships don't necessarily change the world, they are signs of life. They are small sprouts of green where somehow the conditions were just right for something new to appear in the world. The decision for two people to live into one another and for one another, carrying all of the history of the world with them, is no small feat.

Part of the violence of white supremacy is the unrelenting commitment to a given normalcy, to unchanging social spheres and roles and ways of imagining life and love. And white supremacy has sought to usurp and reproduce itself through a narrow conception of marriage. But when marriage becomes a wild space of difference devoted to relationship, when two people choose to be committed to the particularity and complexity and wholeness of this one other person, the veneer of white supremacy becomes unstable, its moorings are loosened, and we begin to see it for what it is: a weak and flimsy idol.

In truth, though, the disruptive possibilities of love are not unique to marriage. Marriage is a place where the fullness of our bodied lives can be shared with another, and in that sharing we are free to be and to become. This does not mean leaving behind race and its joys or its traumas, but in this relationship a space emerges where we can lay it all down and begin to discover what it means for our lives together. Nothing is wasted.

And this is true for any place where people gather and begin to foster a commitment to discovering their own story and making space for the stories of others—a community house, a group of friends, a small group, a bike club. Any of these might also provide some semblance of liberative space for people. One way that a marriage uniquely subverts the violence of race is by resisting the intimate violence that racism exerts every day. What we mean here is that racism is ubiquitous and unrelenting, and part of its power works through its invisibility and ever-presence in everyday interactions. Racism is everything from violent police to credit ratings and mortgage lenders, from silence in response to hundreds of job applications to someone taking an extra look at your credit card.

Dr. Emilie Townes writes of this unrelenting pressure of race as a cultural production of evil. Her response is the power of "everydayness." In this everydayness, we "live our faith deeply."[2] A life of faith is never a life of certainty but a life of discovery and surprise. Sometimes what we discover causes us to repent because we see how we are complicit. Sometimes it causes us to rejoice because our curiosity brings us to see God as present in new ways. Sometimes we can only lament as we learn to see how race is violently inflicted on the lives of those around us.

In our discovery process, we begin to understand the small turns of screws and shifts in balance that perpetuate this evil. Refusing to acknowledge another's pain. Failing to go deeper to discover the larger social history that is connected to a moment in the life of your neighbor or friend. Insisting on lower taxes because *your* tax bill is too high. Voting no on redistributing funds for public education. These are always more than ideas and principles; they are everyday acts tethered to long, long histories.

When we live lives apart from another, we barely understand the impact of the everyday, believing instead that what we know about the world is everything we need to know. But part of the promise of a life together is beginning to discover the ways those very same levers, subtle turns, and questions begin to loosen the bolts of oppressive social structures. No magic bullet or simple policy will overturn white supremacy. But small communities committed to discovery, to beginning to see the lives of those who are different as somehow irrevocably tied to theirs, can begin to create spaces of life in the midst of a racist society.

Together we discover what wholeness looks like, and we garner whatever resources are available to us in order to make that possible. Sometimes this is making sure people have resources. Sometimes it is showing up at a council meeting. Sometimes it is taking care of one another's children. But inevitably these ties lead us not only to being bound with this other person but also to discovering just how deep those cords run in our communities.

In the face of a racialized world, a marriage must be able to acknowledge the legacies of race that permeate two people's lives together. But those same postures of learning—wrestling with one's own formation, creating a space of flourishing for the other, and enacting that commitment in everyday ways—are also practices that participate in the dismantling of oppression.

For us, marriage is about creating a space to discover what flourishing and wholeness might look like. But it is also about creating a space for others, inviting people into our home, to play with our kids, to eat Korean barbecue or homemade fajitas, or to simply be. In our mutual discovering, we have also created a place for people's stories of race or their struggles with whiteness (either their own or someone else's)—even though we ourselves didn't have an established path that we had followed, and didn't have any clear-cut answers. Without realizing it, we came to understand that part of what dismantles racist systems is our clinging to one another, speaking of our histories and our formations honestly, and inviting others to do the same, believing that when we step outside our four walls, we are ready to face the world, to risk, and to create more spaces of possibility wherever we are.

FOUR

It's a Man's World?

Gender and Marriage
from a Man's Perspective

Simple stories have a way of being the most powerful ones. God made Adam and Eve. Adam was in charge because he was first. Eve was made to be submissive because she was second. "Look! Men can lift these rocks! I guess that means women are meant to follow." "Childbirth is 'natural' work that doesn't require the same strength or skill as hunting." "This is man's work." "A woman should be . . ." These simple stories, assumptions, and ways of seeing the world are woven into our lives, pushing or pulling us in a myriad of ways. Lillian Smith called these stories "lessons," and they were spoken over her every day as a child growing up in the South in the 1940s.[1]

But how do these stories work themselves out in our relationships as we navigate daily life together?

As Christians, one of our fundamental beliefs is that humans are imperfect, which means that our freedom and our capacity to love and create give us the freedom to act in ways that are detrimental to ourselves and to those around us. In confessing this, we acknowledge our limitations, the ways we make life difficult or even fail to acknowledge that there are things we could do to make life for those in our midst a bit more whole. Confession is a way of saying that we do not know, but we want to learn. And when we learn, we want to struggle to become people who can see the fullness of God's life in ourselves and in others and in the world, and ultimately to participate in God's presence in the everyday.

Sometimes when we talk about gender (or race), especially if we are someone who benefits from social structures, it can be easy to roll our eyes and say, "Here we go again with how bad men are." And it would be easy to simply nod our heads and go on with our lives. But a life of confession, especially a life of confession that is joined with another person's life of confession, invites us to say, "My life and its flourishing are bound up with the flourishing and possibilities of the one I am with. But their life and my life are connected to these ropes and tethers of history whose strands wind themselves into our lives in ways that I may not be able to see. I want to learn to see—for their sake and for mine."

I grew up in a house filled with women. At any given time, our home included my mom, one or two of my aunts, and my grandmother. I saw firsthand the ways infidelity and alcoholism wreaked havoc for my mother. I saw her navigate the wild swings between inappropriate comments about her weight and utter invisibility when we went to clothing stores.

I sat quietly while my aunts talked about office politics and the promotions they were passed over for, even though they were more than capable of doing the work while also navigating the seemingly impossible line of demonstrating competence without seeming too "assertive." I heard veiled stories about violence and trauma and daily, unrelenting choices to be made. And I saw the ways they made lives for their children, their family, and the people they loved.

I was never the typical boy. I recoiled from locker room talk. I enjoyed long talks with my mom and wrote terrible poetry and wanted nothing more than to be in a relationship with someone. I thought I was a different kind of guy, a guy who was sensitive, a good listener, and willing to help out, hold babies, and change diapers.

But a relationship—the daily presence, the unsaid expectations, what isn't seen—uncovers the social formations that get laid brick by brick in our lives. In spite of all that I knew and had watched the women in my life experience, one simple barrier hindered me from understanding and recognizing what Gail would live with, and from seeing how my manhood worked in the world and in our house:

I am a man.

I know this sounds too obvious to have to write. But acknowledging and beginning with simple facts is the beginning of subverting the histories of patriarchy and their outworkings in our daily lives. This acknowledgment is the starting point because one of the pillars of patriarchy is that men know women better than women know themselves.

This pillar is powerful. It has a way of taking knowledge that should help us to see women differently and instead uses it to collapse women into what *we* see, and nothing more. In its worst manifestations, this gaze reduces women to vessels of sexual consumption, or domestic workers, or people whose identity revolves around reproduction. But even the more benign forms of patriarchy and misogyny distort the truth. They convince us that because we have seen one woman's experience or read this or that book, then we must understand completely—and because we understand, we must not be part of the problem. I am a good feminist. I am one of the "good" men.

As Gail and I began our life together, as I heard the stories of what happened to her at work and elsewhere, I started to see the realities of her life as a woman in this world. But it was also in the course of normal day-to-day life, in the questions and tensions about simple things like cooking and bigger things like kids and jobs, that I had to begin to wrestle with the ways that the patriarchal formations of manhood had shaped me and were working themselves out in our life together.

Invisible Work

The realities of gender have worked themselves out in our home in two distinct spaces: in our domestic life and in our professional lives. The two spaces are related to one another in some significant ways, but each has required its own conversations (and arguments) and ways of navigating toward mutual flourishing.

Gail did most of the cooking for the first fifteen years of our marriage. I would grill meat, and I could throw together some spaghetti or some other dish Gail had given me directions on how to make. Making dinner whenever Gail was busy with church was something I had no problem doing, along with changing diapers and taking care of the kids—so by most standards I was amazing! But in truth, the bar is pretty low for us men.

Things started to shift, though, on a night when I got home from teaching as Gail was getting ready to go to a meeting at church. I asked what the plan was for dinner. She looked at me and said, "Plan? I have been in meetings all week and haven't been grocery shopping, so I don't have a 'plan.'" So that night was a McDonald's night. But it began a conversation about what mutual work looked like. Up to that point, I had been willing to do anything—clean, cook, take care of the kids—but it usually included me saying to Gail, "Just tell me what to do and I will be happy to do it!" Her response was, "But creating the list is also work."

I would love to be able to say that we had a good, healthy conversation and, through our mutual sharing, came to a place of equitable distribution of familial responsibilities. But in truth, this was an argument we had been having for years, and that particular night's conversation was simply the dam bursting. I thought I was already doing a lot. As far as I was concerned, most of the guys I knew did half as much as me. I saw them reading more and writing more and going on long weekends with their bro friends while I was hanging out with our kids. But Gail was the one who felt tired and was trying to keep up with multiple appointments and cooking and house responsibilities on top of her own vocation and career. That conversation had been spinning around in our house for years, kicking up into a storm every now and again, only to settle back into old patterns.

But in the weeks after that exchange, we came to a different place. In part, it was because the demands of Gail's ministry were growing, and she just could not sustain what she was doing. But it was also because I slowly came to recognize that she wasn't thriving and there was something I could do, and that I needed to learn in order to be a better partner to her.

So Gail taught me a few of her go-to recipes, including fried rice, spaghetti, and tuna noodle casserole. I started looking up recipes for other dishes and making grocery lists. But the thing about a grocery list is that I also needed to be attentive to the whole house in a different way. Are we good on toilet paper? Is Gail going to need tampons soon? How are we on Caleb's favorite lunch snacks?

I was slowly being introduced to the "invisible work" that most women perform every day. In truth, it was a sliver of the world, but for someone who did not have to think about these things on a regular basis, it was ponderous at first. I had to think about a theology paper on the dynamics of identity and Christological history in the midst of remembering whether we had enough sugar.

When we had kids, we had begun this juggling act and had each committed to participating fully in caring for the children.

While I was in school, and then eventually when we were both in school, we handed the kids off to each other, worked in spurts, and balanced family and school life on a constant seesaw. But as I began to cook more, I found that there was a fundamental difference between being willing to do what was on a list and being the one who created the list, or even co-created the list.

I began to acknowledge the invisible work Gail had been doing every day. Before I went to bed at night, I had to think about things like what we were going to eat the next day, when I would have a window of time to go grocery shopping, and how or when I was going to make a casserole if Ezra had soccer practice and Caleb had a concert. In some ways, cooking is a minor piece within the large scale of patriarchal systems and violence. But it begins there, in the everyday, mundane realities that have to be accounted for, planned, and made. In taking on more of these responsibilities, I began to see the rhythms of the house differently.

Something else happened along the way. The more I cooked, the more I found that I actually enjoyed it—everything from the prep of dicing onions and marinating chicken to the satisfaction of people you love finding joy in something you made for them. I started looking up new recipes, experimenting with old ones, and trying new techniques. I went from cooking three nights a week to cooking four or five, and eventually to cooking every day. One night I told Gail just how satisfying I found cooking to be. And she said she was glad because she actually didn't like cooking. For her, it was satisfying to eat something someone else had made. For fifteen years, I hadn't realized she had been doing it simply because that was what was expected of her. For all of our progressive sensibilities, we had simply fallen into a social pattern of the woman cooking.

I came to see how much patriarchy had done violence to women and how my assumptions or lack of attention had limited Gail. But I also came to see how much these gendered systems had limited me. As a man, it was not assumed that I would cook or clean or stay home. And wrapped in those assumptions was a whole world of possibilities that I might have found myself gifted for but cut off from. But even more, having responsibility for cooking also allowed me to see my life more holistically, to see that my vocation was not the center of my identity, and to see ways of enjoying and serving Gail and our children that were more fulfilling than I had imagined.

But some realities of a gendered world are not as straightforward as learning to cook and grocery shop. Sometimes the possibilities of working for one another's fullness is bound up in the systemic limitations and biases of industries and communities.

Professional Hazards

"I followed you for ten years. We aren't moving." Gail said it as clearly as could be. We had been in Seattle for a few years. She was finally working at a church that fully embraced her gifts and calling as a pastor. Our kids loved Seattle. But I wanted to take "the next step" and pursue a job at a major research university. I would teach fewer classes, be able to write more, and, if I'm honest, have more prestige. In that conversation, Gail reminded me of our earlier moves, first to Durham when I went to Duke and then to Seattle for my first teaching position. In each new place she had built a life, a career. She wasn't willing to do it all over again.

In each new place, Gail had to fight to establish herself in a vocation that rarely saw women as equals. Women make up only 10 percent of all ordained clergy. And even then, those jobs are more often confined to children's or women's ministries. For all of her talent and apparent gifting, Gail had to prove herself over and over. When we got to Seattle, she had finally found a place that embraced her, where she didn't need to prove herself (as much).

And as fortunate as I was to have a tenure track position (a rare thing in higher education, especially after the financial collapse of 2008), I felt the lure of the next step, of finding my sense of wholeness in my institution. But as Gail was living into her call, I was also getting inquiries and feelers for positions around the country. The lure wasn't just an issue of individual advancement; it was also about being part of a larger system that held more possibilities for me, potentially an easier path for promotion and advancement.

These greater possibilities didn't have to do with my skills or giftings or hard work. The opportunities were available because of the realities Gail faced when we chose to have children and the paths that are closed off when kids are in the picture. We were young when we had children, but we knew we wanted our schedules to align so that one of us was always able to be with them. This was partially for financial reasons, as neither of us could imagine working a job that would require them to be in daycare and would essentially generate just enough income to cover the cost. But it was also personal, as we wanted to be present with them as much as possible. We were both flexible. We shared responsibilities. But the reality was that oftentimes it was just easier for me to work, or for me to pick up an extra part-time job. It was easier for Gail to start off part time to allow her a bit more flexibility. One little choice after another led to my working toward a doctorate and Gail finally being in a full-time position, but still she wasn't seen as a pastor. It was a dead end.

With each of these small choices and our ongoing navigation of larger economic and social realities, the opportunities available to Gail got narrower. And every time they narrowed, it became easier to justify following a job opportunity for me. We were an egalitarian, progressive couple, committed to both parents being present and each person being able to pursue their call and passions. But we didn't recognize the rip currents swirling under the surface of the water. Ten years into our marriage, we found ourselves on a strange part of the beach, not quite sure how we got so far away from what we intended.

As a man, if it was difficult for me to see what Gail was seeing in our home, it felt virtually impossible to see these deeper currents that we were swimming in. In truth, I think Gail probably saw these currents or at least felt them, and that's where some of her frustrations emerged in our arguments about who was watching the kids on Friday afternoon or about my plans to play golf with friends on Saturday. It wasn't that she wanted to keep me from enjoying myself. It was that she somehow saw how these currents were flowing with me to where I hoped to be, while she was having to drive her legs into the sand just to stay where she was, much less move forward.

Discussion Questions

- What are some moments when you've seen opportunities opening up for one person and not the other? How have you made the decision about whether to go for it or wait?

While I loved teaching at my institution, I was hoping I could write more. I would browse social media and eventually drop into that dreaded envy scroll, where everything my eyes landed on seemed to highlight colleagues and former classmates publishing articles and giving lectures. I just didn't have time for the writing I wanted to do. Summer research was actually "Camp Bantum," where I made sure the boys got up on time and did a bit of reading, instrument practice, and maybe some math before they settled in front of screens for the rest of the day. It was cooking and carpooling to soccer and orchestra, managing classes and committee work and institutional politics.

In the midst of these pushes and pulls, something odd happened: I stopped fighting. "This is my life. What does flourishing look like inside of *this* life, not some other ideal version of a life?" When I asked this question, another possibility began to slip in, and a different set of questions started to float to the surface: "Do I even want that ideal life? What makes it ideal?"

When I sat back and actually considered those questions, I began to see the moments of joy and frustration in my field, the things that I loved to do and the things I always regretted saying yes to. I started a mental list and began to see a different measure of success. The picture of an ideal was shifting. In actuality, I hated writing peer-review articles. I didn't want to write multiple scholarly tomes. What it meant to flourish started to look different.

To live a life with Gail was to begin to see the currents pulling her to a place she didn't want to go. It meant digging in my feet alongside her and each of us mooring the other, taking small steps toward a place we were not sure existed. And in that refusal to allow ourselves to be carried away by these seemingly natural forces, I could also see how the current's promise of success and fullness was not what I actually wanted for myself or my family.

In stopping, slowing down, and allowing the contingencies of life to become starting points for how I define flourishing, I was able to see new outlines of a "successful" life. Success is my spouse being able to enjoy and pursue her job without feeling like she is holding me back. Success is my kids knowing I will be home and finding joy in the small presences. And a successful life was actually possible at this little institution because what I had written and how I was teaching were enough. And even more than that, in that place, I had been opened up to a new way of thinking about my gifts and passions and call, apart from the assumptions of my guild or higher education. The contingency of my life had shown me what freedom and wholeness might look like.

Our limited view of what "success" looks like is one of the most profound lies of patriarchal societies. It drags men down even as it crushes women. It can carry us to places that we are not always sure we want to go to. But position Y or promotion Z is the ideal because maleness has become collapsed into vocation and possession. The fullness and success of our life couldn't possibly mean being in a middle management position that allows us to be home when our kids return from school. Fullness couldn't possibly mean working as a stay-at-home dad who keeps things running so his spouse can go to school and pursue their passion, or simply have an opportunity to work a job that can sustain the whole family.

The lie of patriarchy is that somehow our lives are oriented toward freedom and possession and self-determination. And as we scratch and claw for this ideal, we end up overlooking and diminishing the very contingencies that make a full life possible. Doing laundry, caring for an aging parent, dog sitting for a friend, taking a meal to a neighbor who broke their leg—these are not the seemingly heroic gestures of blockbuster movies that shape our male imaginations. But they are the salt of life, the small moments that help us see the people in our midst and learn to savor, struggle with, and recognize our own needs and possibilities as humans.

Subverting patriarchy sometimes happens through grand court cases or marches. But more often, it happens through digging our feet into the sand next to people we admire or love or simply find ourselves in community with and then struggling, step-by-step, toward a world they hope to realize. And along the way we might find that that world has promise for us as well.

Pocket Ministries

The possibility of subverting patriarchy in the world and in our relationships is no better imaged than in the person of Joseph, the husband of Mary, mother of Jesus. In Eastern Orthodox icons, Joseph is often depicted in the corner of the image, seemingly forlorn, sitting without a purpose while Mary lies in the middle of the image, with Jesus next to her. In some images Joseph is being harassed by a serpent or demon whispering doubts.

"Maybe it was a mistake?"

"Maybe it wasn't an angel?"

"What am I doing?"

Can we blame him? He was just minding his own business, making an honest living, following the law. He loved his God and could look forward to marriage, children, a simple life.

But then he gets the news: his soon-to-be-wife is pregnant. He knows it's not his. He's not cruel, but he also knows the law. He's responsible for his purity, for the honor of his name and his family's name. So he commits to divorce her quietly—no scandal. No need to make it worse for her. Her life is going to be hard enough as it is, with a child born out of wedlock and no hope of getting married.

And then he dreams. *She's with child. It's of God. Marry her. Name him Jesus.* He wakes up, and he obeys.

Matthew doesn't record a response. Joseph just listens. That's not the first time he'll have a conversation with an angel—and it's not the first time we see him with no words. Although Matthew does not give us Joseph's words, we can see that something powerful is happening in this moment. Even in Jesus's conception, something is being transformed.

While we might read Joseph's lack of words as strong, silent obedience, we can also see them as a reversal of sorts. In the second creation account (Gen. 2:4–25), it is Adam who speaks and who is encountered by God and shown around the garden. Eve is drawn from Adam's side and speaks no words until her encounter with the serpent.

Sadly, reading the creation of humanity through this story instead of through the first creation account (Gen. 1:1–2:3), where God makes "them" in "our" image, male and female, has been taken to mean that somehow men have priority over women. It has been interpreted to mean that a penis gives men privilege and power, that somehow being the "first" makes us closer to God—even though we were the first thing God said was not good. It is not that this first creature wasn't loved or beautiful. But we might say that this first creature was not truly imaging God while it was alone. To be like God is to be with another who can choose and who can love and create along with us. This is not to simply say these first creatures are symbols of marriage. They are signs of just how fundamental relationship (of all kinds) is to who we are.

But in the incarnation, the patterns of patriarchy are being subverted. Mary is the first encountered, the first breathed into—made alive through the Spirit, implanted with a new way of being and living in the world. In the conception, God is making present redemption and making plain the possibilities of being created in the image of God. Women are not just hearers, apple givers, or children's workers, nor are they secondary in their needs or capacities. Mary is our first preacher, our first priest, our first taste of what it means to be made in the image of God in the first place. And God essentially says to Joseph, "You need her, and she needs you—you are bone of bone and flesh of flesh."

This new birth is going to leave Joseph transformed, pregnant now with a new way of being in the world because now Joseph's life is no longer the center of the mission. Mary's mission is Joseph's mission. In the patriarchal system of first-century Judaism, Joseph is the head; in this new family, his maleness and his vocation are something new. Mary is the breadwinner. Her career and calling is the family business.

In the face of this new life, Joseph has no words—he has no deep insight into Scripture, no cultural analysis, no prophetic insight into the significance of the moment. What does he have? He has a name and a donkey. But without these, God's hope is dead. Without his name, Mary remains destitute. Without a donkey, they remain in harm's way as Herod seeks to kill every firstborn child.

Men have been sold a hope that is dehumanizing—the notion that somehow, we get to be in control of our own lives. Sometimes we don't know the power of what we already have, of the stories and gifts we wield. I'm sure if anyone had asked Joseph whether he thought of himself as a powerful man, he would have said no. And it's true that when compared to governors or rabbis, to the rich men in the village, to boat owners, to soldiers, Joseph probably was not seen as the strongest or wisest or most learned. But this doesn't mean he has nothing to give in that moment. Matthew speaks, for example, of Joseph's respect for the law and his obedience—attributes that are amplified by the social system in a patriarchal society. Even a man like Joseph, with what little power he has, can decide whether to jeopardize his name by associating with a pregnant woman. He can decide how to use his limited resources, including his name. Joseph still has power.

And let's be clear: Joseph's power was not just in his character or in his resources but was provided by the very social system that put Mary in such grave danger. It was not an extravagant power; it was ordinary—as ordinary as the pockets of your pants.

It started off innocently enough. Gail and I were out for a walk and she asked me to put her phone in my pocket. Of course. But out of curiosity, I wondered, why could she not put it in her own pocket? Because they weren't big enough, she said. Huh? They looked like mine, from what I could tell. But then she explained: her pockets were just for show. *What?*

Come to find out, even something as simple and ordinary as a pocket has a history. In this history, women did not need pockets because pockets were where money and other important items were kept. And more often than not, women weren't in charge of their own money. (Virginia Woolf once talked about what the world would be like if each woman had a room of her own—not just pockets.) They didn't need pockets because their clothes were not about use but about image, about projecting an image of femininity, while men's pants were about utility and carrying the means of consumption and production.

Such a simple thing. As followers of Christ, we have to recognize the nature of power in our context. Power isn't really about what you get to do. Real power lies in the things you never have to think about. I can walk at night simply because I want to. I don't have to call a friend and keep her on the line until I get to my car. I don't have to have pepper spray attached to my keys. I don't have to ask myself if these pants are too tight or if people will take me seriously if I wear a t-shirt to teach my class. When I'm in class and I press into a difficult topic, I rarely get a knucklehead who questions whether I know my field. I have pockets.

Joseph has pockets too. He has a status that can protect Mary. Yes, it might mean people whisper about him, but he'll still be able to eat. Maybe he has a little money tucked away. It was enough for the two of them, but now a baby means a bit more insecurity, and of course we know that his marriage to Mary will put him in far more than economic danger. But now, in this moment for Joseph, God is telling him that he's going to need to put his name on the line. He's going to have to bind himself to this fierce, dynamic woman of God . . . and follow her into a life of joy and fear.

We often hear that the weak will become strong and the strong will become weak, that the first will become last and the last, first. But people don't fit neatly into these categories. We are strength and weakness; we have needs and hopes that are a priority and needs and hopes that ought to wait. When God encounters us with the promise that God is with us, suddenly a light appears in our midst and we discover that what we thought was our strength is our weakness, and what we overlooked or thought was ordinary is exactly the thing God sees and says, "I can use that." How beautiful.

As Gail and I have walked together, I have often thought of Joseph and the detours his life took because of his devotion to and love for Mary. And while we don't often think of Joseph as a prophet in the mold of Isaiah or as a miraculous leader like Moses, Joseph's life points to the ways relationships can become inflection points for transformation—not only personal transformation but lives that create spaces of transformation in their midst.

Even after more than twenty years of marriage, Gail and I are still working to see how gender shapes what we imagine for ourselves and for one another. And as we have walked, I have recognized that the most fundamental act of love and devotion I can offer is a willingness to be still, to be wary of the ease with which opportunities come my way, and to be open to the possibilities that this life of contingency is not some act of valorous martyrdom but is actually for our mutual flourishing. But it will always require dissecting the gendered assumptions that float in our midst.

Discussion Questions

- What are ways a space of privilege or power might give you the freedom to go slower or take advantage of institutional bias to create space for your partner?

FIVE

Glass Bulbs and Rubber Balls

Gender and Marriage from a
Woman's Perspective

Making the initial leap into a new life or major decision
can be hard, but what is often even harder is living
with the decision and who each person becomes in
its wake. What if we have a hard time juggling everything that
is expected of us and what we want for ourselves? "Flourishing"
and "thriving" can be tricky terms because of their tendency to
make us and others believe that our life is amazing. But when
flourishing is understood as more than individual happiness,
we begin to see it as a give-and-take, a pushing and pulling. It
may even mean that someone has to give up something, or that
something will fall through the cracks. Many of us call this
impossible pursuit of balance a "juggling act."

In my two and a half decades of counseling couples, I've
found that women who pursue work outside the home have
to account for more of these work-life balance conversations
than men generally do. Women are confronted by this impossible standard not only within themselves but also within

their partnered relationships and among other women. And, depending on their upbringing or theological convictions, many women also struggle to prove their place in the world outside the confines of home. It's understandable, then, that many women feel forced to choose an all-or-nothing life path—either they can't pursue their passion and career path in order to raise the family, or they have to juggle everything and be a superwoman to prove their worth.

Instead, what might it look like to live *for* one another, re-defining flourishing? I can promise you that it will not be the dual power couple and the perfect kids and the smooth upward trajectory. Flourishing means recognizing when one person has had all the opportunities, whether because of gender or privi-lege or something else, so maybe it all needs to slow down for that person. It means the kids might not have to be in the perfect daycare or in daycare at all. It means knowing which balls can fall, trusting that they'll bounce back, and which bulbs have to be carried with care in various seasons of life. (More on these metaphors later.)

As we continue to learn ourselves and the other, we're mind-ful that we live in a world where gender creates and forecloses opportunities. Flourishing and thriving is an expansive, com-munal idea that sometimes requires us to make difficult choices for one person to slow down so another has opportunity. Being a "we" requires us to reimagine what flourishing looks like together.

Do Gender Norms Always Win?

I remember Brian's and my first phone conversation when we were nineteen, both sitting in our dorm rooms in two different schools and different states, trying to make sense of the person on the other end of the line. "What do you see yourself doing after college, or as a career?" Brian asked.

"Uhh . . . well, I'm at this school because I want to be a conductor, but I think I'm called to ministry. My mom was a pastor," I answered.

"Really?" he said. "I didn't think women could be pastors." He said that!

Apparently, I had forgotten about this whole conversation and blocked it out of my memory, until Brian brought it up years later. Whether I'd be a conductor or a pastor, I was certain that I would not be stuck at home, forgoing the gifts and passions I knew God had given me. I had something to offer the world. Brian, on the other hand, replied to that same question not really sure what he felt called to be or do but knowing it had something to do with teaching or ministry. So when we planned to get married the summer before our senior year of college, we decided to spend that year seeking jobs to begin my career, and he would figure things out along the way.

We moved to the Philadelphia area, where I started my first job in ministry as a part-time worship/music director. In the 1990s, very few churches would hire women full time in significant church leadership positions, much less a twenty-one-year-old Asian American woman in non-Asian contexts. It probably wasn't the best decision to move out of state for a part-time job, but I was just grateful for a job, especially that this church would hire me out of college with no experience. Brian landed a full-time job at a private Christian high school. We both also cobbled together part-time jobs as side hustles to supplement our income during those two years. It was a challenging season as newlyweds, being in a new city, with new jobs, a new community (an all-white church, which was new for me), and feeling isolated.

In our first year, when we realized these jobs were not going to fulfill us long term or offer opportunities for growth, Brian applied to a few grad schools, thinking he might want to explore ministry or teaching in an intentional way. He applied to Duke Divinity School. We were waiting and excited at the thought of a transition that could potentially allow us some forward movement and clarity in our careers. Unfortunately, Brian's application packet ended up missing some materials by the deadline that year, so we decided to keep his application on file for the next year.

Then we found out I was pregnant.

Then, nine months later, we found out he was accepted to Duke for the following year.

I realized that our baby boy was going to be seven months old when we moved to Durham that summer. The feeling I had the moment we learned Brian got accepted was suffocating. I was confronted by the thought that, in fact, gendered norms always win. But I couldn't tell Brian how I was feeling. We were going to have a beautiful baby boy! We both wanted a family. In the moment, however, I couldn't shake the thought that even though I was the one who'd had the career on lock from the beginning, as far as knowing what I wanted to do, I now found myself stuck at home with a baby, then two babies, hustling to work my part-time ministry job in those early years after the move to North Carolina. All the while, it seemed like Brian was flourishing.

Don't get me wrong, Brian was also working a couple jobs on the side to help us make ends meet financially as a family of four. During those first few years of seminary, his mother was diagnosed with cancer. She survived two years and died at age fifty-four. We experienced three miscarriages in the first five years of our marriage. Brian's situation was hardly the same as many of the divinity school students coming straight out of undergrad—able to attend to their studies full time, read every single page assigned in class, *and* have the energy to camp out for a few days on the lawn every year in hopes of getting those coveted Duke basketball tickets. But his momentum and visions of opportunity vastly differed from my experience in the years that followed.

I wonder if the notion of flourishing carries different weight in different seasons for different people. As a pastor, I've had the privilege of walking alongside many women and men over the years who are navigating this tension. Who gets to pursue their dream job, their passion project, or just move forward in this season of life? And who sacrifices (even a little) or seemingly takes a back seat to make that movement possible? Any relationship that has its foundation in "being for" the other will inevitably encounter these crossroads; truthfully, these questions and decisions will be engaged over and over again. We might as well allow these hard and honest questions to become good companions on our journey together.

No More Balancing and Juggling

I can't tell you how many times I've wrestled with the words "juggle" and "balance" as a working woman, wife, and mother. Juggle and balance. Seriously. Whether I was at the local park with other moms, or at church with other women, or offering a listening ear to congregants as a pastor, these two words have disrupted my life for years. "How are you going to juggle all of these things?" other women would ask. "You need a better work-life balance." "You can't juggle all of those things without dropping the ball somewhere. Something's gotta give!" "How do you spin so many plates in the air?"

For many women, it's not uncommon to feel the burden of juggling or balancing work, home, relationships, a social life and the social engagements of our family, and the nonstop orbit of our kids' or extended family's needs, all while carrying immense guilt for not being able to do any of these things wholeheartedly. Add to this the reality that in some ethnic-cultural contexts, if your kids misbehave or look disheveled in public, this is assumed to represent the mother's lack of parenting, attention, or care. And, as if all this weren't enough, we have to fight against significant gender gaps that still exist in the workplace, like the lack of fair pay and policies around women's health, as well as cultural strongholds regarding the expectations placed on women to continually shift and adjust to major life changes.

While all of this is true and real, I also believe it's true that many of us have allowed ourselves to get sucked into the lie that balancing and juggling is a faithful way to live. If we look at nature, at creation itself, it's never a juggling act. Life is about cycles. Cycles of life and death, ebbing and flowing, hibernating and emerging, seeding and growth, day and night—otherwise known as "seasons" from Ecclesiastes 3:1: "For everything there is a season, and a time for every matter under heaven."

As I've navigated my vocational aspirations over the years alongside my children's thriving, my partner's hopes, and a constant web of discerning which challenges were mine to carry and which were societal (gender, race, age), I had to figure out analogies that were more faithful than "balancing" and "juggling." As a pastor, I felt it was important to frame people's lives in a way that made space for women to flourish and to hold their male partners accountable. What were the non-negotiables in our lives? And do these stay the same over time? What were projections or pressures placed on us, whether from within ourselves or by others? And do we even realize we're carrying these things? Have we ever proverbially dropped things, only to discover that the world didn't end? Have we ever dropped other things, only to discover tragic ramifications?

Being parents of three boys, we had many years early on when our cupboards were stacked with plastic cups, plastic plates, plastic trays, and rubber-coated silverware. Because children drop things *all the time*. But as the first two got older, it seemed like a good opportunity for us to own some adult things like glassware, mason jars, and ceramic platters. We chose ones that would be sturdy enough for when the boys wanted to use them. And yet, when the boys would cheerfully grab the champagne glasses for our New Year's sparkling cider toasts, my eyes were constantly watching as they would throw one hand in the air to shout "Happy New Year!" while holding their glass in the other. I had to sacrifice a bit of my midnight moment in order to be mindful of their joyful celebration. The analogy became clear to me: During the times when we or someone we love is holding something fragile, it takes a greater level of attention on our part in order to not let it drop. The consequences can be harsh. But at other times, we can relax because we know and trust that the plastic cup or rubber spoon will bounce back. We weren't meant to juggle it all or perform a balancing act. Some things we must give extra care and attention to because they hold some level of uncertainty and fragility in the moment—those are our glass bulbs. Some things we just have to be okay with letting drop because we know they'll bounce back—and those are our rubber balls.

When we've experienced enough ebbs and flows in life, it's much easier to look at the bigger picture and realize there are just some things we carry in different seasons of life that are more fragile than others. I've found that anything new, or things we are potentially losing, or shifts we encounter, carries a little more weight and requires intentional care, whether it's a new relationship, new job, new city, new home, new baby, or new promotion, or losing a loved one, letting go of a dream, or caring for the needs of extended family members. New situations and shifting realities present particular challenges for any person because of the nature of change and uncertainty and because of the fragility latent in pursuing success, making adjustments, or managing new circumstances. These are the glass bulbs we want to be attentive to. Many times, if we let these bulbs drop, the ramifications could potentially be devastating and carry long-lasting effects. The fragility of the glass bulbs is not merely the thing itself but is how these new or shifting realities force us to shift—our expectations, our roles, our time, our energy, and even perhaps the seeming loss or sacrifice of what we had planned. That's what makes these bulbs in various moments of our lives require greater attention than perhaps other things in that moment. Not balancing. Not juggling.

But as with all new and shifting things, new doesn't always stay new. You won't always be a newlywed. Your job won't always be challenging to navigate (for most of us) because you'll become familiar with the expectations and the tasks. Your baby will grow up and no longer need you to feed and burp him every forty-five minutes, which is what it feels like during that season. The intense grief of losing a loved one will slowly ease, and it will be possible to find your way with each new day. And other new things will emerge over time. Perhaps your increasingly seasoned marriage is no longer the thing that's fragile, requiring extra care as it did when you were first navigating life together, but maybe now your second-grade daughter just let you know she is being bullied in class. In this season, your marriage is a rubber ball and your daughter is the glass bulb.

Maybe your boss just let you know that if you don't get another book published within the year, you may not get tenured. It's in this moment that your desire to volunteer as a coach for your son's soccer team becomes a rubber ball, releasing you of guilt and allowing you to be a little more flexible (maybe forgoing being the head coach and instead being a substitute or providing snacks). So for now, in this moment, your attention can be placed on nurturing your job. Or maybe your partner, in turn, can bear the burden of some of the things you used to do for a season so that you can focus more intentionally on your work.

Maybe you decide that your second-grade daughter will not take the bus home every day and instead figure out how to rearrange your schedule so that you can leave work an hour earlier for the rest of the school year and pick her up for quality time. Glass bulb.

Or perhaps you're anticipating your fifteenth wedding anniversary this year, but you know your marriage is fragile, and it has been for a while. Instead of signing your child up for three different after-school activities that require your carpool attention or presence during the week, or instead of going to happy hour three days a week with your coworkers, you'll need to invest those hours in marriage counseling and honest times together to process and confront the reality that your marriage is shifting right in front of you. Trust me. Your child will live through it, and they may even flourish because of only having one activity to manage that school year. Rubber ball.

Life is full of constant ebbs and flows, shifts and changes, surprises and the mundane. Some things will bounce back while other things will likely crack. Wisdom is knowing the difference and allowing yourself to let some balls drop, knowing they'll bounce back.

Mutual Flourishing, Finally

After ten years in Durham, having just graduated with my MDiv and Brian with his PhD, and three sons in tow, Brian was offered a job in Seattle, an area of the country neither of us had ever been to. It was yet again a new city, new community, new job, and new schools. I had been in ministry for fourteen years prior, and I found myself again wondering what my role would be. Brian was starting his first "real" job in his forever career, and our youngest was entering kindergarten. In reality, I was experiencing burnout from the hustle of motherhood, ministry, and graduate school. I thought it might be a good chance for me to reassess what I wanted to do with my call. Knowing that it was a major life change for our kids as well, it seemed wise for me to be the tether for this first year in their transition to a new city. We realized that our children were the glass bulbs in that season. My career could wait while Brian was getting settled in and the kids gained a sense of belonging in this new city.

We quickly found our new church home, and ten months later, it became my new place of employment. I grew to love the job in ways that surprised me. Within two years, I became ordained in the denomination of that church. My career was taking off, and I was growing in my role in ways I hadn't anticipated or even known that I wanted. It was the first time in my career that I felt any type of momentum and a future I could envision, with a deep love for what I was doing. Brian was hustling to make sure the kids' needs were met while I was transitioning from part time to full time to taking ordination classes to shifting into an expansive role as the church was growing. We realized that I was the glass bulb in this season—my calling, my job, my vocational movement, and the necessary attention to it. All of this was our glass bulb.

Years later, when we reached our forties, we had some major life decisions, opportunities, and uncertainties ahead of us. Brian was beginning to receive invitations to apply to more notable academic institutions, and I was receiving inquiries for whether I'd be open to taking lead or senior pastor positions around the country. Wow. But also, "Why Lord? Why now?" Remember, I had finally found my niche and felt like I was flourishing and free for the first time in my adult life.

Brian, on the other hand, was tolerating his job and struggling to find joy and a sense of fulfillment. But he had been committed to it and to us as a family. We were rooting ourselves in Seattle because he knew I was finally thriving in my vocation, our three sons were doing well, and we loved the beauty of the Pacific Northwest. Those years of uncertainty and potential upheaval were extremely challenging for me. As I finally had forward movement in my career and the kids were getting easier and older, it was painful to watch Brian endure his job day in and day out. He wasn't thriving; he was enduring. I kept

GLASS BULBS AND RUBBER BALLS

reassuring myself, "But it's my turn, right? I'm the glass bulb right now, right?" But even if I were the glass bulb, when we really care for and deeply love one another, we want the other to not only survive and endure but thrive. Those years of discernment, of finding ourselves once again navigating whose turn it was to pursue furthering their career or sacrificing, weren't easy, and we didn't always engage it well.

Our anxiety was at its highest when we'd talk about who gets to do what, and when. Opportunities and inquiries seemed to be flowing into Brian's inbox and voicemail at a steady pace. "Could this be God opening doors for him?" we wondered. But something inside of me couldn't get down with any of it. Was I being a horrible and selfish partner? Perhaps. But I was okay with that. Why? Because I knew my vocational calling and movement forward was the glass bulb. I knew that our kids uprooting again was potentially a glass bulb. "We've had to follow you the last two times!" I blurted out in frustration and fear. "We moved to Durham for you to pursue *your* degrees, and we moved all the way out to Seattle for *your* job! It's *my* turn!" I was fighting to not let this bulb drop. Brian agreed, and we tried to stick to the plan that our next big move would be for me, no matter what. Those conversations weren't cute or pretty. There was a kind of callousness that had to overwhelm my heart in order to not let that bulb drop. Would our marriage take a hit? Nah. We were confident that in that season, our relationship was healthy and would bounce back because he had always believed in my call and knew deep down this was my moment.

Fast-forward four years to today. Through a series of painful and unexpected circumstances and a whole lot of patience, tears, anxiousness, faith, and surprises, we find ourselves respectively flourishing where we are today. Both of us are in places and roles that we didn't anticipate but that we are seemingly well suited for in this season of our lives. We're enjoying it for now, as we prepare to celebrate our twenty-fifth wedding anniversary in 2021, but we also know that, in time, something new will emerge that will require care once again.

Sometimes it takes us fighting for what we know are fragile realities in a given season. Women often carry the burden of negotiating the uniqueness of what we know only our bodies can do, often in seasons that seem to conflict with vocational timing and progress that men rarely have to navigate (e.g., giving birth and breastfeeding). More and more women that I know are deciding not to breastfeed but instead utilizing bottles and formula to allow their partners to have access to more areas of care during those early months of child-rearing that are not dependent on the mother's body. Every couple will have to navigate what works for them and decide what are the glass bulbs that require particular care and what are the rubber balls that will bounce back. For many women, their vocational opportunities are often continuously fragile because of the ebbs and flows of life and the very real struggle for advancement we encounter as women. But even in the midst of those realities, instead of holding a posture of "either everything drops or every plate needs to keep spinning," considering glass bulbs and rubber balls may be a more faithful way of imagining what flourishing can look like in any given moment and season.

I know this sounds risky. As women, we tend to think that if we are going to err, we should err on the side of being in control, of not letting anyone tell us that there is something that we can't do because we are women. But that's part of the lie, isn't it? That everything is possible and that we can somehow control all of the circumstances of our lives perfectly and with grace and power? The idea of glass bulbs and rubber balls is simply a realization of what's most true about being human. We are limited creatures who can only walk so far or accomplish so much in our lives. Part of what makes marriage and relationships so tricky is that in our society, too often women are the ones who have to give up or bang our head against the wall of perfection. Everyone, regardless of relationship status, has to grapple with this truth.

But in a relationship, we also have to begin to recognize that flourishing is not a single moment but the accumulation of moments. It is the whole of a life together. When we can trust the one we are with to be *for* us, we can also trust letting go of perceived perfection to find a deeper version of flourishing that makes room for all of us, even if it is a slow process of building.

Discussion Questions

- How have you experienced the pressures of juggling and balancing?
- Have you been told it's possible to juggle life well?
- What are glass bulbs in this season for you that seem fragile, or may require intentional and extra care?
- What are rubber balls that you know can and will bounce back in time if dropped?
- What does this look like for you as a couple or family?
- What might this look like for each of you individually?

SIX

Our Golden Rule

We don't do anything big until we both feel total peace in the decision.

It's a simple rule, really. When we have a major decision to make—having a baby, starting a degree, moving, taking a new job—we don't take action until each person has peace. We commit to being truthful about how we feel, and we honor one another and wherever each person is, even if one of us isn't entirely happy about it. This rule has shaped every major decision in our lives and helped us navigate hope and tension in the midst of difficult spaces.

Oftentimes, it's meant that one of us has to continue in a job that wasn't ideal, or take on a bit more work during a season, or slow down to care for the kids while the other ramps up. But because this commitment lay beneath each decision and had brought us to where we were, we could trust that a mutual sense of peace was a sign of being called to something new. And until we both felt that peace, our call remained where we were.

It would be nice to say we developed this rule through prayer or studying Quaker practices of consensus or because of the example of parents or mentors. But as we discussed earlier in the book, in so many ways we were just making this stuff up as we went along. To be honest, neither of us can quite remember where the rule came from or why it seemed to resonate with us.

The idea of peace, or maybe a better word is "resonance"—a hum that you feel when the notes ring into a chord—has marked our lives together and shaped the ways we navigate through it, trying to listen to and serve one another, and trying to live into what God has called us to be. But to get a sense of how this commitment shapes our lives, it might be helpful to start by looking at how the ideas of peace took root in each of us early on.

Brian

Not having grown up in the church, peace didn't initially have a spiritual meaning for me. My home was a place that swung from uncertainty to joy and back again. My mother was a woman who felt like sheer love, but who was also holding a life of trauma in her body. Sometimes it felt like so much of the pain she experienced was walled up inside of her, as she refused to let it pour out onto my brother and me. But of course it did. She struggled with bipolar disorder, depression, and chronic pain from multiple back surgeries that left her unable to work, which compounded her depression.

So peace was when her body wasn't hurting as badly, or when we had enough money—maybe even a little extra to order out. Peace was hosting extended family and birthday parties. But peace was always thin. I grew up like a finely tuned instrument, able to feel the shift in the barometric pressure. A deeper sigh or a door closed with a little extra frustration would send me around the house looking for something to clean, trash to be taken out, or someone who needed a hug—anything to help ease the moment. Sometimes it worked. Sometimes it didn't.

But peace also looked like drawing or writing a poem. I would spend hours doodling or writing poems. These were ways to cope, but creating something also gave me a small moment of pride that I could look at something I had made and feel it was beautiful or funny or touching in some way.

When I was sixteen, I became a Christian because I was chasing peace, in a certain way. My mother and father had been divorced since I was eight, and my father had always been a source of my mother's pain, even in their love for one another. But when I was fifteen, I came home to the news that he had been diagnosed with stage four colon cancer. He was going to move back in with us.

What I hadn't realized was that in the year or so before this, he had gotten sober, attended meetings regularly, and committed himself to Christ. He had been going to church regularly for a year. When he moved in with us, I could see something had changed in him. In the face of death, he seemed calm, at rest. I saw him reading his Bible and going to church, and in the midst of my fear and uncertainty and sadness, I started following along. I walked to Walden Books and bought my own New King James Version Bible. In those pages I saw a God who had knit us together and was with us. During that time, I also found a community of people, friends, a place where I was seen in ways I hadn't been seen elsewhere, except in my home. Peace was a sense of belonging.

But belonging was always a fleeting thing. In a couple of years, I would come to see the cracks in the church community. I was still wrestling with my racial identity and finding a sense of belonging. Then I met Gail, and peace was like a harbor. I'm not sure peace was ever a perpetual condition; rather, it felt intermittent, almost an interruption. But because I had felt it in those small moments throughout my life, felt it flood in even in the midst of profound fear and loss, I always knew it was there, sometimes close, sometimes distant.

As Gail and I talked about our stories, trying to mine where this idea of peace even came from, we both began to realize just how much our lives had been defined by struggle. We discerned peace in our midst, not because we experienced it often, but because it was so infrequent. Peace stood out. Although we felt the marginalization of others or the lack of belonging for ourselves or the uncertain circumstances in the lives of those we loved, in the midst of it all, we still saw reminders of faithfulness and the possibility of God's presence seen in the people who showed up for us or in biblical stories we heard from week to week. In quiet, persistent ways peace rang in our lives.

No Peace without Trust

We also began to discern peace because we felt the lack of it in our decisions—those moments when we resisted the small voice, or remained silent as another was mocked or treated poorly, or when we filled the discomfort with games or shopping or media. When we were twenty, we couldn't have given you a definition of what peace meant to us or the criteria we would use to figure out if we felt peace in a given moment. As we grew together, we began to sense where that peace rang true in our lives individually and together. We had to have hard conversations when one of us felt peace while the other was still wrestling.

Again and again, we've come to realize that peace was not about the problem being resolved or getting a dream job or being sure about what was going to happen. Peace was about trust that we would be with one another in the midst of it. That trust had to grow over time as our family expanded, as our decisions got more complicated and the ramifications more significant.

Looking back, it is clear to both of us that there is no peace without trust. But trust is one of those feelings that rarely comes with ease and, in truth, probably comes through repetition or mistakes, or a little of both. Whether it's through showing up on time, or washing dishes, or asking how the other person's day was, or getting up to change the baby, or setting the coffee to brew in the morning, trust gets built in the small acts of being present to one another. It happens through little touches, reminders that you're seen or known, or that we're in this together.

And sometimes trust has to fly across a gorge on nothing but thin air because some mornings we wake up and the previous day's frustration didn't dissipate. It dug up something deeper. Trust is that layer of air running under the wings telling you that this person was there for you. Yes, they got mad, but they came back. They always came back. They took a step back and asked questions. They gave you room to be frustrated and vent. Trust is that scary unknowing between the jump and the landing, after you've flung yourself off a branch that was just a little higher than you had imagined.

Peace comes when that repetition, the jump and the landing, has happened enough that even if it was a little higher or the landing was a little rough, even in the mistakes and the unknowing, you each know that the other is committed to walking in the joy or the difficulty together. Trust is the belief that in the end you are walking with someone who is most committed not to the destination but to walking together.

Gail

Searching for some semblance of being "at peace in the Spirit" was common for me growing up. In the midst of chaos, uncertainty, and drama in the house, I've always known peace as something supernatural, because it isn't anything your present circumstances can make real or tangible. Instead, peace is supernatural because it's the way we choose to draw out pockets of possibility and hope *in the midst of* these pressing spaces. When I think about having to make a major life decision at age nineteen—that moment my

115

dad made me choose between honoring his desire that I not marry a Black man and my deep love for Brian—I can still feel the pressing space I was in. I spent the whole night mulling, praying, and considering the decision. What an impossible space to be forced into! I decided to follow my heart and conviction, going against my dad's admonition, only to discover that I would lose twenty-one years of relationship with him because of it.

Peace for me wasn't ever about avoiding conflict or loss, but it was about hoping for possibility in the midst of these things. I've always been struck by the story of Shadrach, Meshach, and Abednego in Daniel 3. As King Nebuchadnezzar demands allegiance to himself and the idols of power, those who refused would face state-sanctioned violence and murder. In response, the three men declare with conviction in verses 17–18:

> If our God whom we serve is able to deliver us from the furnace of blazing fire and out of your hand, O king, let him deliver us. *But if not*, be it known to you, O king, that we will not serve your gods and we will not worship the golden statue that you have set up. (emphasis added)

"But if not." That phrase is everything! Those two verses describe a deeply centered conviction about who God is and one's place in God's economy—a radical peace in the face of idolatry and injustice. Martin Luther King Jr., in the face of anti-Black racism and systemic injustice toward African Americans, gave an entire sermon in 1967 based on that phrase "but if not."[1]

In truth, the peace that Jesus offered throughout the Gospels was always peace *in the midst of*—peace in the midst of persecution (John 16:33), peace in the midst of a world that tells us otherwise (John 14:27), peace in the midst of the storm (Mark 4:39). And the promise of peace is that God doesn't leave us alone or forsake us in the chaos but is intimately with and for those who pursue righteousness and justice.

In elementary school, there was a boy teasing one of my Asian classmates, calling her "eggroll" and making fun of her eyes. He was ruthless. We went outside for recess, and my heart beat faster and faster as I wondered, "Should I do something about this or not?" I don't think the boy even knew I had heard him teasing her. There weren't that many of us. His words about her were words about all of us. But growing up in my family, we weren't taught to use our words to defend or stand up for ourselves, so the only way I knew how to meet the pain was to fight—to use my body.

Like a good friend does, I walked up to the boy and casually put my arm around his shoulder, pretending like I was interested in talking to him. Then as we were walking in step, I tripped him and punch-slapped him. He went to a teacher crying. I went to the principal's office feeling liberated and at peace with my actions, despite knowing that when I got home, I was going to feel the wrath of my parents on my calves with the whip of a broken fishing rod!

Fighting might seem like a weird way to "make peace," but throughout my life, peace wasn't about an absence of conflict but about the presence of equity and liberation. I never felt that there could be peace when there were people being bullied and pressed. Fannie Lou Hamer said, "Nobody's free until everybody's free."[2] Peace to me always meant more room for the underdog, not letting people get beaten down by power. To be fair, I wasn't constantly fighting, but these moments punctuated my life.

When I look back and reflect on my formation, fighting was very much a part of my family life as well. My brother struggled for place and identity at school by fighting his way through; my parents fought their way through poverty and fought to belong as immigrants; and my mother struggled as a woman called to pastoral ministry. For an immigrant family struggling to get by, it was one way we took care of things and carved some sense of space for ourselves. It wasn't ideal. In thinking back, I realize that peace was never a foregone conclusion. Sadly, I knew from a young age that there were people who didn't believe peace was an option for them, and that revelation always pricked something deep in me.

In my faith formation growing up, I remember hearing words like these: "Pray about it until you have peace." "Do you have peace in this decision?" "I don't feel peace." As a child, I was never sure what that meant, just that God can and will give a profound knowing. Over the years, whenever I've found myself in a place where I'm seeking an answer or some notion of peace in a decision, I ask a lot of introspective questions: "Is this a selfish desire? Is this impulsive? How would this affect the family or my colleagues?" But at the end of it all, peace is an immovable feeling that there is something I or we ought to do. Sometimes it just doesn't make sense, but we have to trust.

Peace for me was always connected to holiness—that we couldn't always trust what we wanted or what we thought we wanted in a given situation. We had to ask ourselves questions like, "Is this desire coming from pride? Or from fear?" Sometimes the peace was in the decision, but at other times, it felt like a promise that would come from living *into* the decision. Often, the peace that I felt or wanted to feel meant that I was going to have to do something I didn't want to do, that there was going to be a disruption.

I'm increasingly realizing that peace is the complicated marriage between what is just and what is possible, or what could be. Given the realities of sexism, racism, and homophobia, the opportunities that present themselves and our subsequent decisions about which ones to pursue are never just about how good a person is. But even in the midst of these larger systemic realities, there are people navigating their own histories and living within those systems. Being married for twenty-five years and having navigated the continual obstacles for women in ministry, Brian and I committed to making my job the priority. Over the years, however, I've found myself thinking about this notion of peace, especially in our moments of uncertainty within our respective careers. I often ask myself, "Are we feeling hopeless right now because I am holding on to something that's selfish versus what's right in this moment? What is the decision that is going to bring the most possibility for both of us? Or do we stay on principle because we say the next move is mine, and because that's what we said we were committed to?" Peace in this sense is a kind of "but if not" peace, where we look squarely at the systems and the limitations they create but always ask what can bring life and possibility for the whole.

Throughout my life, whether it was going into ministry, or going to seminary, as well as so many other things I didn't want to do, I've had to ask myself: What have I heard God ask of me, and what ultimately creates greater possibility? Obedience takes courage. For many of us, our yesses have often been labored. But the truth that I've experienced in these yesses throughout my life is that I know God will be with me, even if I don't understand it. I don't always know what God is calling me toward, but as I take that step forward—as scared as I may be—I've learned to trust that God is going to make a way. And for me, it has always happened in the midst of uncertainty. The sentiment that there's "peace in the midst of the storm" strangely resonates with me; I find peace in the midst of struggle—the harder the struggle, the deeper the peace. I wonder, is this what my Pentecostal immigrant parents were speaking of? They were "at peace," not because their circumstances were peace*ful* and without conflict but because, whatever their struggle was that day, God was their light.

Leap of Faith

Early on, we didn't really know who we were. We had a sense of calling but weren't sure what that would look like or where it would take place. And because we had little money and no financial support from family, we couldn't choose whatever we wanted. Sometimes we had to make do with whatever came along. So when the possibility of moving to go to seminary came up, or when an opportunity to take a part-time job as a worship leader arose, the idea of peace wasn't that difficult to discern. It was an easy rule to follow when it didn't seem like there were many decisions to make.

But as we got older, one kid became two, two became three, the part-time worship-leading job became a full-time job, and the master's in theology became something that led to a doctoral program. As I (Gail) was finding my voice in ministry and I (Brian) was being encouraged to think about doctoral work, we noticed that the weight got a little heavier and the roads didn't seem to run parallel to one another.

Over the years, there were more voices, more people, and more communities to account for and listen to. It became harder to be objective because we had a seemingly clearer idea of what we thought we wanted. And when there are more viable options, choosing something that isn't ideal feels like a lack. What seemed like a good plan two years ago begins to lose its luster because we realize we aren't the same people, or we're wrestling with what we thought we would be and who we actually are in a particular moment.

As we've been together, we've come to find that God doesn't always speak in the same way that God spoke early in our relationship. God speaks to us in different ways in different seasons, and every decision had a greater weight when there were more people who were part of our community and the various communities we were leading or involved in. Sometimes peace meant making decisions that made no sense but trusting one another in the process.

Brian

One of our biggest leaps happened about ten years into our marriage. We had bought our first home in Durham, North

Carolina. For the first time, we had rootedness. Gail painted every room. I made built-in bookshelves and cabinets. We made an outdoor patio and dug out every truckload of dirt and laid every stone ourselves. We loved that house.

I was still two years from graduating. Gail was about to finish her MDiv, and I was finishing my PhD. But Gail, as she does, was thinking about the "what ifs," especially what would happen after we graduated. We were starting to think and pray about how to navigate both of our callings and job prospects and cities. "Do you think we should sell the house?" Gail said.

"Babe, that's two years away," I said. "We've only been in the house for three years. We need to let it appreciate. We can just sell it when we move." But Gail had been thinking about the complications of selling a house from far away and the hassles of renting, and she was starting to get worried. I was worried about losing the investment in the house, but in reality, I was thinking, "I've got exams coming up. I have to write my dissertation. This needs to wait."

Every few months Gail would casually bring it up. This is how we tend to work toward decisions. We circle for a bit. Talk for a few minutes, offer a few thoughts. Sometimes we agree. Sometimes we don't. Then it sits again. Usually, with each conversation we find ourselves a little closer than we were before. But this was not one of those times. I didn't want to move.

After a year of short, dancing conversations, Gail woke up one April morning and immediately said, "We need to sell the house."

"Why now?"

"I can't really say." That's when I knew it was serious. I looked at Gail and saw that something in her had shifted. This wasn't about fear of the unknown, or even practical reasons for thinking about a move.

One of the benefits of living by a rule long enough is that you know what the outcomes look like, what it feels like when the decision process or the discernment process was faithful, and when it wasn't. We had made enough of these decisions by that point that we could feel the resonance of peace in one another.

We could also trust one another when we felt like we didn't have peace about something. One of the things I had learned about Gail in our first ten years together was that she can feel the Spirit, and while she doesn't force it on people or on the family, there is something about what she can see in a moment that would be dumb to not listen to.

That morning, I saw it in her eyes and felt it in her spirit. God was doing something in that moment. Unfortunately, that moment was also a week before Gail's final exams and my comprehensive exams. So in the midst of school, finals, papers, field ed, multiple jobs, and being a TA, we got our house ready to sell. We cleaned walls, sold furniture, and fixed dented corners. And with three kids—ages nine, seven, and three—we got ready to keep our house immaculate for the foreseeable future.

We put the house on the market on a Friday. On Monday we had a contract. A month later the economy collapsed and the housing market cratered.

For the next year, the five of us lived in a one-thousand-square-foot townhouse, buried in boxes. But we were able to make enough off the house to be debt-free (except for student loans) for the first time in our lives. We were also unknowingly preparing for more confined houses that we would find in Seattle. And we were able to move with no strings.

We did not realize any of this in the moment. For us, peace in that moment wasn't a list of positives that outweighed the negatives, or the next step in a carefully prepared plan, or even an indescribable calm that descended upon us. Peace on that particular morning was the fruit of hundreds of conversations and experiences that allowed us to trust one another, knowing that what we were seeing or feeling in that moment was real.

Peace allowed us to listen to God's prompting in us and in one another. Peace came in the trust, not in the calculations.

Do You Trust?

Selling our house in the midst of one of the busiest, most stressful times of our lives was not easy. It wasn't life or death either. It was just one example of a process of communication, self-reflection, and trust that has marked our lives together. For every moment when I (Gail) woke up with a call and I (Brian) was ready to work it out, there were countless other moments when one of us wasn't so sure. There were times when the waiting didn't feel holy or courageous or sacrificial. Sometimes waiting meant believing something in the other person that wasn't entirely clear in the moment.

What started as a rule—"We don't do anything big until we both feel total peace in the decision"—was, in actuality, a hope. Calling it a rule suggests that there is a level of certainty about what happens when the rule isn't followed or when it is instituted after a series of mistakes or problems emerge. But our rule was born out of a belief in one another, a desire to trust one another. And that trust had to be worked at. The hope would only become a rule after lots of trial and error.

If we were to talk to our younger selves, we might point out the places where we got it right more than where we got it wrong. We could trust ourselves. We might ask ourselves to be a bit more patient with one another. But who knows what we would have been able to hear in the midst of so little money, and kids, and major decisions, and what felt like so few options? And that's so often the case, right? We never really feel like there are limitless possibilities in front of us.

For us, the golden rule was a hope, but there were some tendencies that allowed it to become something more than a slogan, something that has continued to shape us and has allowed us to choose one another while still feeling like we were both continuing to grow. For peace to be possible, we found ourselves asking some fundamental questions about ourselves and about the other person. What do we trust?

1. Do we trust the other person's ability to hear God? We both came from traditions that described Christian life in terms of call and movements of the Spirit. We both had testimonies of how we had seen God move in our lives. But where we saw that move and how we trusted it were often very different. Growing up in Pentecostal traditions, I (Gail) heard God speak through Scripture, but also as a firm and unyielding move within my spirit. Once I've heard it, there's no going back and no waiting. For me (Brian), God's call was a sounding stick tapping out in front of me, looking for solid ground and a path forward. Hearing it is painfully slow and feels like I am bumping into more wrong turns than right. It's like smelling for good air, leaning, and following. But what happens if one person hears a call clearly while the other isn't so sure? Or if there has been a call working itself slowly to the surface for weeks or months or years, but the other person hasn't felt a sense of certainty yet?

When you begin to trust, you are trusting that the other person might be hearing God too. And somehow, because you were called together, to be a "we," you trust that the call will never be about only one person hearing. The call will be clear when those moments of clarity ring together and allow you to walk into each decision having heard it for yourselves and in one another, even if it was not necessarily the timing you would have expected. Trusting one another is also trusting God, that somehow this person next to you is shaping what you hear and what you are called to be in ways that you cannot yet understand. So you allow your lives to be open to what God is saying to you, knowing that God speaks to both of you in different ways, and in her own time.

2. Do we trust that the other is being self-reflective? It's one thing to hear God. But what if the other person just doesn't like change? And what if it's not that they don't hear God; it's that they just can't hear God through their fear? Sometimes you might think you hear God, but in actuality you kind of always feel like a second fiddle, and you don't want to go somewhere feeling like the other is the main player. What if your fears are valid? Or instead, what if they are rooted in family histories or patriarchal ideas about what a man or a woman should be?

We don't always know ourselves. If this book has tried to show anything, it's that we change over time. We come to understand ourselves in new ways, and we discover old patterns are not just "how we were born" but might have something to do with how we've navigated feelings of isolation or rejection. As we grow, we also learn more about how our body works in the world.

When we need to make big decisions and find ourselves disagreeing or sensing that we are in different places, we have to trust that where we are in a moment isn't necessarily where we will be in a few weeks or months or years. And this doesn't necessarily have to do with someone changing their mind. It has to do with whether we trust one another to ask questions of ourselves and where our fear or uncertainty or hesitation is coming from.

Over time, even when one of you is in a space that is not ideal, or you are both in spaces that are not ideal, you can trust that the other person has and is doing their own work to ask questions, pray, wrestle. In the end, trust in self-reflection is trust that the other person is open to change. It is trust that as we get older and experience more, we will have a different perspective on ourselves and the world, which will shape how we face new opportunities and new challenges. You will not be the same people in five, ten, or fifteen years. But will you be people who have learned and grown in ways that allow you to see yourself and the other person more truthfully? Or will you be people who carry the pain of trying to stunt growth and wrestle time until it bends and breaks, leaving shards in your lives and in the lives of those you love?

3. Do we trust that the other knows themselves? While we have talked a lot about change and listening and adapting to another person, there are limits. We can't be the person the other wants us to be if we are not wired for that. This doesn't mean we don't try to accommodate a person we love or try to stretch to respect or hold or work with the other. But it does mean that there will be aspects of who we are that remain fundamentally the same, and we know it.

I (Brian) am a pretty cautious person who has a deep aversion to change. When I enter a new space my first instinct is to find a routine, cultivate some spaces of familiarity, and just sit and be "home." But I didn't always know this about myself. When we first moved from Durham and Duke University to my first job in Seattle, we were excited to have a job and to be in a beautiful city, but I was unsettled. For the first few years, I thought it was because of my institution, or the teaching load, or the city, or the fill-in-the-blank. I was constantly looking at new job postings, and Gail knew I was unsettled. I felt like I heard God "calling" me to a new job. But Gail was not so sure. As we circled around these possible jobs and the question of whether to apply, her refrain to me was constant: "How do I know you won't just be unsettled wherever we end up?"

I was convinced she didn't really understand my frustration or my professional hopes. But what she was really communicating was that she wasn't sure I really knew why I was unhappy. And she was right. But it would take years for me to realize this. Ten years later, in a dream job, with Gail in her dream job, I found myself with the same sense of unsettledness. But I had no good excuses. As I walked around my new institution and found myself gravitating to the same coffee place, the same restaurants, the same walks, I began to sense just how hard my body was pulling toward a sense of normalcy. Change made me anxious and uncertain, and when I am anxious and uncertain, I don't ask questions of myself, but I find flaws in my environment, and once I find them, my brain can't see anything else.

As I realized this, I remembered my first few years after moving from Durham. The institution and the city weren't perfect, but the biggest problem was that it was not familiar. And I didn't understand myself enough to know just how deeply that shaped how I heard God's call, how I saw myself. So when we say we need to trust that the other person knows themselves, it doesn't mean a complete knowing. But it does mean that we need to know ourselves enough to acknowledge there are things we don't know or are trying to discover. It also means that we need to trust that we know ourselves enough that when we say we are worried or uncertain, it comes from someplace that is real. We have to honor and hold the other person in the spaces they occupy, and we can't ask the other to be something they're not, to believe something they don't believe, or to be ready for something that they simply are not ready for.

When you are able to do this, you are opening yourself to the miracle and the power of the moments when the other person says they are ready, and you know just how much of a leap of faith or act of courage that yes is. You can trust that the other person is saying yes (or no) out of everything they are in that moment, given what they know about themselves and about who they hope to be.

4. Do we trust that the other wants us to flourish? In a lot of ways this is the hardest one, the trust that feels like the biggest leap of faith, because it's not always clear. Years of small moments can mean misinterpretations, unspoken frustrations, and hurts that build like a film on a window, obscuring everything.

And for this trust to work, it has to be true.

We don't always want what's best for the other. Sometimes this is because we can't separate what's best for them from what we think is best for us. Sometimes it's because what's best for them might mean something less than ideal for us. Sometimes it's because we don't really see the person we're with. We haven't become a student of their habits and small joys, talents and gifts, struggles and daily victories.

But assuming you've made commitments to each other and have already begun to wind significant aspects of your lives together, you can start by trusting that each person at least *wants to* want the best for the other person. When you trust that the other person wants the best for you and wants you to thrive and find joy, then you can begin to make space to ask what that "best" might look like in a given moment.

Without this kind of trust, there really can't be peace, and we can't trust what that person says about what they are hearing from God or the honesty with which they are working through their own questions about who they are.

Let's be clear: this trust that the other wants the best for you is different than them saying they can give you the best or be perfect in every situation. Maybe a better way to say it is that they want the best for you and want to make it a reality to the greatest extent possible for them at that moment.

This is a trust of mutuality. It binds the previous trusts together in a way that allows two people to move beyond simply negotiating trade deals or workloads. Trust that the other wants you to flourish means that you also have to open yourself and your hopes for fulfillment to others. To say that another wants you to flourish is to acknowledge that your flourishing needs this other person in some form or fashion.

When you begin to open yourselves to this, you also begin to see that what you understand to be flourishing can sometimes be surprising and different from what you first thought.

128

In the previous section, I (Brian) mentioned Gail's uncertainty about my unease with my job. Her question about what would really make me happy certainly had some connection to her own satisfaction and sense of rootedness in Seattle and in her job as an associate pastor. If this had been the only reason I could see for her hesitancy, it would have been sufficient. For her, as a woman, finding a church that would celebrate her gifts and make room for her to live them out was so difficult. And I was committed to supporting her in that call, even if it meant a less than ideal situation for me.

The problem was, I didn't make it very easy. I was clearly unhappy and in lots of little ways communicated that unhappiness. I didn't blame her, but how could she be happy when she knew I wasn't? Here is where this aspect of trust becomes really important. If I had believed that Gail only wanted to stay for her happiness, I have no doubt that a sense of resentment would have crept in, a quiet waiting and pining for "my turn." In our years together, Gail had shown me that she was willing to take risks, to start over, to try something new for the sake of my call or for a sense of vocation I was drawn to. Whether small things or big decisions, I saw her trust.

Throughout our relationship I have always been sure that Gail believed in me and wanted me to flourish in my calling and in my life. It wasn't simply that she wanted to stay where she was happy. She was really not sure that I would be happy or that I would flourish in a new job, for instance. So when she asked if going to another institution would really bring me peace, I had to pause, reflect, and trust that she was hearing from God too. And then I had to begin to ask myself some real questions about the moments where I had been most fulfilled in the past months and years.

As I reflected, I came to realize it wasn't the formal academic papers and settings that gave me the most life. It was teaching in churches. It was creating in new ways. The whole time, Gail had been watching and walking with me and seeing where I lit up and got excited and where I dragged my feet. I just hadn't seen it yet. But to see it, I needed to fundamentally trust that Gail wanted me to flourish.

These patterns of trust take time to cultivate. They don't emerge overnight. They begin in the everyday decisions like where to eat out, who to invest time in, where to serve together. Whether in the small things or the large things, we are always navigating different perspectives, wants, priorities. We are wired in different ways and have different histories and fears and hopes that we carry with us. Cultivating trust begins in these small moments as we ask deeper questions of why we are willing or hesitant to do something and how we sacrifice or don't sacrifice for the other person. And as we start to see where the seeds of resentment or frustration emerge, we have to be willing to ask those questions alongside each other.

Our golden rule began as something of a whim, a nice idea that we thought might last a while. But it has become something that not only guides our decisions but also has shaped how we come to decisions and how we live into them, even when things get hard or don't go as planned. And the trust that is cultivated along the way allows us to enter those hard spaces together, as a *we*.

Discussion Questions

- What is a foundational commitment that you share with your partner?
- How does that commitment inform not only the decisions that you make but also how you navigate the life that those decisions create?

SEVEN

Covenant for Community

When I (Brian) was a new Christian, hungry for a sense of purpose and eager to know how I ought to follow Jesus, a well-meaning mentor took me to a Promise Keepers conference. At the Robert F. Kennedy Memorial Stadium in Washington, DC, I was surrounded by thousands of men looking for a similar sense of direction. Speaker after speaker taught us what it meant to be a leader in the home and a "tender warrior." They called us not to abdicate our responsibility to lead our households.

These messages didn't seem to fit with the way my mother had taken care of us and raised us. But we weren't raised Christian. So maybe this was the Christian way, I thought. It would take some time to understand the history of marriage and family that Promise Keepers and similar men's movements were trying to maintain.

The history of marriage and family is long and complicated. Polygamous marriages of ancient societies, arranged marriages, economic systems, gender roles, and children—all have shaped what marriage is and what its purpose is from culture to culture. Even in the Bible, marriage is not a fixed ideal. As just one example, Jacob had to wait to marry Rebekah until he first married her older sister, Leah—and this doesn't count his concubines, all of whom bore children who would become the twelve tribes of Israel.

There was a time in the US when the family was considered the cornerstone of a community. In antebellum society, the purity of women's lives was seen as protecting the very future of Southern culture, even as enslaved people were not allowed to marry or their marriages were broken up for economic purposes. The Great Depression and the two world wars complicated the roles of men and women, with men heading off to war and women entering factories. The 1950s saw a resurgence of the nuclear family as a bastion of American identity and even national security. That vision—a vision rooted in whiteness—would eventually reach me in that stadium forty years later.

The conception of the ideal family—husband, wife, 2.5 children, nice little house, white picket fence—was an attempt to define the ideal American identity and the respective roles men and women ought to occupy. Shows like *Leave It to Beaver* and magazines like *Good Housekeeping* and *McCall's* reinforced the images of what a marriage looked like and what its purpose was.

This image was always a fantasy; it rarely looked this way in real people's lives. It was often a rigid, unyielding framework that trapped men and women in prescribed roles without regard for their unique gifts and callings. For those white bodies who could approximate the ideal, the particularities of their gifts and callings would always be snipped and folded until they were squeezed into the limited molds of masculinity and femininity that this idea of marriage tried to maintain.

But this ideal was also used to diminish the love of Black people and communities (especially single Black women) and to forbid marriage across racial lines. It stigmatized couples who could not have children and single women who didn't see themselves in the role of housewife. It was utter violence to people of the LGBTQ+ community, whose love and lives were never imagined within this "ideal" social life.

Given all this, it's worth asking, "Why bother with marriage? What does it add to the world?" It's a question we hear more often these days, especially among young people we serve in our church and classrooms. Given the high rates of divorce and the ways that many couples enjoy fruitful and full lives without marriage vows, their suspicion is warranted.

So why marriage? And what would fruitful marriage look like? How does it add anything to the world?

We still believe that marriage is a vital and powerful way of living and joining lives. Marriage isn't necessary for God to transform communities. It's not the pinnacle of human life or the cornerstone of society. But marriage is *a particular way* of participating in God's work in the world. And it's *one* important way we are all reminded that we cannot do this work without being bound to another. We have to choose one another again and again. We have to choose God again and again. We have to learn who we are and who the other is in our midst. And the flourishing that emerges in that space will make room for new people, new models, and new ways of seeing the kingdom of God, which will change over time. The possibilities of marriage are never only about the individuals who constitute the "nuclear" family or the maintenance of cultural norms.

The idea of sharing your life with someone is powerful. Someone who will be there when you get home. Someone who will wake up with you and ask, "Did you sleep well?" Someone who will cry with you or run errands with you. This idea of companionship and sharing ourselves with someone is such a fundamental aspect of human life.

But marriage is more than companionship or friendship or having a live-in partner or a sexual playmate. All of these relationships are possible without a legal agreement or a religious ceremony or covenant. When we begin to think of companionship, friendship, sex, and living life together in terms of covenant, these relationships take on a different hue and begin to make space for something unique in the world—something difficult but beautiful.

Covenant Changes Everything

Covenant is not necessarily a marriage, but a marriage is always a covenant. Some are understandably suspicious of invocations of covenant, and we understand that, especially in a world where institutions have often abused the idea of covenant, of commitment and fidelity, using these bonds as means to control and determine people. In theological terms, a covenant is more than a contract, more than a set of terms that each party must fulfill in order to be in compliance.

Covenant is a way of being in the world that says, "I choose not to be who I am without you." This rhythm of choosing, of being with and binding with, is the earliest sense of God's creative work, of God pressing God's own breath into dirt and clay to create what Phyllis Trible describes as "earth creatures," androgynous beings that bear something of God in their bodies and souls.[1] With God's breath within them, human creatures have the possibility of saying back to God, "Yes. And I choose not to be who I am without you." And they are able to say and live into the world around them, "I am like you and I need you, and you need me." This rhythm of mutuality and need is part of the first human being's likeness to God. It was not good for this creature to be alone. Without the other that is bone of bone and flesh of flesh, this creature is not like the Triune God, not fully what it was intended to be. So they each wake up one morning to see another who is like them but is not them, one who can choose and love, one whom they must struggle to learn.

134

This rhythm continues in the creation of Israel, a people created from two "grains" of a people. God promises them, "I will take you as my people, and I will be your God" (Exod. 6:7). It's a promise of presence, of braiding God's own life and identity into them. And in the incarnation God echoes Adam's song in Genesis 2:23: "I will be flesh of your flesh and bone of your bone" (paraphrase). I will always be God and human. You are like me. I am like you.

And threaded through all of this is love: God's desire to share God's self with us, and God's desire for us to live with God and one another.

What rings in all of these aspects of covenant is the idea of a relationship that has permanence and meaning beyond itself. Two creatures imbued with the *imago Dei* were not to mark their superiority to creation around them, but to show how deeply God and creation are interwoven with one another. These earth creatures are of the earth and *for* the earth. Israel's life is not simply for God's play or pleasure, nor is God's creation of Israel for the sake of Israel's dominance over the earth. God speaks God's name through these people, refracting something unique and particular through their life and longing and through God's faithfulness to them. In God's relationship with them, God also relates and is present to the world in ways that speak uniquely.

Any notion of covenant that only speaks to how it benefits the participants is merely a legal agreement, not a theological or Spirit-filled presence. In God's life, covenant is a way for our lives to point beyond ourselves. Marriage as covenant is the beautiful struggle to cultivate a space where God works, where each person can discover and grow into the fullness of who they are, but also where that discovery cultivates life in their vocations, in their home, in their friendships and service, in their parenting, and in their caring for parents or uncles or nieces or cousins. And it is in the very permanence of covenant that the possibilities of life emerge in unique ways in the world.

135

We believe covenant is an important facet of Christian marriage. In a world where every aspect of our lives is seemingly customizable—our Spotify playlists, our Netflix feeds, our social media follows—the idea of remaining connected to and in relationship with a person who doesn't meet our changing needs or tastes can feel antiquated.

And this social pressure is coupled with an increasing and well-earned distrust of institutions. Too many Christians and church communities have alienated and abused their members. Christian communities have theologized the exclusion or subjugation of women and LGBTQ+ people. Outside the Christian realm, further reasons for distrust of institutions abound. Businesses shutter offices and lay off or cut the pensions of lifelong workers. Government feels like a playground for the wealthy and well-connected. Over 60 percent of marriages end in divorce. Too many marriages are violent or dysfunctional or stiflingly pedestrian. What can be trusted? What can one devote one's life to? How are we to believe in the possibility of mutual thriving?

It makes sense to react against institutions and ways of life that reproduce so much pain, but these failures and distortions are not all that remain. Covenant has its gifts and power. While the possibility of choice is alluring, isn't it also overwhelming at times? We have access to the possibility of everything, and yet nothing seems to meet our needs. We move from job to job or from city to city, and while we discover new things in each place, the roots never have time to grow. It begins to feel easier to keep moving rather than discover the depths of a place (or a person).

A covenant relationship is one that roots us in the world with *this* person and not *that* person. This rootedness can be difficult as we try to navigate who we are and who we are becoming alongside this other person who sometimes sees us and sometimes doesn't, and who is growing in their own ways. But the rootedness can also be a gift. As we grow and work and toil, even in our mistakes and unknowing, this person tethers us, allowing us to find the water and nourishment that is deep in the ground where we have been planted together, rather than uprooting ourselves and trying to plant in new places over and over again.

Why Marriage Matters

While we are trying to hold up the possibilities and beauty of marriage, we also want you to hear it again: marriage is not the be-all and end-all. Marriage is one point in a constellation of relationships that make up our social fabric. Some of the fundamental aspects of marital relationships are present in all relationships in their own way—things like mutual respect, trust, sticking by, learning, and being transparent. Whether in friend-ships or in parent/child relationships or in relationships with close colleagues, these are habits and virtues that we need to cultivate in order to build deep, meaningful bonds with people.

So how is marriage different, and why does it matter? When we entered that little church twenty-some years ago, we entered as individual people. At any point before those words were uttered, we could have turned back and said, "I don't think this is the right decision." And we would have left as people who used to be engaged. One or both of us might feel bitter, or sad, or relieved about that outcome, but neither of us would be an ex-spouse.

In the legal and religious ceremony of marriage, our com-mitment to one another becomes public. We become an entity, a small little community that exists inside of and for the larger community. In a way, the public oath is a part of this transfor-mation. We commit to one another and are joined by a pastor or a judge or a person recognized by an authority beyond the two of us, and we make an oath to be committed to one another, to love, to hold, to stand by, to care for.

What makes a marriage different from a friendship is the power of covenant and the legal and spiritual bonds that are formalized through a religious community and/or the state. While these bonds can be broken, they are irrevocable in the sense that these two lives, and all the lives that are connected to them, will never be the same. The intertwining of daily life, the intimacy of sexual lives, perhaps the sharing of children and finances—all of these threads weave two people together to become something different than friends. The two have become one, bone of my bone and flesh of my flesh, as Genesis states.

But part of what makes this public declaration of fidelity and devotion and care so powerful is not only what the oath means for the participants. This public commitment is also powerful because it invites accountability. This couple is not only a new body for one another; they are a new body for their community. They are inviting the community to hold them, to support them as they begin this life together. And even as the community helps to support them, they also are creating a home that will serve the community by becoming a new space of life in the midst of the community.

Just as a lawyer pledges an oath after passing the bar exam, or a doctor pledges the Hippocratic oath upon completion of their degree, the public marriage declaration is an entrance into a larger body that the couple is connected to and that is connected to them. The power of the oath lies in its capacity to transform the identities of each person. Whether with a name change or a ring, it changes us. In the same way, the dissolution of that relationship also leaves a mark on us, making us widows or *ex*-husbands or *ex*-wives. Whether there are children involved or not, there are ties that bind us to that person that are sewn and stitched into the daily intimacies of life together that do not fade away.

One way to think of covenant is like the spines of a basket, the structure of thicker sticks that thinner branches are woven through. The spine, as the structure of the basket, is not what makes it a basket. Yet without that structure the sticks are no use for carrying anything. But that structure also bends the sticks together, toward one another, allowing them to move in and out of the other branches until a space begins to form, a shape that can hold, that can carry.

The permanence of covenant, of that structure that can feel like it limits us, is also what makes space and purpose possible. In our years of marriage, it has not always been bliss. While we are flattered by the #powercouple and #relationshipgoals monikers, the truth is that we wrestled and pressed and chafed throughout the years. For everything we are proud of, there are stretch marks and scars big and small, trust that had to be healed and restored. In those moments when we weren't sure we were going to make it, when we each started to quietly do the calculus in our heads of what life would look like without the other, what brought us back was this deep sense of covenant. Not the legal sense of divorce or obligation, but covenant in the sense of, Who am I without this person? Bone of my bone and flesh of flesh: I choose not to be who I am without you.

When we do the math and try to unravel the basket, we find that our shape has bent toward the other. We are encircled, entwined with one another, and if we are honest, who we are, both in our difficulties and in our joys, was not possible without this other person. So we stay. We listen. We learn. We wait. We grow. We talk. We allow one another to be reminded of the journeys and the transformations and the kernels of who each of us was and always will be.

There is something freeing in the ways covenant ties us together. It calls us back again and again to one another. And with each return, we find our dreams to be wider than we might have imagined. Or we might find that our dreams and our hopes are already realized when we take stock of who we are and who we get to share it with. Within this spine of covenant, we also begin to find the freedom to discover, to change, to become in new ways.

A Community of Relationships

We've mentioned that both of us lacked models. In an ideal world we both would have been able to build on parents and families who formed us into ways of loving and living. And having to piece together ways of walking together in life wouldn't be the whole story. In truth, though, our life was also made possible by people who walked with us over the course of months and years. Some were newly married couples. Some were single people who found small spaces of life in our home and who came alongside us to watch kids or bring food or encourage us on our journey.

In these relationships, folks also gave us small bits of wisdom or caused us to slow down and ask questions of ourselves. The possibility of learning and growing also meant we had to risk actually revealing the truth of our life together. When we were at Duke a couple stayed with us one night a week instead of doing a long commute during the week. Most nights this was a wonderful time of cooking, hanging out, or studying with friends.

But as the weeks went on, the ordinary rhythms of life revealed the crags and rough patches that couldn't be thrown into the coat closet until guests left. Sometimes little disagreements or frustrations spilled out. On one of these nights our friends sat with us. They had only been married a few years. We had been married twice as long and had two kids. What could we possibly learn from them? But on that night, we needed them to help us hear each other, to help keep us from devolving into the usual patterns. At first, we were a little embarrassed. But as each difficult hour passed, we had to let our friends into the disagreements and hurts and disappointments, and even more difficult, we had to reveal our shortcomings as people. They stayed up with us until 4 a.m.—and after a few hours of sleep before starting a new day, we were able to keep moving, to see each other again, and to remember who we wanted to be to one another.

Single people have also poured into us in ways we can't measure. We have learned of new restaurants and hot spots in town that we would never have found on our own with our usual 4:30 p.m. dinner. (Eating out with three young kids is no small task!) But even more than social networks and babysitting, the single people in our lives helped us to remember small joys, to recognize that our little life was not ours alone and that there were realities people faced every day beyond our tiny apartment while we were just trying to get from naptime to bedtime. They connected us to a world we would have too easily driven by. One of our single friends came over for dinner after trips to India and talked to us about her work with trafficked women. Another friend organized protests after yet another killing of a Black person by police. Another would sit and tell us about the inner workings of corporate America and the challenges of being a Black woman. Our marriage needed these people and their gifts and experiences and struggles. Their lives would inform how we imagined our vocation.

This community has been especially welcome and helpful as we have raised our three boys. While each of them is similar to us in their own ways, we also realized early on that the two of us didn't have all the resources or experience or insight our kids needed. Oftentimes friends who shared similar interests with our children were able to be someone they could talk to. Sometimes it was hand-me-down audio equipment for a child who was just getting into recording.

But most often it was someone who wasn't inside of our daily, incremental, just-trying-to-get-to-naptime life who could remind us of the wonder of our children. Our kids are amazing, don't get us wrong. But we often get so caught up and fixated on the frustrations and rough patches that it is hard to see the strides, the victories, the amazing people those little children were becoming. In truth, we needed this for ourselves; we needed people in our lives to remind us that we are real people. In some cases that meant letting them see the closets and the rooms not meant for guests. And we also needed people to remind us of the wins, of just how much life was running through our little marriage.

There is no relationship that is sealed off from the world. Just as the marital relationship is a nest of stories and histories woven together, marriages are also caught up in a vast network of relationships. The relationships in this ecosystem feed and support each other, all the relationships learning and growing from how the others exist in the world. Yes, in our marriage we tried to create spaces of life and rest for people along the way. And we believe that our mutual flourishing could create a space for others in our respective vocations and in our lives with each other. But this life was also made possible by all the people we found ourselves alongside. We all fed and ate, offered and received. Our marriage would be very different without these people in our lives. Marriage is always a communal journey, for us and for those we meet along the way.

Marriage serves the community in its collective life. And it serves the community in that it allows each person to flourish wherever they are, in or out of the home. But marriage is only one of the baskets feeding the neighborhood. In the same way that ecosystems require biodiversity in order to thrive, communities also thrive when we recognize the many ways people relate and commit to one another—whether as friends or family or neighbors or colleagues. Each of these, when oriented toward the possibility of a thriving mutuality, allows all of us to grow and discover, to create and sustain small cultures of mutual thriving and flourishing.

In the permanence and daily intimacy of life together, we grow. Our roots reach deep into the soil, seeking nourishment and life, and weave into one another, allowing everything we see above the ground to bear fruit. But it is also covenant that allows us to see that our flourishing is bound up with the other. Part of the gift of a life together is that when one of us gets an amazing job opportunity, the question is also an opportunity for the other to take stock and reassess their vocation. Our lives are intertwined. And this is a gift because it means that the time when we have to wait, or the risks we both have to venture into, or the compromises one of us must inevitably make, these realities are also teaching us.

In that ebb and flow of pressing or slowing down, of having to live our life wound up in the life of this other person, we also begin to find new ways that our lives and our bodies do work in the world. While I (Brian) might have thought that working at a small liberal arts school wasn't doing much for me professionally, Gail's presence leading worship or preaching was connected to our life together. My life with Gail pressed me into new ways of inhabiting my manhood, which gave me the freedom to sit still (as best I could)—and even that sitting still speaks in the world, just like *not* following the dream job can also create in the world.

Within the spine of covenant and trust and commitment to one another's flourishing, something amazing can happen: you discover that your lives are opening up possibilities for others. In the freedom of being bone of bone and flesh of flesh, you are able to fail and grow and change, knowing that this person has committed themselves not only to who you are but to who you will become. And in that space, those who live in your home, who you work with, who you live next door to also are shaped by your life together.

Sometimes the hard part of living a life day in and day out with someone is that we miss the growth because it is too subtle. The daily grind or to-do lists begin to cover over what was once the beautiful grain of an oak table or the shine of a favorite picture. Or the frustrations of a world that seems to beat us down can still weigh on us at home, even in a place that should feel safe. So we have to fight to make the smallest bit of room for ourselves, and before we know it, the home is its own kind of competition. And because we have lost sight of the beauty of those people who are in our life or feel like we can't depend on this person to join their life to ours, we miss the small changes and transformations that are beginning or that are possible.

But a life of commitment to one another will never be the accumulation of completed plans or a predetermined picture of the perfect couple or perfect family. In truth, a flourishing marriage is measured by the degree to which each person is able to live and grow and discover their call, their passion, their whole selves because of whom they share their life with. We hold the plans lightly because we never know what comes or who we are becoming along the way. That hope and faith in the other's possibilities and in our commitment to them is the joy of a life together. The power and possibility of marriage is the gift of a relationship that makes space to fail, to enjoy, to change, to not need to be perfect, and to live into a life of learning. It all goes in the basket. It all gets used, creating opportunities to nourish and grow and cultivate life in all its varieties if both people are willing to live into the other. That's the gift and the challenge of choosing *us*.

Discussion Questions

- What does your marriage mean for your community?
- What are ways that creating a space of flourishing for your partner might also create space for others outside your home?
- Marriage isn't only about creating spaces but also learning and receiving. How do the single people in your life model love and flourishing?

Acknowledgments

Writing a book on marriage while quarantined together during a pandemic was harder than we thought and more rewarding than we could have ever imagined. This book would not have been possible without our editor, Katelyn Beaty, who believed we had something valuable to share, who walked with us as we conceived of the book, and whose thoughtful comments helped to clarify what we hoped to convey. To everyone at Brazos Press and Baker Publishing who helped with editing, copyediting, designing, marketing, and all the other details that went into making our book come to life, thank you.

We were always loved. Growing up in homes that were filled with turmoil and uncertainty, our parents did the best they could. Each of them loved us as best as they knew how. We lost them too soon, but even now, we can see small ways that their lives and legacy are present in ours.

To our three favorite humans in the world, Caleb, Ezra, and Joseph—aka Caba, Ezbo, and Junebug—you continually inspire us to live into our best and fullest selves. We pray that our lives have become small seeds of imagination and dusty trails of possibility for you in the face of all the naysayers and boundaries you will encounter along the way. But more than anything, thank you for letting us think that we were the dopest parents for as long as you did, and for already planning how you'll take us into your homes when we don't want to pay rent anymore and have no teeth. #ChoosingUs #squadBANTUM

Not having the luxury of our parents being around for us, our understanding of family evolved and expanded over the years. Part of what made it possible for us to be where we are today was a community of people who walked with us, tangibly supported us, and deeply demonstrated their love for us and our children throughout our lives together. There were countless people who were like family for our boys while we were in classes at Duke, at meetings after church, in music rehearsals at night, and away on overnight out-of-town trips when we both had speaking engagements, interviews, anniversary getaways, and those most challenging hours of labor and delivery. Our community's presence made our lives possible, giving us small moments to pursue our callings or reconnect with one another as we fumbled our way toward this life together. We especially want to thank Tanvi Mohan, Leashia Pope, Christina Williams, Amey Victoria Adkins-Jones, Carrie and Jonathan Tran, Minhee and Eugene Cho, Joanie Komura, Deanne Liu, and Roxy and Matt Hornbeck for the ways you helped care for our boys when we needed it most.

To our Regroup, for the privilege of getting to walk with you in all of your various stages of young adulthood, we say thank you. In navigating everything from singleness, to engagements, to married life, to parenthood—you were willing to be community to one another and to us. While we hosted, we also learned. Your lives are a constant source of joy and encouragement for us.

In addition to walking with younger couples, we have also learned from watching couples who are four and five steps ahead of us. While we have had the privilege of admiring many couples and partnerships from afar, we want to especially show love for Willie and Joanne Jennings, who heard us in our individual struggles over the years and showed us what choosing the other looks like in the everyday; and to Brenda Salter McNeil, whose life and love have demonstrated what friendship looks like when we choose mutual flourishing, continually breaking boundaries together.

Notes

Chapter 3: Race and Belonging

1. Gretchen Livingston and Anna Brown, "Intermarriage in the U.S. 50 Years after *Loving v. Virginia*," Pew Research Center, May 18, 2017, https://www.pewresearch.org/social-trends/2017/05/18/intermarriage-in-the-u-s-50-years-after-loving-v-virginia.

2. Emilie Townes, *Womanist Ethics and the Cultural Production of Evil* (New York: Palgrave MacMillan, 2006), 165.

Chapter 4: It's a Man's World?

1. Lillian Smith, *Killers of the Dream* (New York: Norton, 1994).

Chapter 6: Our Golden Rule

1. Martin Luther King Jr., "But, If Not," sermon, Ebenezer Baptist Church, Atlanta, Georgia, November 5, 1967, available at https://youtu.be/0-kgkeuNOB4.

2. Fannie Lou Hamer, "Nobody's Free until Everybody's Free," speech, July 10, 1971, Washington, DC, National Women's Political Caucus, in *The Speeches of Fannie Lou Hamer: To Tell It Like It Is*, ed. Maegan Parker Brooks and Davis W. Houck (Jackson: University Press of Mississippi, 2011), 134.

Chapter 7: Covenant for Community

1. Phyllis Trible, "Eve and Adam: Genesis 2–3 Reread," in *Womanspirit Rising: A Feminist Reader in Religion*, ed. Carol P. Christ and Judith Plaskow (New York: HarperOne, 1992), 74–83.